Crimson Ramblers of the World, Farewell

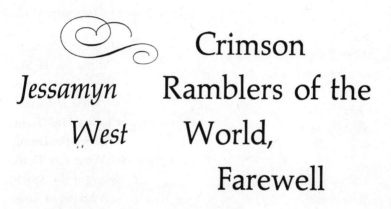

Jessamyn West

Crimson Ramblers of the World, Farewell

Harcourt Brace Jovanovich, Inc.

New York

"Mother's Day" appeared originally in
The New Yorker. Other stories appeared originally in
Harper's Bazaar, Harper's Magazine, Mademoiselle,
and Woman's Day.

c. 2

To my Irish girls,
Ann McCarthy Cash
and her daughters,
Lisa and Molly

Contents

Crimson Ramblers of the World, Farewell

Up
a
Tree

I called Harold Fosdick, the attorney, at about four o'clock. I thought of him because he was the one my mother had gone to see when I was fourteen or fifteen. I was afraid that attorneys, like bankers, might quit work early and that Mr. Fosdick would already have gone home.

"This is Eugenia Calloway," I said when his secretary answered. "I'd like to speak to Mr. Fosdick if he's in."

"Oh, Miss Calloway," his secretary said, with that special something in her voice I was beginning to be accustomed to hearing. "He's with a client just now, but I'll have him call back in a short time."

He called back at once. "Eugenia," he said.

He didn't really know me well enough to be calling me Eugenia. I'm almost nineteen years old, and so far as I know he's never seen me except for that one visit to his office. But I was glad to hear my first name. I'd been "Miss Calloway" all day, and I was glad to have someone speak to me as though I were a friend or a relation.

"What can I do for you, Eugenia?"

"Nothing, maybe," I said. "I'm just calling to ask you about my legal rights."

3

Mr. Fosdick was silent for a second or two. Then he said, "Ted Hughes is your father's lawyer, you know."

Of course I knew that. "I don't know Mr. Hughes personally," I said.

"You don't know me."

"I was with mother that time when she came to see you. You were very nice to her."

Under different circumstances he might have said, "I'm always nice to the ladies." But the circumstances weren't different. "Your mother was an unusual woman, Eugenia." No one was going to contradict that. God knows I always thought so myself, and still do, though in a different way.

"All I want is some information. It might not even have to be from a lawyer."

"If I give it, it'll have to be from a lawyer, I'm afraid."

"Okay. What I want to know is, do I have to see all these reporters? Have they any legal right to question me? Have they any . . ."

Mr. Fosdick broke in, as if I were in court and testifying, "Legal right? They haven't even any *human* right."

"Then I'm not required to answer. . . ."

"Required to answer? Eugenia, you're not a child. You surely know a reporter is nothing but a man hunting news. He has no more right to ask you . . . about your mother's death . . . than he has to ask you . . . Well, he has no right. Spit in his eye."

"There're too many of them. I don't have that much spit. How can I keep them from pounding on the door?"

"Move away from there for the time being. I'd think you'd want to anyway."

I didn't want to move away from there. "Where would I go?"

"Don't you have any relatives?"

4

"You know who mother's relatives are. Out in Riverside County."

"Well, you wouldn't feel at home there. Where are your father's people?"

"Back east. If he has any. He never mentioned them."

"Move into town to a hotel. A hotel could protect you from intruders."

"I want to stay here. And I want the reporters to stay away."

Mr. Fosdick was quiet for another few seconds. Then he said, "There's a lane runs into your place from the main road, isn't there? The house is at the back of the ranch?"

"You weren't ever out here, were you?"

"Not since you've lived there. But that ranch is a lot older than you are. How old do you think those eucalyptus trees are?"

I didn't want to talk about the eucalyptus trees, so I didn't say anything.

"There should be a barricade, at the entrance to the lane. 'Private Property, Entrance Forbidden.' That would take care of the reporters."

"I don't know how to build a barricade."

"Isn't there anyone there with you?"

"Not unless you count the reporters."

"Well, they're not going to build you a barricade. That's a cinch."

"They're not here now. They've gone back to town to file their stories. Or to get something to eat. Anyway, I'm alone, now."

"I'll send my yardman right out. He'll build you a barricade and put up a sign. That should take care of the reporters. Have you already talked with a lot of them?"

"I've really only *talked* with one."

"Smith? The young fellow from the *Star*?"

5

"How did you know?"

"He's sympathetic. And nice looking. He's the one a girl *would* talk to. What did you say?"

"I don't remember, exactly. But quite a lot, I'm afraid."

Afraid? I *knew* I had talked to him a lot. I had been dying, it seemed, to talk to someone. Especially Smith, once I got started. Three days had gone by, and except for Mr. Hughes and the reporters there had been no one. Three days and all that wondering and remembering. Trying to put two and two together. And trying even harder not to put two and two together.

I read somewhere recently that a person at twelve has all the intelligence he is ever going to have. I believe it. I could have dealt with this at twelve just as well as I can now. Perhaps better. At twelve I knew exactly what was right and what was wrong. Or thought I did. Now I'm not so sure. Also I now know that it is easier to love the dead than the living. That confuses me. And I know that pity can bind you closer than love. You feel that you owe more to pity than you do to love. Love gives you joy; pity, pain. And isn't what pain says more to be trusted than what joy says? Pain says you have cancer. Joy says he loves you madly. You're prejudiced in favor of joy, aren't you?

Mr. Fosdick said, "Eugenia. Eugenia. Are you all right?"

"I'm okay. I was thinking."

"You've got plenty to think about. I grant you that. Look here, I'm coming out in the pickup with Tony. While he's putting up the barricade, I'd like to talk to you."

I was tired. "I've been talking all day, Mr. Fosdick."

"That's one of the reasons I want to see you. I'm a friend of Ted Hughes."

6

"I didn't say anything to hurt Mr. Hughes. Or Father."

"You said you didn't know *what* you had said."

"I don't *know* anything that could hurt Father. So it doesn't matter what I say."

"Have you seen your father?"

"Since he's in jail, you mean?"

"That's what I mean."

"No."

"Why not?"

"He said he'd rather not just yet."

"That's strange. Well, I'll be out in an hour. I've a man here I have to finish with. Then I'll pick up Tony and be right out."

"Okay."

"I'm not coming as a lawyer, you understand. I'm coming as a friend. As someone who knew your mother."

"Okay, I'll be here."

"Meanwhile, don't talk to any more reporters. Not even Smith. And don't let them clamber around that platform."

"You don't have to worry about that. The police are taking care of that. Mr. Fosdick?"

"Yes?"

"Do they have a right to keep me away from it?"

"Yes, they do."

"It's on our property. It's practically a part of my home."

"Well, it's a peculiar part now. I wouldn't think you'd want to go up there now. I'd think wild horses couldn't drag you. Now you stay put where you are, and I'll see you in an hour."

It was two hours. I knew it would be. The client would take more time than Mr. Fosdick had expected. It's fifteen miles between here and Santa Ana, where his office is, and when he got home he wouldn't be able to locate Tony at once. After

7

that he'd have to buy lumber for the barricade. So I could just relax.

I had told myself and told myself to stop looking at Mother's picture. Stop peering over it with a magnifying glass like some mad old Sherlock Holmes. I had to use a magnifying glass because the picture was a snapshot, and though good of Mother, it wasn't very clear. It was good of Mother because it wasn't taken by Father. When he took a picture of her, she was self-conscious. She knew he didn't like her looks, and she was too proud to bridle and smile for him and try to look attractive and appealing. (What she was, I now see, was downright starkly beautiful.) This snapshot was probably taken by her brother, Uncle Eloy. I think the strand of leaves hanging over her head was part of the bougainvillea vine which covered the tank house at the Souza place. She knew Eloy liked her, so she was relaxed and smiling. Facing Father was like facing a firing squad for her.

The beautiful woman in the picture was a woman I had never seen before. When she was alive, she was like a painting, so close to me that all I could see were blobs of paint and brush strokes. Death had moved her far enough away so that I could see her true outline. She had a strong face, with high cheekbones, heavy brows, and a nose that was large, but neither sharp nor long. In the snapshot there is a shadowy smile at the corners of her mouth. Her face is manly but beautiful, like a tender Indian chief's, or a great resolute Egyptian queen's. Her hair, clipped together at the back, is hanging down like the switch tail of a black racing mare. She was thirty-eight when she died. Three days ago. I don't know how old she was when this picture was taken. Twenty-eight, perhaps. If Katharine Hepburn had a stronger face and was madrone-colored instead of pink and white, she'd look a lot like Mother.

I had been shoving the picture, after I looked at it, to the very back of the drawer of the library table, promising myself not to look at it ever again. I hadn't appreciated her when she was alive. What was I doing now, gazing and gazing? Pretty soon I would be kissing her picture and crying, "Never leave me, dear Mama. Forgive me, dear Mama." Now I put the picture and the glass on the top of the table. Okay. So I hadn't appreciated her when she was alive. Never thought of her as an Indian chief or an Egyptian queen in my life before. Thought of her instead as someone Father and I had to put up with. If death taught me better, well, better late than never. Such thoughts wouldn't do Mother any harm now. And they might do me some good.

"Good-by, Mother," I said. "I'll be back before dark."

This was as crazy as staring at her picture through a magnifying glass. Crazier. When Mother was alive I never told her anything. Father and I were in cahoots together. Talking to her seemed disloyal to him. And Mother never asked me any questions. Sometimes I resented this. Other mothers wanted to know what time their daughters got in and who they were out with and when was their last period. I wanted to be worried over a little. Maybe I was. But Mother never said so, and I wouldn't ask. So we were both lonely, I guess; though I had Father to talk to and she didn't.

It was a little after five when I went outside. In mid-October with daylight saving, the light is still strong, but beginning to slant, at that hour. It was unnaturally quiet and clear; Santa Ana weather, the hush before the strong dry wind blows up the canyon from the east. Our ranch is at the very edge of the Santa Ana canyon, beyond what used to be the town of Olive. Olive was just beyond Orange. But everything has run into everything else now in Southern California, and beginnings and endings are all mixed up.

Our ranch is still a ranch because Father, being a doctor, hasn't had to subdivide. He doesn't have to make money ranching. In fact, he can lose money ranching, and it helps his tax bracket. Though that isn't the reason he has kept the ranch.

The place began fifty years ago as an olive ranch. Most of the olive trees have been replaced by avocados now. The olive trees that are left are gnarled and scaley. But they bear good crops still, and Mother cured her own olives in big stone jars of brine.

It seemed lighter outside than it really was because our house was so dark. It was built about the time the olives were planted and has never been remodeled, except for the bathrooms and kitchen. It's old-style California with a screened porch on all four sides. That's one reason for the darkness, though it would have been dark anyway because of the redwood paneling inside. Old-time Californians liked it that way. That was the point, they thought, in coming indoors: get away from that hot glare. Being Easterners (not Mother, of course), their eyes weren't adjusted to so much sunshine. Around the house are all the trees the old-timers planted for shade and coolness, peculiar kinds that didn't grow back east. Pepper trees, with trunks gnarled as the olives. Peppers have tiny little dry red berries. When the wind blows, a clump of pepper trees sounds like a tangle of rattlesnakes practicing buzzing. There are palms of every variety, of course. When a Santa Ana blows, the palm fronds clash against each other with the sound of scraping timbers.

At the east end of the ranch, next to what's left of the old grove, is a big double row of eucalyptus trees, planted fifty years ago as a windbreak. Everybody planted eucalyptus windbreaks in those days. Mostly they've been dug up or cut down now. They get in the way of subdivisions. People say they are dirty because they drop their limbs sometimes in storms. The few ranchers who are left don't like them because eucalyptus saps water from the soil. Father didn't have to worry about any of these things. So our windbreak still stands and is a landmark for miles around. It can even be seen from out at sea. Mother loved it. So do I. No other tree as large as the eucalyptus gives itself so easily to wind; or is so open to the sun. When the sun shines and a Santa Ana blows, a big eucalyptus shimmers and glitters like a bonfire of green-white diamonds.

I walked down toward the windbreak, slowly, breathing in the sharp aromatic eucalyptus smell. In the old days people with lung disease were advised to live near a eucalyptus grove. Doctors thought the smell was healing. The Indians still pound up leaves to make a kind of poultice to use for chest colds. The trees don't smell medicinal to me: they smell fresh and free, like the old days Mother talked about and the open country she knew.

The platform was toward the south end of the row of trees. There were two policemen there. They sat on upended orange boxes, with a third box crosswise between, which they used as a card table. They had put their cards away when I came down that morning. I don't know whether it's against the rules for policemen to play cards when on duty or whether they were afraid I'd think they weren't paying proper respect for the dead.

I looked up at the trees at that end of the windbreak and at the platform. I didn't intend to go near the policemen again. They couldn't do me any good, and all I did was to make them uneasy. They sat at the foot of the ladder that leads up to the platform. The platform is built between two trees, seedlings, I suppose, which grow a few feet away from the double line of the real windbreak trees. Mother had it built six or seven years ago. I don't know who the Police Department thinks would want to go up there. I do, but they wouldn't expect me to want to. And I can get up there without using the ladder. I can shinny up to the platform between the two trees, and the police would never know I was there.

Police brutality? I don't suppose the most aggressive men are chosen to sit in olive groves to watch bird-watching platforms. These two men would look okay in checkered aprons baking cookies. They have their revolvers on the orange-box card table like old-time TV gamblers. I don't know what they would do if I started climbing the ladder. They're too portly to climb after me. Would they shoot me in the leg? That would be brutal but maybe they would consider it in the line of duty. Enjoy it, maybe; I don't know.

While I was watching them, one of the men stood, then picked up his pistol. "You're not allowed down here, fellow," he called. He put his pistol in his holster, but he had showed that he was armed and meant business.

"I'm not coming down there. I was looking for Miss Calloway."

"She's right here in front of you."

"I can see her now."

I recognized the voice. It was Smith, the man I'd talked too much to. I turned and walked back toward him.

"Hi, Smith," I said.

"I've got another name," he said.

"I know. Don or Ron or Jess or Steve. I don't want to know it."

"What makes you so mean to men?"

"I'm not mean to men."

"Just me?"

"You're a reporter, aren't you?"

But he was right. Brush them off at once, then you can console yourself by thinking, Well, what did you expect from someone you treated like that? No one's going to fall for a mean-mouth like you.

"Do you hate all reporters?"

"Of course not. I don't know all of them. But I talked too much to you."

"That's why I came out. To show you what I wrote."

"I don't want to see it."

"This isn't anything about the case. In this, it's what you told me about buzzards."

"Buzzards are in the case."

"I suppose they are. This is a special piece, though, just on them. It doesn't mention the case. I wanted to check some of the facts. I tried to quote you exactly."

"I'm in the case. How do you think you can be writing about me, and about buzzards, and make people think that's all you're talking about?"

"I don't suppose I can. I don't care, actually. I want it to be a good piece of writing about buzzards and about you."

"The *Star* is a lousy paper. If your piece is good, they won't use it."

"It can be good about buzzards. Buzzards aren't political. They're human interest."

"Human or inhuman?"

"I saw a piece of yours in the *Yucca*. It's not much good either."

"You're frank, anyway."

"I didn't mean what you wrote. I mean the *Yucca*."

"What do you expect? It doesn't pay. And it's conscientious. Somebody there reads every word I send them."

"Where else have you been published?"

"Nowhere. But twice in the *Yucca*. What do you read it for if it's no good?"

"I read everything. Would you like to hear the buzzard piece?"

"No."

"I'll read it to you, and if you don't like what you hear, you can walk off. It's nothing but what you told me."

He began reading before I could say a word.

" 'Buzzards live the year round in the eucalyptus windbreak at the east end of the Calloway property. They don't nest there. Their nests are in the rocky hills still farther east. But the eucalyptus windbreak is their home. They soar in at dusk after their days of hunting food are over. In October, for some reason naturalists don't understand, hundreds of buzzards congregate in one spot for a fly-in.' "

"I didn't say 'fly-in.' "

"I know you didn't."

"I would never say that. It sounds too cute."

"I'll take it out. 'The windbreak on the Calloway ranch is one of these congregating spots. The buzzards don't get together to mate or to hunt. They do nothing but fly in crisscrossing patterns, so tight you'd expect twenty collisions a minute. They miss by a feather's breath.' "

"I didn't say that."

"I know you didn't."

"It's okay, though. It's the truth."

" 'It's a beautiful sight. They aren't flying to get anywhere. Or to kill anything. Just for joy. Just for pure joy. They don't even fly; they soar. In perfectly still afternoons, with no wind to support them, they find updrafts which send them, without their moving a wing, skyward. They fill the air with black scissors. All they cut in two is sky. All they snip off is joy.' "

"That's pretty fancy for the *Star*."

"You said it."

"Okay. What else did I say?"

14

"You said, 'A couple of hundred birds will decide at the same time to light. All of them at once will slide into and among the eucalyptus leaves and limbs where there isn't any opening to be seen. The trees seem to open up for them, the leaves to lift for them to enter, and the limbs to stiffen to hold them once they've landed.' "

" 'Leaves lift and limbs stiffen.' Sounds like Swinburne."

"You said it. There's only one more sentence. 'And all this without a sound.' "

I didn't intend to cry.

Smith said, "I didn't intend to make you cry."

"It's okay. I've wanted to and couldn't."

"Couldn't?"

"I didn't have the right. You don't have any right to cry for someone who's gone when you've wished a thousand times he was gone. *She* was gone. If you've wished she was gone, you should rejoice when she is gone."

"But you don't?"

"No. Of course not."

Smith gave me his handkerchief. "Why did the buzzards make you cry?"

They were floating homeward at that minute, sliding down the sky from the south to the trees.

"I never saw a buzzard until my mother spoke of them. I didn't hate them the way some people do; they just didn't exist for me. Mother would stand about where we are at twilight to watch them come home. I don't know how old I was when I first went out to stand beside her. She said they were beautiful. I told her they ate dead meat."

"So do we," she said.

"They eat rotten meat," I told her.

"They don't kill it."

"Neither do we."

"Somebody does for us."

"Somebody does for the buzzards."

"The buzzards don't pay them to do it. Nobody dies because of a buzzard."

"Is that why you like them?"

"That's one reason. Another is, they're beautiful."

"Beautiful?"

"Watch them fly."

I did and I saw that they were beautiful.

"And they're so quiet."

"Is that better than singing?"

"There's screaming and squawking, too. No one wants to be quiet but a buzzard."

"If you could be an animal, would you choose to be a buzzard?"

"I am an animal. We're all animals. The buzzards are good animals."

"May I put this in my piece?" Smith asked.

"No. You can't put anything else I say in the paper either. Otherwise I'm going in the house."

"I promise you. She sounds like a wonderful woman."

"She was."

"But you didn't like her?"

"No. I was ashamed of her."

"Because she was half Indian?"

"Partly. Most people thought she was Mexican. She didn't look Indian. Not like the Sobobas anyway. Have you ever seen a Soboba?"

"No. Not and know it, anyway."

"Well, look at me. Pudding shape, pudding face, pudding nose, pudding mouth. That's a Soboba."

Smith didn't contradict me. How could he? He said, "I never heard of a Soboba with red hair."

"No, I've got Calloway coloring and Soboba shape. It was just the other way with Mother. Soboba coloring and a face like her father's. It made her a beauty. But I didn't know it when she was alive. They called her a greaser at school. When you're ten years old, you hate having a greaser for a mother. She did queer things, too. She didn't like a lawn. She liked a yard she could sweep. So we don't have any grass. She didn't like to work inside. So she shelled peas and things like that sitting out in the yard. She washed out in the yard. Herself, I mean. She went fishing and brought fish home in a gunny sack."

"Where could she find any fish around here?"

"Down at Newport. She would sit all day on the pier along with kids and old men and Negroes."

"And your father didn't like this?"

"I didn't like it. I don't think it made any big difference to him."

"There must've been something that rubbed him the wrong way."

"I think he didn't like so much devotion."

"That's a queer thing not to like."

"Maybe you've never had too much."

"That's right. But I can't imagine not liking it."

"Polishing your shoes?"

"Okay with me."

"Waxing your car?"

"No complaints."

"Calling you to the phone when other women call?"

"Ideal."

"Well, doctors are different. They like something to fight. They wouldn't be doctors if they didn't. They want to fight

17

and win. Mother was already *won*. She wasn't a challenge any more. She accepted Father completely no matter what he did. He was her husband, and what her husband did was right. I never heard her complain about anything."

"Even the women?"

"She was his *wife*. They weren't."

"What do you think?"

"I thought that Father and I were putting something over on Mother. 'Us Calloways.' That's the way I thought of Father and me. Us Calloways against the redskins. Mother was an outsider, and Father and I put up with her. I was trained that way. It began when I was too young to know what was going on. But I can remember when I was six, going along with Father to call on ladies. I had a nap or played with the puppies while he doctored the lady. That's what I thought he did."

"In a manner of speaking," Smith said, "I guess he did."

"What makes doctors so irresistible?"

"They aren't."

"Father was."

"He'd have been irresistible as a grocery clerk. If you look like a professional football player, you don't have to be a doctor."

"How do you know what he looks like?"

"There've been plenty of pictures of him in the papers. Besides, he took out my tonsils. *And* my appendix."

"You must've been a sickly kid."

"No. Doctors pushed such things when I was a kid. And my folks had the money."

"Father's way past stuff like that now."

"I know. Open-heart surgery and so forth. Why did he marry your mother if her devotion got on his nerves?"

"Me. I was on the way. *That* kind of devotion didn't get

on his nerves, ever. He didn't know she had the other kind yet. He was a poor nobody and she was a beautiful Indian maiden. I don't *know* that. Maybe it was a shotgun wedding. Maybe her relatives out on the reservation threatened to bury him in an anthill. There would've been other women no matter who he married. Only, another wife would have divorced him. Mother wouldn't. She loved him. He was a fine man and her husband, and she was proud of him and proud to be his wife. And a woman expected a man to be manly."

" 'Being manly.' Is that what your mother called cheating?"

"She didn't *call* it anything. That's how I think she felt about it. He was her husband, and it was for life."

"So your father had to . . ."

" 'Had to.' I didn't say a word about had to. I don't intend to talk about my father."

"You talk about your mother."

"She isn't in trouble. He is. Besides, she wouldn't want me to talk about him."

Smith said, "Maybe you *are* a Soboba."

"I told you I was the exact shape of a Soboba."

"Okay. Yes. You did. Okay. What about the buzzard piece?"

"What 'What about it'?"

"Is it okay with you?"

"Don't quote me."

"If I don't quote you, I don't have anything."

"You say what you want to say about buzzards, and I'll say what I want to say."

"A lot more people read the *Star* than will ever read the *Yucca*."

"You know what a lot of people want to read. I don't. You give it to them. But not Mother's buzzards. They're too good for a lot of people."

Mean-mouth again. But not to put Smith down. That's what I truly felt. The sun had set. To the west the sky was red and gold, and buzzards were silently sliding home to the trees. In the east the sky was pink, and against it Old Saddleback was grape-bloom blue, but as solid looking as the big mountains, Baldy and Wilson. Smith was watching the buzzards, too.

"I'll give you a can of beer if you come up to the house." It was about the first invitation I'd ever given to a male since I was sixteen. I expected Smith to have a date in town. Instead, he said, "Okay, that would taste good."

We were halfway to the house when Mr. Fosdick turned into our lane, stopped to let Tony out and to put down the lumber for the barricade.

"There comes a man who told me not to talk to you," I said.

"I'd better be on my way then."

"You show me your buzzard piece, and I'll show you mine. If I ever write it," I said.

"It's a deal," Smith said. He started his car, but waited for Mr. Fosdick to drive in before he drove out.

I took Mr. Fosdick into the living room. I showed him to our best chair, the fumed-oak Morris with the brown corduroy cushions. It was old, but in a way it was modern because it had an adjustable four-position tilt-back. Mr. Fosdick didn't sit. He turned a full circle, like a man in a museum trying to make up his mind what to look at first. Then he took off his specs. When he did that, I remembered who he had reminded me of when Mother and I called on him. He hadn't changed a bit and he still looked like the same man: Woodrow Wilson. I had been studying American history then and had spent a whole week seeing Wilson's picture in the chapter on World

War I. The horn-rimmed spectacles were wrong, of course, and with them off he looked more like the President.

"My God, my God," Mr. Fosdick said.

Mr. Fosdick used the name of God, Christ, Jesus, Heaven, Hell, the Devil, and damnation very often. I wouldn't exactly call it cursing. It was more as if he felt himself the resident of a universe where there were more powers and personalities than were visible, and that this was his courteous way of letting them know that he was aware of them and was trying to include them in his life. He certainly included them in his conversation. In some ways it was embarrassing. I felt like an eavesdropper to someone praying. This shows how different it was from real profanity, which would have made me mad. I wouldn't care to be cursed. And there is no obscenity that disgusts me.

Mr. Fosdick patted his chair all over as if it were a horse before he sat down. "Jesus, sweet Jesus," he said. "I never expected to see a room like this again. I didn't know there was one like it left in California."

"What's so queer about it?"

"Mission furniture. Redwood paneling. Leaded-glass doors to the bookcases. Grass rug. Eucalyptus portieres between dining and living room. Clock held up by lions' heads. Why, hell, Eugenia, you must know all this. It surely hasn't been changed since the day Gene bought it."

"It hasn't."

"Why didn't he modernize it?"

"He didn't care. He wasn't here half the time. And Mother thought it was wonderful."

"After the reservation, I suppose it was. Why didn't you change it?"

"I didn't have the say around the house."

"Who did?"

"Around the house . . . Mother."

"Eugenia, I didn't come out here to talk about the furniture. How are you? How're you feeling?"

"I don't know. I'm changing. I don't feel the same as I did at first."

"Do you remember the day you came to my office with your mother?"

"Yes. That's why I called you."

"I've never forgotten your mother. I never will. And not just because of that damned idea she had."

"It wasn't such a damned idea. And she had her way, finally."

"Not exactly, I wouldn't say."

"She got there. That was what she wanted. A book influenced her. Did she tell you that?"

"A lot of people told me that."

"Mother's whole life was changed by that book, about how Californians were buried."

"It was Americans, not just Californians."

"Americans. Mother didn't think it was fair that undertakers should make the rules about how persons were buried."

"Well, my God, who said anything about fair? But Christ Almighty, her ideas were a lot worse. Who could put up with thirty-foot platforms all over the country with dead bodies stretched out on them?"

"The Indians could."

"Not *her* Indians. The Sobobas never went in for anything like that."

"She was a half-breed. She didn't have to be tied down by what any one tribe did. All Indians were being discriminated against, she thought."

"Nobody's going to dispute that. If your poor mother were alive today, she could have people organized and burning down mortuaries so that Indians could have platform burial again. My God, they're tearing down whole universities now for less. Soul food and Swahili! Jesus, how do *they* stack up alongside something important like how your ancestors were buried?"

"Mother would never have done anything like that. Organized or torn down or burned down. She wouldn't even protest. She was shy. She was born to endure. She was afraid to go to your office that day without me."

"What good could you do her? You were nothing but a kid."

"I was Father's daughter. And I was white. And she thought I was smart. I know now that's what she thought. She saved every one of my report cards and every composition I ever wrote."

"You probably were smart. Probably *are*. You're Gene's daughter."

"I'm Mother's, too."

"She was plenty smart in her way. Except for that idea of hers that a lawyer would be able to fix it up so she could be on a platform and be eaten by buzzards instead of worms when she died."

"I would prefer it myself. Wouldn't you?"

"After I'm dead, I don't care what eats me."

"She cared."

"What did your father think of all this?"

"He didn't say. Nothing, I suspect. He lived his life and she could live hers."

"Up a tree was okay with him?"

"I never heard him say it wasn't."

"What did he say when she had that platform built?"

"Nothing. It was for bird watching."

"Buzzard watching."

"They're birds. She watched them. So did I."

"Did your father ever climb up to that platform?"

"Not that I know of."

"He must've once."

"You believe that?"

"It's nothing I want to believe."

Mr. Fosdick put his glasses back on, began to cry, and had to take them off. "I don't want to believe it. Gene was my friend. I'd a thousand times rather be where your mother is than where Gene is."

I watched Mr. Fosdick polish his glasses.

"Eugenia," he said, "you are one-hundred-per-cent Indian. Here your mother's dead, your father's in jail accused of her murder, and I'm the one doing the crying."

"I never was encouraged much to cry when I was young. Mother didn't believe in it, and Father was never around to notice. I'm sorry Mother's dead. But being in jail doesn't mean you're guilty."

"You don't get there without damned strong evidence that you belong there."

"They haven't much evidence against Father."

"Mrs. Crowther swears that Gene said on his way back to town that he'd see that his wife didn't cause them any more trouble."

"She never caused Father trouble."

"She wouldn't divorce him. That's trouble if you want to marry someone else."

"He didn't want to marry anyone else."

"Mrs. Crowther came out here with your father, and he told your mother . . . Well, you heard it all. You were here."

"When they started quarreling, I left."

"Your mother and your father?"

"Mother never quarreled with Father. Father and Mrs. Crowther."

"What were they quarreling about?"

"I don't know. I tried not to hear."

"Did your father threaten your mother?"

"No. But Mrs. Crowther did. Maybe Mrs. Crowther killed Mother."

"Mrs. Crowther has an alibi from the minute she got back into town. Your father hasn't."

"Maybe I killed her."

"Don't be blasphemous."

"There were times when I wished she was dead."

"Fortunately, you didn't tell anyone that. And fortunately, she wasn't found dead after you said it. Where did you go when you left the house?"

"I took my bedroll and went out to spend the night in the hills."

"Alone?"

"Sure, alone. I'm no hippie."

"Did anyone see you?"

"I don't know. I didn't see anyone."

"When did you get home?"

"Next day. About noon."

"Was your mother here?"

"No."

"Weren't you alarmed?"

"No. I didn't ask her when I wanted to go someplace, and she didn't ask me."

"Where did you think she was?"

"Uncle Eloy's. Out by San Jacinto. That's where she goes when she leaves for a while. That was Sunday night. I phoned Uncle Eloy on Tuesday. He hadn't seen her."

"Then you called the police?"

"Yes."

"Why didn't you call your father?"

"I didn't know where to find him."

"Did you try his office?"

"They didn't know where to find him."

"And the police couldn't find her when they came?"

"No."

"But you did?"

"Later, yes."

"How did you know where to look?"

"I didn't. I went up there by chance."

"You didn't see your father carry her up there?"

"I wasn't here. I told you that. She was a big woman. How could he carry her up there kicking and screaming?"

"She didn't have to be kicking and screaming when he carried her up. Though he was a strong enough man to have done that if necessary."

"How did he kill her?"

"Who knows? What can you tell from bones that have been stripped bare? He knew that. And he knew that I'd come forward with evidence that some years ago she'd seen me about being buried on a platform."

"Buried on, not killed on."

"Okay. Buried. There must have been a lot of buzzards up around that platform for a couple of days. It's a wonder you didn't notice them."

"This is the time of year buzzards from all over come to these trees."

"To the trees, maybe, but not just to that platform. But you didn't see them?"

"I don't spend my entire time watching buzzards."

Mr. Fosdick took off his glasses again. I don't know why he wore them. When he seemed to want to see something particularly closely, he took them off. He leaned forward and looked at me as if I were a strange animal. Or a page of print in some language of which he knew only a few words. I was standing in front of him. I had never sat down since he came in. I felt more alert standing up. He had stopped swearing. I remembered that when Mother and I had gone to his office there had been no swearing. Perhaps he saved swearing for his social life, but when it came to business, he was all business.

"Did Ted Hughes send you here?" I asked. "Or maybe Mrs. Crowther?"

"You called *me*, remember?"

"I haven't said anything to hurt Father."

"You certainly haven't. I'll tell Ted that. Why don't you go up to see your father?"

"I told you that, don't you remember? He doesn't want to see me. He said he wouldn't talk to me if I came."

"You'd think he'd *want* to see you."

"He's probably ashamed of being in jail. How can they keep a man in jail just because of what some woman says? Probably she was trying to get even with some other woman when she said it."

"They couldn't keep him in jail. Except that the wife's dead, and he said she'd cause them no more trouble. And there's no other explanation. Is there?"

"Maybe not. But don't you feel sorry for him? His wife dead. And the woman he was going to marry, according to you, accusing him of murder. Don't you pity him?"

"My God, yes. He was my good friend. I've shed tears for him. That's more than I've seen you do."

"Well, he wasn't a very good father. Let's face it. He kept me from loving my mother."

"Eugenia, come home with me. This is no place for a girl to be staying alone after what's happened here."

"Nothing's happened here."

"You weren't here. Remember? So how do you know? Come

home with me. My wife would be glad to have you. Clarice will be home from Pomona. She must be about your age."

"She's my age exactly. No, I don't like to be in town. This is home."

"Okay then. If you need me, phone, and I'll be right out. Tony's barricade should be up by now, and you shouldn't have any more trouble with reporters."

An hour or so after Mr. Fosdick left, I went down the back way to the south end of the windbreak. The Santa Ana that had been threatening was already beginning to blow a little. There was a small moon, short of full quarter by a night or so. I could've made the trip in pitch dark, but the pale moonshine plus the stars of a clear night made the way plain—besides making me feel more tranquil and peaceful than I had for days.

I could have climbed right up the ladder. One policeman was nowhere to be seen. The other, stretched out on his sleeping bag, was dozing. I was barefooted. Though I did not like to be called the daughter of a greaser, I liked to play at being a hundred-per-cent old-time Indian, who could move noiselessly through a forest never slipping on a twig; and able to make an owl's soft hoot, absolutely owl-like, but recognizable as a signal, too. I gave the hoot then, to try out the cops, but the one I could see never so much as twitched.

So though I could have climbed the ladder, I wanted to go up the hard way, and out of sight, for practice. I wanted to see if I could still do it. People never expect me to be agile because I'm so stubby. They are mistaken. I am agile. I can put my head to the floor and look at you upside down and backward from between my legs, the way a baby can. A baby is not tall and thin either.

The way up to the platform, on the back side, without us-

ing the ladder and out of sight of the police, was by a moun-
tain-climbing maneuver. You go between the two trees that
hold the platform, back against one tree, feet against the other.
The trees are exactly the right distance apart for inching up
that way. It's no trick to reach the platform, but it's a little
tricky getting onto it. For a second you hang by your arms
thirty feet in the air.

The platform is about six by six. You can stretch full length
on it, either direction. I lay down flat on it facing Saddleback
Mountain. There was enough of a Santa Ana blowing to rock
the platform gently. Above were the dark forms of the buzzards roosting. They look so much smaller roosting than they
do flying. They are mostly wingspread and feathers. I have
never held a live buzzard, but I think they would weigh less
than a young chicken. Without feathers they would be almost
nothing.

The last time I had been up to the platform I had used the
ladder. There had been the first tiny thread of a new moon,
which is shaped like a eucalyptus leaf. Mother believed, and so
did I, that you will have bad luck if you don't see the new
moon the first night it is in the sky. It is also discourteous not
to give your attention to something that is making a start. I
looked at the new moon that night, because I knew Mother
would want me to; but I could not see much luck in it. I said
to it, "Prosper, prosper, new moon," though I had never done
that before and was disgusted when I had heard Mother, a
grown woman, talk to the moon as if it were alive and had
ears. It was a part of her queerness; and when you're young,
the last thing you want is a queer mother, a mother who talks
to the moon and puts fish in a gunny sack.

Somehow I had believed that the buzzards would be cere-
monious when they stripped the flesh from bones set out for

their feasting. Mother had talked that way, as if they were as dignified and professional as undertakers; only not hirelings. But they had scrambled her bones, pushed them every which way. In my mind I truly believe I thought they would arrange them as neatly as a corpse in a silk-lined casket. I expected to be able to lie down beside Mother, she on one side of the platform, I on the other, and together we would rest there and remember and decide what to do. She was not even all there. Some of her bones had been pushed to the ground. I went down and brought them all up. That was what she had wanted, to be in the sky, not on the ground. But there was no use trying to arrange them as they had been when they were covered with flesh. She wouldn't care about that, and, besides, I didn't know how to do it. The thin thread of a moon had left the sky by the time I got back on the platform. It was warm, and I stayed there all night, sometimes sleeping. I was asleep at first light, and it was the buzzards, creaking a little as they levered themselves upward, that awakened me. I lay perfectly still, wondering if they could tell that I was alive. They swooped low across the platform but never stopped. My flesh was alive and Mother's was gone. I went back to the house, and after a day had passed I phoned the police to tell them what I had discovered.

This was a different night. Mother's bones had gone to where she had never wanted them to go, to an undertaker's. But first she had been where she wanted to be. Father wouldn't let me talk to him, but I understood that, too. I didn't really want to talk to him or see him. I didn't care if the silence was between us forever. Except for him, I think I might have loved Mother *before* she died. Maybe not. Anyway, he had fixed it so the love I had once had for him had changed to pity.

I lay on the platform, the wind rising, the platform swaying rockaby, and the cop who had been dozing snoring now, full out, tired of silly tree watching and of pretending that he *was* tree watching.

Out of habit, not thinking, I felt around to the back of the far eucalyptus where a limb had dropped off leaving a hole as deep as two hands and as wide as one. When I was learning to smoke, I had kept cigarettes there. Mother kept binoculars there, a pencil, a pad of paper. She wasn't just a buzzard lover. She wanted to remember what they did, how many were in the sky at once, and so forth, like Thoreau. I let my hand lie in there touching Mother's things that had meant nothing to me when she was alive. "Mother's bird-watching junk." And I could have been up there with her learning with her when she was alive. And I would have been, too, I think, except for Father, who made me *his* child and not hers. But above everything that she loved, birds, the new moon, me (I now believe), she loved Father.

I went back up to the platform very early the next morning. The cops were both there, not even pretending to watch. Sleeping like hounds, twitching and grumbling with dreams. I stayed quiet until sunup. Then I called down to them.

They hopped out of their sleeping bags with only their shorts and undershirts on. Before they grabbed for their pants, they grabbed for their holsters.

"Put on your pants and don't shoot," I said. "I'm Eugenia Calloway. I've found some of Mother's things up here I'd like to have."

"There is nothing up there," the first one who finished said. "That platform has been gone over with a fine-tooth comb."

"They're not on the platform."

"What are you doing up there?" the tall Sherlock Holmes–looking one said.

"I am being where Mother was."

"How did you get up there?"

"Climbed," I said.

They'd been sleeping like skunks, so what could they say? They had to say something.

"It's forbidden."

"Why?"

"That's none of our business. Or yours."

"I'm not trying to break the law. That's why I told you what I'd found. I could've sneaked it out."

"What did you find?"

"I didn't take the stuff out. What I can feel is Mother's binoculars."

"Out? What's it in?"

"A hole in the tree."

"You come on down," the boss cop said. I came down the ladder as if I'd gone up that way. Carefully, too, like a clumsy young lady. The plump cop, agile like me, did the climbing.

"I don't see anything," he called down.

"Feel around in back of the big tree," I told him.

He began to bring out objects—binoculars, pencil, notebook, a package of Life Savers, some Kleenex, and the big plastic bottle with just a few red capsules rattling around in the bottom.

Down on the ground, the two cops looked at their treasure trove, especially the plastic bottle.

"Is this medicine your mother took?"

"She didn't take any medicine that I know of."

"Seconal," said the tall man. "Sleeping pills. Did you ever see this before?"

"You don't have to answer," the plump cop assured me. "Anything you say can be used against you."

"We oughtn't to be saying anything ourselves."

"Nothing being said is official. This isn't a big city. We're all

32

neighbors here, so to speak. This girl's father relieved me of a kidney stone once."

"I've seen the bottle before. It was in the medicine cabinet. Father took a sleeping pill sometimes when he'd been working too hard and was too strung up to sleep."

"Was it full or empty when you last saw it?"

"Almost full. Father was no drug addict. I don't think he took a pill once a month. You can ask him," I said.

The scholarly-looking cop, now that he had his pants and jacket on, was leafing through Mother's notebook. It was a plain flappy-backed twenty-five-cent book. The binoculars were expensive, but the notebook was small and cheap, big enough to hold buzzard facts, but small enough to fit snugly into the hole.

"Your mother was quite a buzzard authority," he said.

"Yes, she was."

He came to the last page that had been written on, about two-thirds of the way through the book. He stood staring at the page he had come to. The plump cop and I stepped closer to have a look. The page was blank except for two words. Three, if you count "good-by" as two. It looked like mother's handwriting—and it didn't; her writing, if she was writing in the dark. Or was sick. The words were, "Good-by. Hello."

"Everything else is buzzard stuff," the tall man said wonderingly, as if he had been reading a cookbook that suddenly started to print obituaries.

"I think we'd better get this in to town," said the Dr. Watson of the two.

One should have stayed, I thought, to guard the platform, if that was what they'd been doing. Maybe they thought the platform wasn't so important any more. Whatever they thought, they got on their motorcycles, leaving me, their sleeping bags, and the buzzards stirred up by the noise of their cycles and circling wildly, alone in the clear early-morning air.

The funeral was three days later at ten in the morning. Mr. Olmstead came over at nine with a big spice cake his wife had made and four combs of honey. He kept bees and he always brought Mother honey because he said that without her trees his hives would be empty. Eucalyptus honey is a little strong, deep amber-colored, but very good if you don't use too much. Mr. Olmstead looked like a Pilgrim Father, tall, wrinkled, and worn to the bone. He was a rancher trying to make a living ranching. He and Mrs. Olmstead and Mother liked each other. The Olmsteads were bee fanciers the way Mother was a buzzard fancier, and they made jokes when they got together, saying that they were going to talk about the "birds and the bees"; which of course they really did.

I suppose I showed my amazement at the amount of honey he'd brought. And the size of the spice cake.

"We thought you'd need it for the folks who'll come in for lunch after the funeral."

I hadn't planned to have folks in for lunch. "It don't need to be a sit-down affair," Mr. Olmstead said. "But your mother's relatives will be here, and they'd like to have a cup of coffee and talk, I expect."

And Mother would like them to. "It's better the way things have turned out," Mr. Olmstead said. "Not good. Nobody could say it's good to die at thirty-eight, but it's better this way. I'm glad for your sake."

"It's the way Mother wanted it," I said.

The funeral was just a graveside ceremony. Mother had been born a Catholic; I don't know how much she'd lived a Catholic—more than I knew, perhaps. Perhaps her sticking to

Father had been as much a part of her Catholicism as anything else. Anyway, no matter what she was born or how she had lived, she was being buried a Catholic. And if you have to be taken down from the birds and the trees, that is a good way. The ceremony seemed bird-old; and the priests were black as buzzards and red-nosed in the chilly morning air.

The burial ground is an old one on the hillside beside the first adobe church in these parts. It's not much used any more. The tombstones bear the old Spanish and Mexican names Yorba, Sanchez, Ortega, Sepulveda, Novano. Now there would be a new name: Inez Souza Calloway.

There were twenty-seven people there. Half of them, almost, were Uncle Eloy's family. I stood with them. Uncle Eloy had got the whole Soboba works: squat body, round face, small steady eyes, dark skin. I stood as close to him as I could. He was a good man, a school-bus driver, and my mother had loved him dearly. When he took her picture, her love for him showed. The Olmsteads were there, of course. Smith was there. Mr. and Mrs. Fosdick. Father's lawyer.

Father never once looked at me. I looked straight at him. I wanted to catch his eye. I don't know what I would have said with my eyes had I had the chance. But I didn't get it. He kept his head bowed and his eyes on that box of bones. He knew why he was there instead of in jail; and he knew why she was there. Knowing these things, I suppose he couldn't look at me.

It didn't make me sad to have Mother's bones buried. Her flesh had gone where she wanted it to go. And I think she might even have been glad to have those old words said above her bones. After the casket was in the ground and the earth placed on top of it and the words about dust and earth and ashes had been said, I did what Mr. Olmstead had suggested; I asked people to the house—the Olmsteads; Uncle Eloy's family; Mr. and Mrs. Fosdick. I didn't ask Smith, but he marched right along with Uncle Eloy's kids as if all that talk about buzzards had made him one of the tribe.

I didn't ask Father either. After everything was over, he did look at me. And I knew, from that one look, that he would never again set foot in that house. He walked away from the graveyard fast, so fast that his lawyer, Ted Hughes, who is shorter than he is, had to trot to keep up with him.

I looked one last time at the grave. After a Santa Ana has blown itself out in the fall, it often clouds up to rain. It was doing that now. The first fall rains in California are a benediction. Everyone loves them. "Rain, rain," I said, like Mother talking to the new moon.

My cousin Gertrude Souza was waiting for me. She is fourteen years old and about six inches taller than I am already. She wears mini-skirts.

"I never saw anyone buried before," she said.

"Neither did I, Gertrude."

We walked toward the cars together, and she said, "We are first cousins."

"From now on," I promised her.

There
Ought
to Be a
Judge

The girl watched and listened, and afterward she remembered. At the time, it was nothing so much: a rainy night, a boy hunting for some people he had lost, and then, after drinking the whisky her father gave him, speaking of them. At the time, she only watched and listened; later, the lonesomeness set in.

It was a warm May night; at dusk there had been a light rain, and now at nine there were bursts of distant thunder. The windows were open, and the girl could smell the laid dust and the wet lilacs. It was the kind of night when young people think something should happen, and the girl let the new petticoat, in which she was setting insertion, lie on her lap while she listened; but there were only four sounds, and none of them said, "Now he comes," which is the sound for which girls listen. Her father's breathing was a steady noise, and the flick of turned pages in the book he read came regularly, too. Besides these there were the distant rumble of thunder and the wing flutter of two moths circling the lamp. Since no more was to be heard, the girl picked up her sewing and added to the room its final sound: that of the delicate clip clip of her thimble against the needle.

The boy entered without knocking. The room was a hotel sitting room, and there was no real need to knock, but most people did.

"Is this the Kokomo House?" he asked.

Her father looked up from his book. "That's what the sign says," he told the boy.

"Are you Jacob Suttle? The proprietor?"

"I am."

The girl could tell that her father was feeling a little testy, but the boy didn't seem to notice it. She saw at once that the boy had foreign blood of some kind; his black hair had that high gloss pure whites don't often have, and a penny laid against his skin would have been lost. He was a big fellow, but lean through the face so that the bones below his eyes caught the light.

He walked over to her father's chair and said, "Has a man by the name of Elias Overfield been here?"

Jacob Suttle closed his book on his finger. "No," he said, "there hasn't."

"Nor a girl by the name of Missouri Overfield? A tall girl with red-brown hair?"

"No. No Overfields, man or girl."

"Look it up," the boy said. "Look it up in your register. You might've forgot. They came north. I figured they'd reach Kokomo the third night."

"Son," said Jacob Suttle, "there's been just five people stop here this week, all men and none Overfields. That's an unusual name, and I'd remember it."

"I figured they'd be here," the boy said, and the girl saw he was going to faint, but he managed to land in a chair instead of on the floor. The upper part of his body fell across the center table, and if her father hadn't snatched the lamp away, it would have been sent flying.

"Get the whisky, Hannah," Jacob Suttle said, but the boy sat up and said, "I'm all right."

"Do as I tell you, Hannah," her father said, and the girl brought the whisky bottle and two glasses, and her father poured three or four fingers in each glass. The boy held his glass in his hand for a while, staring at it, then tossed the drink down his throat as if he were pouring it out the window.

"That'll make you feel better, son," Jacob Suttle said. "That'll make you forget your troubles." But it didn't. It made him remember them.

"There ought to be some place in the land where there was a judge," he said, "who could tell you exactly what was right and what was wrong, and I would go to this man and tell him everything and let him judge."

"Well, son," Jacob Suttle told him, "I'm no judge of right and wrong, but you can tell me if you want to."

The boy poured himself another tote of whisky. "For three days," he said, "I've been thinking how a stove poker would feel in my hand and of the sound it would make landing on that bony old head of his. One good big splintering sound, then the old fool would be quiet, keep his mouth shut for the first time in his life. No more preaching for him and no more ruining my life."

The boy reached again for the whisky, but Jacob Suttle put the bottle on the floor. "You'd ought to think twice before you talk murder that way."

"Murder," said the boy. "If I could tell someone who knew right from wrong, he wouldn't call it murder."

"Listen, son," said Jacob Suttle, "I can see you're not used to whisky, and more 'n likely you're saying things you'll blame yourself for in the morning. Now I've got a room here where you can rest, and by daylight things'll look better."

"If you don't want to listen . . ." began the boy.

39

"What's your name, son?"

"Joseph Fane," the boy said.

"Joseph, if it'll ease your mind any, I want to listen."

Jacob Suttle took a match out of his vest pocket, put it where he'd left off reading, closed his book, and laid it on the table. The girl settled her needle along the edge of the insertion, folded the petticoat she was making, and listened.

"I'm the teacher at Maiden Creek," said Joseph Fane, and the girl understood that was a place the boy thought they'd know, and she saw it somewhere to the south, a white building shining in morning sunlight, and, inside, Joseph Fane, dark and grave, instructing his pupils.

"This was my first year. The Saturday before school opened, I was cleaning the place, tacking pictures on the wall, writing exercises on the board. When I'd finished, I walked down to the branch to wash up before going to my boarding place for supper. It was about sundown, and the sun slanted through the willows along the branch bottom. It'd been a hot afternoon; birds would tweet once or twice, but night bugs and tree toads hadn't opened up yet. I was washed and standing looking up at the school in the quiet when I heard hoofs in the beech mast along the woods trace.

"First I saw just a patch of white now and then as the horse came opposite a place bare of leaves, and finally the whole horse and the girl who was riding him. Missouri on Old Moon.

"Look," the boy asked, "do I sound drunk?"

"No," Jacob Suttle said, "I wouldn't say that."

He asked another question. "There's got to be a first time, hasn't there, that a man meets the girl he's going to love?"

Jacob Suttle nodded. "I wouldn't deny that."

"The first time," the boy said, "could be at an oyster supper and she sluicing out the oyster stew. Or hoeing corn with the evening sun shining through the little hairs on her arms. Or maybe he'll see her first walking down a dusty road at nightfall holding the hands of her little brothers, and calling to their old dog, who's run off to the wood lot. Those would all be good ways, but if a man could choose, how could he choose better than to see her come through green beech trees riding on a white horse?"

The girl listened for her father's answer, but Jacob Suttle said nothing, so, her heart beating fast to be speaking of love, she herself said, "Yes, that would be a good way," and she saw that the boy heard her voice with surprise, as if only then realizing there were three persons in the room.

"I walked up the rise," he said, "and met her before the schoolhouse. I asked her to light down, but she wouldn't. She had to get back to cook her father's supper. They lived alone and he depended upon her. She told me she wanted to start school on Monday. She'd graduated last year from Maiden Creek but couldn't go off to school because of being her father's housekeeper. 'I hear you've got a box of new books,' she said. 'If it's agreeable to you, I'd like to go another year and study out of them.'

"I told her she could. I told her I'd give her special studies from these books so she wouldn't have to go over work past and done. So she thanked me and slewed fat Old Moon around and rode back down the trace the way she'd come."

I wonder, the girl thought, was she a person like me? If it had been me on Old Moon, would he be speaking of me now, saying she was a small thing with a big braid of yellow hair?

"I've covered many a page with poetry about Missouri," the boy went on, "but the first I ever wrote, that starts

She had the dark and wind-swept beauty
of the hills from whence she came,

is as good as any. There was something wild and free about

Missouri's looks. Indoors, she'd always lounge against a window looking out, and outdoors, she'd always be lifting her eyes to the clouds or treetops. Her hair was brown, but under the sun it would light up like a bonfire, and her eyes were the color of the sand that lies in the bends of Rush Branch."

The girl leaned forward as if she were saying, Look, look, there are other ways of being pretty, too; but the boy went on about Missouri.

"There was nothing about her I didn't love—except her father, and for no good reason, and maybe what I say now is hindsight. He was a short man, wide as a door, with tow-colored whiskers. He was a good farmer and stock raiser, out early and late with his crops and beasts. He was a smooth talker, except that sometimes he'd put a word in a sentence that didn't make sense there. But discounting him, everything about Missouri was to my liking—every single thing—the way she had of taking up the carpets in her house and dousing out the whole place with hot lye water so's the house always smelled like clean-scrubbed wood, and the way her face would mirror what she was reading, so if you knew the book, you could always tell by her look what part she was at.

"And Missouri loved me and was to have married me this summer. And that," the boy said, "is enough to say of our lovemaking. A man's love-making is about all he's got in this world to call his own, for sure. I wouldn't tell more to help my cause with any judge in the land. If he couldn't see from what's been said how beautiful Missouri was and how I loved her, more wouldn't help."

The thunder was fading away; the moths, unable to kill themselves because the girl kept small pieces of screen on top of all her lamp chimneys to save them from the flame, still fluttered hopefully; a light gust of wind shook the roof.

Jacob Suttle looked across the table at the boy. "Nothing

here," he said, "so far as I can see, to make you want to lay a stove poker across anybody's head."

"That's to come," the boy said. "Old Man Overfield always had a hankering after protracted meetings. He never went up front or made any manner of profession, but he'd sit on a back bench, and when the preacher said, 'Brethren, we've all sinned and fallen short of the mark,' he'd groan and say, 'Amen to that, brother. Amen.'

"Did you ever hear of the revival preacher Jerd Smith?" the boy asked.

"I've heard the name," Jacob Suttle said.

"Last week Jerd Smith was holding meetings at Bethel. Old Man Overfield was set on going, and Missouri wanted to go, too. Missouri wasn't seeking salvation, but she likes to see people and to join in the singing. So on Wednesday night I drove them over in my buggy.

"The church was bulging with people, and we had to find seats nearer the front than I'd like. The big hanging lamps overhead were aswinging a little, and that coming-going kind of light didn't make people's faces any prettier. Then out from a side door, tripping and treading, came this Jerd Smith, dressed in a black coat and wearing trousers so tight you could see his leg muscles work as he walked. His red hair was shoved straight back from his forehead, and his face was white like that of a man who is never in the sunlight. His eyes had a faraway look, as if he'd just come out of the Lord's presence and could barely see us here on earth yet. He leaned over the pulpit, and in a voice so quiet and gentle you had to strain your ears to hear it, he made some announcements.

"Everybody was sitting on their chair's edge looking up at him. Was this the man they'd heard about? The man who'd had more 'n one woman talking in tongues, and who'd leaned over an old farmer saying, 'Confess, brother, confess,' until the

43

farmer'd owned up to a long-forgotten killing? He was that one, and they knew it and they judged him like a storm by the silence that comes before it.

"Then, still quiet, he gave out a song to sing, and he led it low and sad. Next he read his text, 'Repent ye, repent ye, for the kingdom of God is at hand,' slow and yearning at first and then bearing down so that the repent ye's clanged like a plow-share hitting stone. People were beginning to get the shakes now, some moaning, some crying out, others kneeling by their chairs with their faces hid.

"Mr. Suttle," the boy said, "it was in my mind to get out of there then, and I'd be willing to admit to any judge I did wrong not to do so. Something put it in my mind to clear out, but there I set and didn't break away, and that was wrong. In-stead, I looked at Missouri, and she was far away, the ruckus going over her head. But Old Overfield was leaning forward, his face red and his eyes popped out like a man about to have a stroke. I laid my hand on his arm and opened my mouth to ask him if he wouldn't like to go out for a breath of air, but he pushed me off and said, 'Keep your hands off me. I ain't fit to touch.'

"Then this Jerd Smith starts the song that ends up 'Why not now,' and every time he said the word 'now' he tossed his songbook to the ceiling, where it made a sharp crack like a drumbeat. Then he'd stop his singing and tossing and say low and sweet, 'Why not now, friend?'

"It was when he was doing this that Old Man Overfield jumped to his feet, grabbed Missouri by the arm, and, before I could make a turn to stop him, ran toward the front shout-ing as he went, 'Got to tell the Lord. Got to lose my burden.' "

Jacob Suttle looked over at his daughter. "You go on to bed, Hannah. Get on, now. You should've been there an hour ago."

Hannah knew what her father was thinking: that the boy

was going to say something she shouldn't hear, and Joseph knew it, too. "What do you take me for?" he asked in a voice curling out like a shaving. "A man like Jerd Smith, rejoicing in sins? A man like Elias Overfield, gone soft in the head? I'm not going to tell you what Old Man Overfield had to say. That old sin, long ago done, repented of till the poor old coot wasn't the same as other men. No, sir, I've got no mind to tell you what Old Overfield had to say. Too many people's already heard that. No, sir. That belongs to Old Overfield. Ask him, if you've got a mind to hear it."

Jacob Suttle said no more about going to bed, and the girl leaned back in her chair.

"But I have got a mind," the boy went on, "to speak about Missouri. Her father led her up there under all those eyes and shouted out the things he had to say. He was happy, I reckon, ranting and foaming, and people hanging on his words, but my Missouri, she who'd always held her head so high, never down-drooping or woebegone, there she stood. And I was so near to her in feeling I could tell how even her bones felt crushed, ready to mix themselves with earth, never walk upright again, never answer to any certain name. What her father was saying was like a dream to her, the way a sickness when you're young's forgotten as soon as you put a foot out of bed. And there she had to stand while every person lived it all out again in her father's words.

"I tried to get to her, but they held me back, and finally a few came to their senses and tried to quiet the old man—but not Jerd Smith, not that preacher. He stood there, his white face twisting, saying, 'Praise God, praise God,' and it struck me that like as not one reason he liked preaching was because he could taste all manner of sin that way, without taking any blame himself.

"It was when he reached down to bring Missouri up to a

45

place beside him on the platform—make a holy show, as they say, of her—that I broke away from those who were holding me. I don't have any idea what I was saying, but they yelled blasphemy at me, and somebody clunked me on the head.

"This was the last I knew. When I came to, the meeting was over and Missouri and her father were gone. Lit out without a sign of where they'd gone to. And I don't blame Old Man Overfield, or Missouri for going with him. How'd they hold their heads up thereabouts again after what Overfield had confessed about the two of them. The man I blame is Jerd Smith—and if I don't find Missouri, he's got to answer to me. And there's no judge of right and wrong in any land who'll hold me to blame for what I'll do."

The boy stood, and Jacob Suttle rose, too, urging him to stay the night and take some rest, but the boy wouldn't hear of it. "I've got no time to lose," he said. "I've had word of a couple like Missouri and her father working northward. I'll head for Peru and maybe catch them there."

"What's to come of your school?" Jacob Suttle asked.

"The school?" the boy repeated, as if surprised that any thought should be given to it. "The country's full of school-teachers, but I'm the one who loves Missouri." He picked up his carpetbag and walked, swaying a little, toward the door. The girl stood, her sewing in her hands, watching her father bid Joseph Fane farewell. Jacob Suttle came slowly back into the room, slowly turned down the lamp, then, with a sound like a sigh, blew it out.

"Headin' for Peru," he said, "and nothing but two swallows of whisky to go on."

The girl heard him stop at the bottom stair. He spoke musingly, as if he had forgotten she was his daughter, as if she had become another person, a real person to him.

"Reckon he'll ever find her, Hannah?"

She answered him like a real person. "No," she said, "he'll never find her."

She stayed for a while stock still in the warm darkness, then put her sewing on the table, took up a match from the cup beside the lamp, and went to the mirror which hung in the panel between the two windows. She lit the match and held it so that her face was reflected white and soft in the shadows. She had never before regarded herself so closely.

Was it a face that could be remembered? Did it lie like a pond lily upon the dark and shining surface of the mirror? Would he possibly remember it, saying another way would be to see her the first time, sitting small and quiet, her sewing in her lap, listening to the sounds of a May night?

Would he? She went to the still-open window and leaned out. There ought to be a judge, and he would surely see that she would never have left Joseph Fane. No matter what had been said or who had heard it, she would never once during her whole life have left his side.

Gallup
Poll

When the prune season is over, Nick and I go up to the city to look at the people. That is our real need, to let our prune-conscious minds see faces once more; remark on eyes and hands, observe the motions they make, the messages they convey; imagine the worlds they inhabit. Imagine the fog- and wind-swept apartments, the grassy peninsula estates, the sprawling homes of professors' families across the bay, all filled with people who have never seen an unpackaged prune.

After we check our bags, we go straight to the St. Francis cocktail room. Perhaps you've never been in it. It's really a funny room, though you don't notice that at first; at first, only the people and the soft lights and the drinks: Dubonnet rubies, Daiquiris like bleached emeralds, and rubies and topazes together in the Old Fashioneds.

You see yourself, too . . . after long absence, in the very beginning you see, more than anything else, your own progress. The clusters of laughing people—women with their coats hanging carelessly over the red leather chairs; the men, papers folded, forgetting the headlines for thirty minutes. They're all there, but in the beginning strictly as background for you.

But after you've found your seat and are no longer a person

arriving, you notice, once again, the room itself. The ceiling is the most peculiar, really. When first you look up at it, you have the feeling you might be on the wrong side of the bed, Beauty-rest mattress over you instead of under you. Then after the second drink you see what that ceiling is really like: it's like the lid of a de-luxe coffin. All that richness; you'll probably never see the like again until . . . Well, forget that.

"Old coffin lid over me again," I said to Nicky.

"Over us all," Nicky said.

"Men don't know it, though," I told him. "Not the way women do." Not the way I do. Some may, I suppose. Next to us were two men drinking wearily, their legs stretched out hampering traffic.

"I had a letter from Bob," one said. "He's at Fort Ord. Don't know how long he'll be there, though."

"How old is he now?"

"Twenty."

Beyond the two men were a man and a woman. They were so unaware of anyone except themselves that they invited inspection as a picture does; their intensity, their absorption in each other placed them on a plane emotionally remote from us, so that it was possible to watch them as if they were acting a scene from some formal and half-remembered play.

I went on to look at other people. I was greedy for faces, and before I went back to the prune trees I wanted to see them all, not just this one man and woman; or the three in uniform standing at the bar, or the girl with the dreaming face, or the sad, orating businessmen.

Nicky still stared at the engrossed couple.

"There's nothing so remarkable about those two," I told Nicky defensively.

The man was pleasant-looking, dark and young, you couldn't honestly say more—though his face was what women call

49

"poetic." That doesn't mean he looked like Keats, or had Byron's proud, sultry front. It only means his face made you feel the way poetry does; as if you were hearing a voice you loved read, 'O western wind, when wilt thou blow," or "My heart is like a singing bird."

The man was very young, twenty-two or -three at the most; he had on the uniform of a Navy flier, with those ribbons and stars that denote service, and perhaps awards, but which I can never interpret.

The woman—perhaps her face was poetic, too, though I don't ever remember hearing a man say that of a woman. Although they write poetry about women.

"There is the face," I said to Nick, "which could have launched the thousand ships."

Nick had been looking, too. "It has, it has," he repeated dreamily.

Well, yes . . . it had . . . but it could again. Couldn't it? Couldn't it?

"You don't call a woman in her thirties—even her middle thirties—old, do you, Nicky?"

My husband smiled at me. "No," he said. What else could he say? I'm thirty-eight. "That's the flower. The crown and flower, really. But it's fifteen years beyond twenty."

"Her hair—that color's real," I told him.

It was a kind of silver mist. Mist with the sun shining through it. Can you remember Jean Harlow? It was hair like that. She wore a black dress, plain, simple. That was right. It would have been a pity to distract the eye by a single ornament from the lines of her figure; but, though her dress was right, and hair and carriage distinctive, still there was something . . . disheveled about her.

The boy was doing the talking; she was doing the drinking. Not for the drink's sake, though.

"She drinks the way Mays chews gum," Nicky said.

I nodded. The boy was leaning toward her talking, talking, his dark mobile face flushed and intent. All his words were there in the room—only there were so many other words, too. I wished for some kind of word filter so that I could sort his out.

"She won't say yes, and she won't say no," Nicky said.

"They're talking about how it'll be when he's gone."

"She's not talking," Nicky reminded me.

"She's thinking, though. Thinking how it's going to be when he's gone. No phone ringing. No car in front of the house. Nothing but the letters."

Now and then the woman let the tips of her fingers touch the boy's brown wrist.

"She'd better cut that out," Nicky said.

She did. She leaned over and picked up her gold purse, opened it, and took from it what looked like a little leather engagement book. Slowly she began to tear out pages, easily and neatly, taking her time. The boy no more than glanced at what she was doing, then went on talking.

"He wouldn't care if she took down her hair and started combing it," I said.

Except when she took a drink (she used both hands for tearing out the pages), she tore out pages; and even while she drank, her free hand kept working on a loosened page.

"What's she up to?" Nicky asked.

"I don't know. Maybe saying 'yes, no, yes, no.' Whichever the last page is will decide it."

She came to the last page. Then she took out a little silver pencil and began writing; on each page she wrote something—not a word, more than that, a sentence, maybe two. Not a single word, anyway. When she'd finish one page, she'd fold it neatly and write her sentence, or perhaps two, on the next. The boy finally reached over in a mechanical sort of way, his eyes still on the woman's face, and picked up one of the folded sheets. She unloosed it from his fingers and smiled at him. It was the sweetest smile, the first time I'd seen her smile since I'd been watching her. She wasn't tense any more; it was as if—oh, I don't know—as if there wasn't anything more to worry about. She spoke to the boy, evidently to ask for another drink, because he ordered another Martini—what she'd been drinking. The boy wasn't talking now, just watching her write, as if the movement of her hand was as beautiful to him as dancing, or flying.

"She's the French teacher at Balboa High School," Nicky said. "She's writing out exercises in the conjugations of irregular verbs for her classes tomorrow." He leaned back satisfied.

"What the hell," he said suddenly, sitting up straight.

She had left the table, the little pack of folded papers in her hand, and was passing them out, one to each person. She did it calmly and naturally, as if she were giving people napkins at a cocktail party. The people who got the pieces of paper unfolded them, read, stared at the woman, read again, fell into a buzz of talk.

The boy just watched her, completely bemused. Whatever she did was right with him.

Nicky acted bored. "Gallup Poll woman," he said. "Do you favor bombing Hanoi?"

I wasn't bored. I was afraid she was going to pass the papers only to the people on the left of her table. If she had done that—I don't know, I think I would have gone over to someone and asked to see his paper. I felt I had to see what she had written; but finally she started circling our way.

Nicky stopped pretending. "Oh, Lord," he said, "I hope they hold out."

They did. She gave Nicky his first.

"Thank you," she said in a low voice.

"Thank you," she said to me as she put a slip in my hand. I looked at her closely. Her eyes were gray. She didn't seem to see me at all.

Nicky and I finished reading at the same time, and without a word exchanged slips. They were identical. Each read, "Will you please write here how old you think I am. Don't flatter me."

Nicky said, "Thirty-six."

"No," I told him. "No. Not a day over thirty-four. And don't write that. Can't you see what she's doing, Nick? She's said to herself, 'If they think, if the majority of them think, well, not more than five years older than he is, I'll say *yes*.'"

"Sure, I see that," Nick said. "That's why I'm going to write the truth. I'll give her the benefit of the doubt. I'll write thirty-four instead of thirty-six."

"Write twenty-five," I said. "That's all she needs to be happy. They'll go away, they'll be happy together. Just your making a change in one number, writing a two instead of a three can do that. Such a little thing to do to make a woman happy."

"Aren't you happy?"

"I am. I am happy. That's why I·want her to be. Look at her."

She was sitting at her table with a numb, waiting look, drooping a little, as if frightened at what she had done.

Nick was counting. "She'll be happy, all right—if this poll can make her. There's twice as many women here as men. She'll get her vote, all right."

"Write thirty, anyway," I said.

Nicky didn't say anything. He just wrote. I wrote "Twenty-five." Then I crossed it out and wrote "Twenty-four."

One of the men at the table next to ours started collecting

the papers. "No use keeping the poor girl in suspense," he said. I could see what he had written on his paper. "Thirty-four."

"He's jealous," I told Nicky. "He can't bear to think she'd prefer a boy."

"It's not that," Nicky said. "It's us versus that ceiling, versus that tufted lid, trying to hold it up, keeping it from closing down on us. All of us, the boy *and* the woman. Defying it, squeezing out one more hour."

The man had made the rounds and put the little stack of papers, folded again, in front of the woman. She opened them slowly, as if afraid of what she might read, putting one to the left, one to the right of her glass. The stack on the right was soon much the higher. She didn't even bother to look at the last three or four slips, but leaned across the table, put her hand in the boy's. You couldn't hear a word she said, of course, but what her lips said as she leaned toward the boy was, "Yes . . . yes . . . yes."

"They'll be in Reno by midnight," Nicky said mock glumly, as they left.

I laughed. "In spite of you."

Nicky put his hand in mine. "Not in spite of *me*," he said. "I wrote twenty-two."

That was overdoing it. I know our ten years' difference shows, but I couldn't have borne it if he hadn't given her a vote of confidence.

"Ceiling unlimited," Nick said, lifting his glass to the elaborate coffin lid.

I looked up, and it really did seem as if the lid had lifted, that there was more space and time to live in. "Here's to their happiness," I answered. "And ours," I added under my breath. It's not a subject Nicky likes me to harp on.

Alive
and
Real

"See what the children are doing, will you, Meredith?"

Meredith Johnson sometimes had the unworthy suspicion that his wife thought up useless little tasks for him simply because the sight of him comfortably established and at ease while she still had work to do irritated her. Now, no sooner had he finished his Sunday lawn-mowing, fuchsia-watering, and car-washing, and settled himself in his deep chair by the radio, prepared to read and listen, than Alice called to him from the kitchen. After a little, above the clatter of her preparation of their late lunch, she called again.

"Meredith," she said, "Meredith."

Meredith made a slight noise in his throat to let Alice know he had heard her. Nothing, he hoped, either positive enough to commit him to any action or so contradictory that it might precipitate a discussion as to whether or not the children needed looking after. They didn't, he was certain. They were six and eleven years old, and what harm could possibly come to them on a twenty-acre suburban orange ranch, he could not imagine. Had they lived in the city, or had the ranch fronted on one of the busy boulevards, the situation would have been different, and no one, then, would have needed to remind him to keep an eye on them; but the orange grove was as safe as, or safer than, any wire-enclosed, sand-bottomed play yard, and besides, he had seen Tim, Sara, and the three Benton kids less than half an hour before, headed, with some contraption they had made, toward the arroyo at the back of the ranch.

He had stood holding the hose with which he was sprinkling the fuchsias and watched them until they, somehow aware of being watched, had hastily put a tree row between themselves and him. He thought he had never seen a picture that represented half so well childlike innocence and that complete absorption that only children can achieve as his two and the Benton three made, hurrying, brown-legged and shining-haired, down the quiet tree rows. Earlier, the May morning had been hazed over with a light shimmer of mist off the Pacific, but the sun had burned through it, leaving air, trees, even mockingbirds, towhees, and children—it seemed to him—unusually bright and fair.

The sun caught the fine spray from his hose and set it adazzle; hummingbirds darted toward it, uncertain whether it was flower or flood; drops hung from the hibiscus at the side door, more resplendent than jewels. The quiet Sunday morning lay like a calm hand upon the land. He, Alice, the children, the ranch, the morning itself, and the whole of their wonderfully lucky life together were, for the moment, caught up and suspended out of harm's way, a transparant and shining bubble.

Ordinarily, life was fragmentary. It was shreds and particles. It was tasks, obligations, worries, pleasures, all so mixed and, while each persisted, so sharp and pressing that one never caught sight of the whole life. Above all, it was not often that one was able to catch sight of oneself in the center of that small and satisfying world. The experience for Meredith Johnson was so unusual and so beautiful that he tried, by concentrating upon it, to prolong it. Remember, he told himself, remember. Remember the bubble, and inside it the five kids, your two lanky redheads and the Benton three, round and brown as buttons; remember the house and Alice in it, softly opening and shutting doors; remember the orchard, trim as a garden, and you yourself here sending this multicolored spray down onto the flowers. For a minute he was able to hold not only this vision of his own small world, but also the millions of others like it, stretching across the earth, all the beautiful, shining, private, early-morning bubbles of the earth's thousands of families. Then the children, with that sense of guilt that watching breeds in the watched, turned about suddenly, saw him, thrust whatever it was they were carrying in front of them, and darted behind a tree row.

The whole vision had broken down then. With that sudden movement, the fragments had returned; but even now, half an hour later, something of that feeling of wholeness still persisted, so that he wanted to sit quietly reflective, not go whooping about up and down the tree rows in order to be able to report to Alice whether the kids were playing the new game they had invented last week, called "I Patent the Jewels," or had reverted to their old stand-by of "Run Sheep Run."

He cocked an ear toward the kitchen and heard Alice moving about there once more, rhythmically, refrigerator door opened, refrigerator door closed, faucet on, faucet off, and he thought he could perhaps get his radio on quietly enough not to bring her in. He knew exactly which station he wanted, so there need be no hunting, nothing but the preliminary click and the smooth voice of Austin Loomis gaining in power as the radio warmed.

He clicked his radio on, and though there was actually no way this could be done more quietly at one time than at another, this, he thought, is one of the quietest clicks I ever managed. As Loomis' voice poured smoothly into the sunlit living room, he gentled its accustomed resonance to a kitten's purr. The actual dropping of the bomb was some hour or more away, but Loomis was already there, already describing with his easy but never merely facile eloquence the island, the peaceful Pacific waters surrounding it, the disposition of the doomed ships, even the reactions of the tethered and probably doomed goats.

Meredith Johnson was privately (except that he sometimes mentioned the fact to Alice) of the opinion that he had a sharper visual imagination than most people, and now he thought he could not have seen better had he been there what Loomis was describing so vividly: the sparkle of light on the white crests of breaking waves, the flash of planes overhead, the dark impassive growth of the tropical island. And he was able to feel, too, the waiting tension of all those gathered there: the young men (the doers) and the old men (the planners).

He supposed that perhaps unconsciously his awareness of what day this was had made, by contrast, the felicity of his moment of seeing so great. As a day of wind and rain makes the hearthside snugger, so knowledge of that experiment half across the Pacific had enhanced his own feelings of peace and safety. After a time he scarcely listened to Austin Loomis' voice at all. The sonorous words became no more than a dark, forbidding weather of the kind best suited to make his surroundings assume their most cheerful aspect.

Outside the big picture window, the palm fronds moved with the gentle, homesick sound of a gate closing. Meredith, listening, remembered the farm in Kansas where he had been born. They had had a gate weighted with window pulleys there which had had just such a melancholy creak when closed or opened. He hadn't heard the creak of that gate for twenty-five years; and when he had, at the age of ten, the sound hadn't seemed in the least melancholy. It had been, instead, very cheerful, saying, "Someone is coming," and, hearing it, he had sped to a window, if it were winter; or if it were summer, to the gate itself. Now the dry complaint of the palm fronds, the squeak of the remembered gate, the somber drone of massed planes, as Loomis enlivened his descriptions with some realistic sound effects, merged in Meredith's mind. Kansas, California, Bikini: they were all there together.

Listening and remembering, he had forgotten Alice, and she startled him when she came in from the kitchen, busy with her familiar postkitchen exercise of rubbing lotion onto her hands. She evidently had known all the time that he had not gone out to see about the children, for she glanced at him without surprise, then walked across to the picture window.

"Has it happened yet?" she asked.

Meredith had had no idea that Alice knew about the experiment.

"Half an hour more," he said, "if they're prompt."

Alice finished her hands and turned away from the window. "You'll just have time then to go out and see about the children." She sank down into the big chair by the window and let her head rest against the chair back.

"You tired, Alice?" Meredith asked.

She looked tired. She had a fair, oval face, which weariness easily smudged, and the soft skin appeared darkened now, almost dented, as if something in the day had bruised and hurt her.

"I don't know why I should be," she said. "I've put twelve cupcakes in the oven and one pot roast on the stove. Nothing in that to do in a healthy young woman." Alice smiled, and all the smudges were erased, and the dents were smoothed out.

Then she sighed, leaned back again in the chair, and folded her hands, as if with one hand she carried sympathy to the other.

"I do wish you'd go check up on the kids, though," she said, not opening her eyes.

"I don't know what in the world you think could happen to them," Meredith told her. "They're far safer out there than . . ."

Alice interrupted him. "I'd much rather go myself than argue about it. It would be a lot easier."

"Okay, okay," Meredith said, and snapped off the radio.

Now that he was going, Alice was ready to give in a little, too.

"I admit it's just curiosity on my part," she said, "but they're up to something, Tim and Sara and those Benton kids."

"Up to something," Meredith repeated in the tone parents keep for that special something.

"Oh, no," Alice said, "nothing like that. It's just that they've got my curiosity aroused with all their mumbo-jumbo and darting around hiding stuff."

"Hiding stuff?" Meredith remembered how quickly the children had got out of sight whatever it was they carried that morning.

"Something they've been making," Alice said.

"Well, there's no harm in that," Meredith told her. "Kids are always having secrets."

"I don't think there is any *harm* in it," Alice said. "I'm just curious. But Sara thinks there's harm in it. She wouldn't say her prayers last night. She said, 'I'm too wicked to pray to the Lord, Mama.' And she wasn't a bit happy about it either. You know how much Sara likes praying to the Lord."

Meredith did know. Whether this was because the Lord, of all the people Sara knew, was the only one who never said,

"Hush up for a minute, can't you, Sara?" he couldn't say, but Sara's nightly prayers were long and thorough.

"The poor kid," he said, and got to his feet. "They must really be up to something. I'll creep up on them."

"Oh, you don't need to creep," Alice told him. "They don't actually think we're able to see them, anyway. They'd carry this stuff they were working on—cardboard, strings, I don't know what all—about one-third hidden, right past me, as if either I couldn't see two feet beyond my nose or, if I could see, I wouldn't have sense enough to make out what they were up to."

"Maybe they're making kites," Meredith suggested.

"It'd take more than a kite to cut off those nightly talks of Sara's," Alice said. "No, it's something they think is wrong— but think we'll never catch on to. Because they don't believe we're actually real and alive. Us grown-ups," Alice explained, smiling at Meredith, "us parents."

Meredith stood up, slapped his thigh. "I'll teach those kids who's real and alive around here," he said. "I sure will."

"Well, hurry back," Alice told him, "or you'll miss it."

"Miss what?" Meredith had forgotten, for the moment.

"Oh," he said, remembering. "The big blast. Don't worry. I'll be back for that. I wouldn't miss it."

He went down the road for a distance before cutting in through the Benton orchard. In that way, without any creeping, he could come unobserved upon the children, where they did their usual playing, in the eucalyptus grove on the Benton side of the arroyo.

The day had turned very warm and still. He slowly walked down a tree row, sizing up the Benton crop as he went. It was lighter than his own, though there was not a thing in his own heavier set of oranges for which he could give himself credit.

He and Benton had exactly the same kind of soil, sprayed, fertilized, and irrigated at the same time, in the same way. It was just a piece of luck. Still, he rejoiced in it somewhat. It was a part of the morning's special pleasantness. Just as when he had watched his kids and Benton's, earlier, he had thought, I'm glad mine are the rangy redheads instead of those brown dumplings of Benton's.

At the far edge of the Benton orchard he was brought up by a sound, a sound that rippled his scalp a little. Had he been walking through an African jungle instead of a California orange grove, he would have thought himself about to come upon a small but earnest band of savages, chanting grace before they popped the missionary into the pot. What he heard, and stood listening the better to hear, was not singing; but then it was not speech either. It was a chant, he supposed, a child's approximation of the liturgical and ritualistic; and it was not so much the raw, thin, naked sound of the children's uncertain voices as something in their voices that stiffened the beard on his unshaved Sunday face.

Standing there in the quiet orchard, listening, he thought, Maybe the kids are right; maybe I'm not real. Then he did what he had said he would do. He crept up on the children, moving from tree to tree, whatever noise he made covered by the sound of their own ungodly and barbaric nonsense. He stopped not six feet from the children and, peering from behind a big ragged eucalyptus, was able to see them all plainly. There they stood, the five of them, his own Tim facing the other four and acting as some kind of conductor, or master of ceremonies, for their chorus of gibberish—if it was gibberish, for Meredith had too much to take in all at once to be certain about every detail. First he heard the children, then he began to see them, and last of all to see the object toward which the children lifted their strained, attentive faces. Seeing it, his first thought was that they were playing at lynching a man, for suspended from the lowest limb of one of the small eucalyptus trees was a cardboard man, or something in the shape of a man anyway, something with a trunk and head, with two arms and two legs—but with a tail, too, and horns; sharp, curved, evil, and unfaunlike horns.

Meredith Johnson caught his breath. This was no man. This was the Prince of Darkness himself. The cloven-hoofed devil, the Black Prince risen to power. This was devil worship and these were his communicants. No wonder small Sara had given over praying to the Lord.

Tim had about his neck a sacerdotal scarf, and he intoned the services from a small black notebook, and his congregation answered with frightened conviction; Sara, her face white, hands clenched; twelve-year-old Joanie Benton, her eyes narrowed, skin taut across her cheekbones; the two younger Bentons, round-eyed and sweating.

"Most holy devil," his congregation quavered in reply.

"Prince of Darkness."

"Prince of Darkness" came the shrill echo.

"Ruler of earth."

"Ruler of earth."

"And all above the earth." Tim's voice cracked here a little, and there was a slight break in the rhythm of the service, but the children whispered, "And all above the earth."

"Most holy devil."

Meredith gazed in pity. Perhaps it was funny, this devil worship, but he didn't think so, and it certainly wasn't funny to the kids. He remembered how, when he had been younger than Tim, he had himself made a brief trial of tree worship. The tree he had chosen had been a grisly old black locust, the sole tree left standing in what was called, because of it, the "tree field," on that distant Kansas farm. He had gone out at dusk, knelt down, and said, "Our tree which art on earth, hallowed be thy roots and branches, thy treedom come. . . ."

It had almost killed him, that prayer to the tree, and afterward he had been sick at his stomach and had lain on the ground and hoped that God would smite him so that the memory of his unfaithfulness might be blotted out. Still, it had been a trial he felt he must make, a thing he must find out about God and trees, no matter how much he suffered. And it hadn't been funny, and if what the kids were doing now was funny, then death was funny, and sin, and the worn-out heart, and the broken earth.

"Most holy devil," the children answered.

"In dust . . ."

"In dust . . ."

"We humble ourselves before thee."

In dust they humbled themselves, Tim leading them. They went down on their knees with the sudden bonelessness of children and laid their foreheads in the dust.

As the children so abased themselves, Meredith moved forward to say something, do something—just what, he was not sure, but something that would put an end to their painful play-acting.

What he did do he was not then, or ever afterward, able to account for; he was not able to understand what in himself or the day could possibly have prompted him to step behind that cardboard figure so that when the children lifted their heads from the dust, they saw not the harmless devil of their own construction but a new devil, a devil alive and real—one whose gaping mouth was filled with sharp white teeth and whose empty eye sockets framed eyes bright and menacing.

But unexplainable as it was, that was what he did, and that was why the children, his own two and the Benton three, screamed so on that fine Sunday afternoon.

64

I'll Ask
Him to
Come
Sooner

At five-thirty the pressure of the day in a sanatorium is at its greatest. The day's routine is over, but the night with its routine has not yet come, and there is left a bare, uninhabited space in which the mind cannot live with ease. It would seem, Flory thought, that all of us together, wishing, desiring ardently, could push the clock's hands ahead, could accelerate the sun—but no, the next hour and a half, when the sad day that began so long ago, in darkness, with the night nurse making her final rounds, is not yet ended, must be endured.

Flory's supper tray still rested on the bed, pinning the bed-clothes across her thighs. She lay looking at the respectable curves they made. A year ago they were planks, two-by-fours, now they looked like young trees, solid and rounded. A year ago, she thought, I was sick, much sicker than I knew, but I was good, and I was believing—and now, whom do I believe in? Whom trust? Not myself, surely.

A year ago, far advanced tuberculosis had meant nothing to her. It simply sounded like the ultimate of its kind, and that of course was what she had always wanted in everything—A plus on her papers, jumbo olives, the forty-foot diving plat-

65

form, fires that roared to the chimney top. When she had arrived at the Vineyard, she had felt infinitely scornful of those in bed with incipient t.b., and those with moderately advanced cases were as dull as ditch water to her—tepid, tepid. She had believed the thing to do was to be desperately ill, hopeless indeed—go to bed, obey the doctor's orders, and get up cured. And by some miraculous chance, that was about the way she had done it. Oh, Jesus, she thought, how foolish and believing I was then, and how sick and how good.

The doors of the nurse's dining room began to bang. Bates never pretended that this t.b. business was anything but hell for all of them. Bates's attitude, indeed, was that the patients had a slightly better time than she, for they, by one exit or another, often escaped, got clear of the Vineyard Sanatorium completely, while she stayed on.

She trod in, a solid clump-clump. No tippy-toes or whispers for her. "Well, Miss Shaw," she said, "I see there wasn't any of this delicious meal you could resist. Stewed tomatoes, baked potatoes, tapioca pudding, all down the hatch. I thought Herman did a particularly good job on the tapioca tonight, didn't you? Every fish eye as transparant and rubbery as in life."

Flory wished she could say, "Bates, stay with me. Stay till seven. I need you, Bates, until a little after seven"—but she couldn't do that. The sanatorium recognized only physical needs. Bates would stay if she had a hemorrhage, or if her pleurisy needed taping; but this—this other didn't exist for Bates and the Vineyard.

"Bates," she said, "can't anything be done about the time from supper until seven? Couldn't it just be done away with, Bates? Couldn't we just eat our suppers and then have it night, time for bed lights and books?"

"That time," Bates said, matter-of-fact as ever, "is for you to rest in. That's what you're here for, Miss Shaw. Complete bed rest. No TV's then, no books, no writing—rest, and if you like that sort of thing, think."

But what about, Flory wondered. What are we to think about? Remembering is not for us—to recall a life other than this, the life we had before, when— Oh, no, no. It is too painful, it is scalding. And to plan. What can we plan? As far as the next X ray. That is as far as we can get in planning, and to do that takes a crazy optimism; we all die between X rays. There is only this world, this little private world of the sanatorium, of the present, that it is safe to think about. And it isn't safe for me any longer.

"What do you think about, Bates?" she asked.

"Well," said Bates, "I was thinking about the lobster I had last night at Lucca's—and about going home to Maine this summer."

"Remembering and planning," Flory said. "Remembering and planning."

"If you've finished with that tray, Miss Shaw," Bates said, "I'll take it along. This is Wednesday night, you know—husbands' night. I've got to get all the wives into their best bed jackets. The husbands will all be here at seven sharp—all except Marguerite Delaney's; he'll be late, as usual, I suppose."

Flory laid her hand across her eyes and held her mouth firm.

Bates stood with the tray deftly balanced. "All you spinsters lie here and pine on Wednesday nights, I suppose, at the sounds of billing and cooing going on. But you're really damned lucky. Not a wife here doesn't have an eight o'clock temp on Wednesday evenings."

"Yes, that's right," Flory managed to say. "We lie here and pine, but we're damned lucky."

"You don't look it," Bates said, and went out, catching the screened door neatly with her toe so that it closed without sound. When she had gone, the heavy silence of the after-supper hour settled down like ashes about the sanatorium, until it was buried deep as any Pompeii. Soundless as any Pompeii, forgotten as any Pompeii.

Flory lay neatly in her bed, her supple brown hands on top of the blue spread, loose and easy, her breath coming evenly from the diaphragm, as she'd been taught, and tried to send her mind into paths where no pain lay. If any such be left to me, she thought. Through the great glassless windows of her room she could see the homeward-bound cars thread the boulevard of the valley below—black rods of movement, they were, from that height, like tubercle bacilli moving along some super-bronchial tract. Must I see everything in terms of disease, she thought. And then for a moment, noting the homeward-bound cars, she saw her own apartment as it had been at five-thirty, when her workday had ended: the curtains, lifting, lifting in the languid little wind that blows down city streets at that hour; the sun gilding her books; a few petals dropped, while she had been away, from the apple blossoms her mother had brought in from the ranch. Her apartment—ah, but it was hers no more, the books packed, the flower bowls empty, stacked in some dusty box. She was gone out of that world of the living to this middle world, this place where you could look neither forward nor backward, this place where even the present had become intolerable to her, this September evening, this husbands' night.

When I first came, Flory thought, I believed in everything. When Dr. Hedges brought me my X rays and had to pull my blind down at the head of my bed so that I could see them properly, he always put his hand on my breast to balance himself—and I always decided it was an accident and was embarrassed for him. And when the janitor boy said he would put a special mixture on my floor for two dollars a month extra, I believed him and paid it.

I thought I would make friends here, too—yes, I believed even that. I knew no better. The first winter in the infirmary, where none of us ever left our beds, the others were only voices, only a variety of coughs. Then, when the rains were past and our beds were pushed onto the long porch, I saw the faces behind the called messages, the coughs choked down, the midnight crying.

Helen Morton, from Virginia, whose face was as soft, gentle, and dusky as her voice. Helene Broka, with her little snubbed-up hazelnut face, laughing, laughing, and saying, "You'd have thought they'd have thought of the sour grapes that would be picked here when they called this the Vineyard Sanatorium." And Laura, with her tender, eager brown eyes, who was determined to live. Laura, who was so reasonable, who never complained, drank twice the amount of milk required, and never once lifted the heavy bag of shot from her chest. But she didn't understand she wasn't living in a reasonable world, or fighting a reasonable disease. Felice, Laura's opposite, her red hair and feverish blue eyes blazing. "To hell with the rules," she'd say. "Where have they ever got us? What He most enjoys"—He wasn't God, but some power, evidently more powerful than God, who planted t.b. in people's lungs—"is to see us follow the rules, deny ourselves everything, and get worse and worse."

I didn't know any better than to make friends with them all, love them all. Then I got stronger and stronger—every picture better, sed rate going down and down, cavities closing—and every single advance was like a disloyalty to them; was like marching ahead and leaving wounded companions behind. They were happy for me, but there was a shadow in their eyes when they said the congratulatory words, as if I had selfishly grabbed something of which there wasn't enough to go around. No, they couldn't get well with me, but I had to die with each of them, each one.

And even then I didn't learn. When I left the infirmary, when I came here to Culbertson, when I could walk every noon to the dining hall for my dinner, then you would have thought, wouldn't you, that the time had come to be a little realistic, a little literal?

But no, then I had to talk with Marguerite, to long to do something for her. I walked by her room every day on my way to dinner. I noticed her first because of the beautiful bed jackets and dressing gowns she wore. All red—every shade of red; deep velvety reds, almost black; orange reds like changing leaves; pink reds like a cat's tongue. They were so beautiful and brilliant you hardly noticed the girl inside them. She was so pale it was almost as if she wasn't, and I wondered at her wearing them. Blood reds in a sanatorium where there is already too much sight of red. Usually she had her hair braided back from her face, but once in a while it lay uncombed on her pillow, a great fan-shaped swirl of black silk. She used to smile at me as I went by, and then one day she said, "Hello," and I sat down for a minute to talk to her.

"I've been noticing your beautiful bed jackets," I said. "They're gorgeous. You must like red."

"No," she said in that little whispering voice she used not to stir up a cough, "it's my husband who likes red. I wear them for him. I hate red. You know how it is when you have fever—you like cool colors. Mist blue, mint green. Don't those colors sound good to you—and cool?"

"Yes," I said, and noticed her face had, already so early in the day, the transparent white of high fever. "But red's a good color for your hair."

70

"That's what Delaney says."

"Delaney?" I asked.

"My husband."

"That's an unusual name."

"Oh—it's his last name. His first name's . . . well, he doesn't like it . . . so everyone calls him Delaney. I wish Delaney could see you."

"Why?" I asked.

"Because you look so well. Delaney says it's foolish to stay here—that I'm thinner every time he sees me. But I think I ought to stay. The doctor says it's my only chance. Though I don't want to, of course. It would be a lot easier to give up and go home with Delaney. I worry about him."

"Isn't he well?" I wanted to know.

"Delaney, sick!" She started to laugh, but a cough stopped her. I tried not to see or listen as she used her sputum cup. "No, it's not that," she said. "He comes up every Wednesday night. You must have seen him—he has to walk by your room to get here."

"Maybe," I said, "but I wouldn't know him."

"He's the best looking one," she said, and managed a little twinkle. I thought then that was just a thing wives say—here in the san, where a male anchor in the outside world might seem their only hold on reality. I didn't know it was the literal truth, an understatement. Not here alone, not here alone, Delaney, is your face most beautiful.

"You were pretty sick when you came here, weren't you?" she asked.

Yes. Yes. Now I knew what to say—exactly. When I first came, my greatest joy was to watch those fat, those stalwart ones walk down the path to the dining room and to be told the story of their progress—she came with two cavities; she had empyema for six months; she's had a thoracoplasty—and then,

71

then to see them waddle and laugh. They were the articles of my faith.

"Yes," I told her, "yes, I was."

"How much did you weigh then?"

"A hundred and three."

That made her gasp. "Really," she said, "really. Were you a hemorrhage case?"

She was. I'd been told.

"Yes," I said, "yes, I was," and felt like a veteran with wound stripes.

"And now?"

"Nothing for a year."

"Not even streaking?"

"No, nothing."

Her little face, almond-shaped, and pale, like an almond blanched, somehow became focused, concentrated itself, came forward out of hopelessness into living. I was her faith made manifest. Her belief, living, breathing, in a blue robe. "Stay here, get well." Ah, it could be done—it had been done.

"I wish Delaney could see you," she said again. "It's so hard to stay here when your husband wants you to come home. To think you should stay and yet . . ." She broke off. "But it wouldn't do any good to get well and then find out . . ." No, she couldn't say it. "It's so hard for Delaney to get up here. Wednesday nights are the only time he can come. He works every day, and Sunday he always plays golf. He has to think of his health, too, you know. Oh, it's awfully tedious for him, and sickness upsets him so."

I began to hate this Delaney. Crazy name. Upsetting Marguerite, dividing her mind, dressing her in red. Jesus, Jesus, I'd like to tell that handsome boy a thing or two, I thought.

How long afterward was it when I had my stiff neck? It doesn't matter. It was almost seven, I know, and I lay trying to lose myself in the movement of the leaf shadows across my white wall, anything so as not to look forward—into uncertainty—or backward—into the lost, when Bates came in.

"I'll massage your neck," she said. "I've got a few minutes. Why didn't you tell me? I wouldn't have known anything about it if Mrs. Delaney hadn't mentioned it."

"It's nothing," I said. "How's Marguerite this evening?"

"Worse every day," she said. "I've just finished helping her get ready to put on her act for her husband."

"Act?" I asked.

"You know—make-up, quilted red velvet bed jacket, perfume, nails done. He wants his senses titillated. All five of them. And she's fool enough to want to do it for him."

She kneaded my neck with her hard fingers until I sweated with pain—but I was glad even for a stiff neck, some harmless pain which could be thought about without danger. At seven the husbands began to arrive—most of them had been waiting below at the gardener's cottage for the gates to open—and within five or six minutes there were no more footsteps on the graveled paths, only a murmur of conversation from the rooms about me, and an occasional baritone laugh, forced and abrupt.

Until suddenly there was a woman's sob, a great, heavy, racking cry, as if a sorrow had been held back until it had mounted into a wave no barrier could resist. Crying is no novelty here—even that anguished cry, I thought I had heard before.

"God damn that Delaney," Bates said.

"Is that Marguerite?" I asked. "Is he making her cry?"

"Yes," Bates said. "Making her cry as he does every Wednesday night by being late. She gets all dressed, and waits and waits. Listens to every footstep, sees the others go by. They only have an hour together anyway—and he's always fifteen to thirty minutes late. By the time he gets here, she's cried all her make-up off, is coughing so she has to use her sputum cup every other word. And Delaney doesn't like that, so he sits and looks at her coldly."

"Does his work keep him?" I asked. "Is there any reason?"

"No reason except his damn cursed selfishness," Bates said evenly. "He's some electric company official. Worked up from a lineman, Mrs. Delaney said. Used to shinny up poles. It's God's pity he didn't fall off one."

Every time Marguerite's crying quickened, Bates pinched my neck muscles harder—but I didn't mind. I felt just as she did.

Then a black Porsche came through the Vineyard gates and swung into a vacant place among the cars at the foot of the hill. A tall man jumped out, and by the time the car door slammed, he was up half a dozen steps.

"That's Delaney," Bates said. "Pretty early for him."

I sat up in bed; he had to walk past my window to get around the corner to Farnsworth, where Marguerite lay. After he climbed the steps, he was out of sight under the wisteria pergola until he came out just across from my room. It was August then, and the evening light, though it had lost all color, was as clear as shadowless water. Delaney came through it like a shadow himself, dark as night, dark as Marguerite. He was all in white, a white rough sweater, and white ducks, as if he'd been playing tennis. By some chance he was looking directly into this room, directly at me. He didn't smile or lower his eyes, but gazed and gazed—and so did I.

"Well," said Bates when he had passed, "selfish-looking bastard, isn't he?"

"Yes," I said. "Yes, he is." And he was. He had that fine, indrawn look of one who thinks of himself alone, a look of reality and concentration. None of himself was lost in regard for others, but all adhered closely about a central core of self-regard. Those who go about loving others, suffering for a cat smashed by a roadside, or a town bombed, or a man imprisoned, lose something of themselves. They spread themselves thin, loving—and suffering. Ah, but not Delaney, not Delaney; he was solid—solid and real. Solid in this separate world where almost everyone, through sympathy, loses his identity.

But I hated him, too. As much as Bates. Hated him for making Marguerite suffer. For I am a tubercular, and all tuberculars are, in a sense, in league together against those who are well.

Yes, I hated that easy, domineering stride, the black curly hair, the crooked nose, the long torso of the wrestler, the feet toeing in a little—even though these were the things I had always loved most in a man. I hated them in this selfish Delaney.

Wednesday evening after Wednesday evening I heard Marguerite crying—and Wednesday evening after Wednesday evening I saw this black Delaney come striding casually, giving me long, slow looks as he went by. And I gave him long looks in return, looks that said, You selfish beast, don't think that I don't see through you and scorn you—late to your wife and eying another woman as you come.

"Look," I said one night to Bates, when it was almost too dark to see Delaney go by. "Some night I'm going out and give Delaney a punch in the nose. Yes, I am. I'll give him another dent in that crooked nose of his. I'll trip him as he comes up the steps, push him over, and he can lie there in the dark with a broken leg and learn what it means to lie and suffer alone."

"You seem to think a lot about Delaney."

"No," I told her. "No, it's Marguerite I think about. I talk to her almost every day, you know. She cries so much. She's so thin. Someday, Bates, you'll go to her room and find only bones, bird-thin bones inside her long red robe. That's all you'll find, Bates. That and her long black hair. And it will be because none of us has cared enough to help her."

"Help her?" Bates asked. "How could we help her? I get her into her red bed jackets every Wednesday evening. I dampen her mascara. I brush her hair. I tell her to take it easy."

"It's not that, Bates," I said. "She'll die dolled up as fast as dowdy. Someone's got to tell Delaney to come sooner. That's what she can't bear—waiting for him. Lying there waiting for him. Thinking every step she hears is his, rising to it, brightening her eyes, all of her blood gone to her ears to listen—and then the footsteps going by. I'm going to ask him to come sooner, Bates. I've been thinking about it. I'm going to ask him."

And Bates said, "I can see you've been thinking about it—you tell it as if you were the one who was doing the waiting."

It was something to think about—and I had thought about it. How I would hear his car grind to a stop on the gravel, late. Hear the door bang, the footsteps of a man hurrying, whose weight never touches his heels, and how I would be hiding in the deep shadow of the pergola—gotten out of my room without a single nurse's missing me. How I would take the edges of his coat in my hands (he wore a coat now the nights were cooler). I would take the rough coat edges close enough to my mouth so that he could hear me whisper, "Listen, Delaney, you must come sooner." I thought about it a thousand times. I learned to fill the time between supper and seven with it. I would do it for Marguerite. I never got further in my thinking than to say, "You must come sooner, Delaney." After that the picture blurred, the film broke.

But still I didn't do it—though every night I heard Marguer-

ite cry, I said, "I'll ask him to come sooner." Then my new
X ray showed no progress since the last one—fibrosis standing
still; and next door in Olney the engineer from South America
died. He'd only been here two months—and had malaria as
well as tuberculosis—but he'd seemed well until his terminal
hemorrhage. He waved to me when he sat up while the nurse
made his bed. He'd sent me over some of his books and I'd
sent him *Bliss* and *The Garden Party*, and I'd planned how,
when we were both better—oh, yes, I was a little in love with
him, not having said a word to him, having seen only his sun-
blackened face, his sun-bleached hair. But you must love someone here, be real to someone besides yourself. Then, the whole
of one night, the lights on in his room, the cars coming and
going on the driveway below—and in the morning his mattress
and pillows hanging out of a window in the sun. And that
evening Marguerite crying and crying, waiting for Delaney's
footsteps.

All week I thought about it. Death touching all about me,
and I not lifting a finger to stop it, as apart from life as if it
had already left me. So I said a week ago, "Tonight, tonight
I'll tell him to come sooner." I was waiting in the pergola, just
as I'd planned, deep in the shadows where the wisteria leaves
are still thick overhead. I heard the car door slam and the footsteps springing just as I had known I would hear them; and
just as I had known I would, I pulled his face down close so
that I could whisper, "Delaney, you must come sooner." His
hands against the small of my back were heavy, and when he
held me close against him, he was as solid and real as I had
known he would be, and his face against mine was as I had
felt it before—in a dream, perhaps. "Sooner?" he said. "Sooner?
It's you who are late. I've waited weeks."

There was a sound of cars on the driveway below. Flory sat

77

up in bed. "Oh," she said. "Bates ought to stay with me tonight until a little after seven. I need her until after seven." But even while talking to herself, she was getting out of bed, getting into her dressing gown, and listening, listening for the sound the Porsche would make as it slid to a stop on the graveled parkway of the san.

Hunting
for
Hoot
Owls

I remember the exact hour at which George accomplished what he had set out to do two years before. We were living where we do now, in Saskatchewan. It was three-thirty on the afternoon of Thursday, October 28, 1958. In this latitude, at that hour and in that month, it was almost night and nearly winter. There was still light, of course, but it slanted in like the indirect lighting of modern homes with nothing visible to proclaim its source. It was a clear cool light, compact, as if shrunken by the cold. There were still a few bleached leaves on the willows down by the lake; not many, and the few that were left were dropping fast. There was no wind, and the leaves dropped straight down as if weighted with lead. It made me feel deaf to hear no sound when they landed.

I remember all this so distinctly, I suppose, because of what George said when he opened the door. I had been standing at the window of the living room (also bedroom, dining room, and, at the far end, kitchen) watching George come up the path from the spring. The lake, at the upper end, was freezing over, and, as it did so, more and more small animals came down to the spring to drink. The spring, too, would soon freeze, but meanwhile George had gone up after lunch to box it in so that for the time it lasted it would be a little clearer than what we had been drinking.

Even though I didn't then know what George was going to say when he came in, I gazed at him like a mind reader filled with premonitions. I mean I really looked at him. After thirty-five years of marriage, a wife only occasionally sees her husband. This doesn't mean that he's as unexciting as the furniture, any more than that he's one with the stars. It does mean that most eyes, after a certain amount of seeing husbands, be it of furniture or stars, no longer see with much curiosity or attention.

But I really saw George that afternoon, as he came up the pathway. It was the change of background that made him visible. In Southern California amidst other school men, George didn't stand out—but here under the immense gloomy trees, with the black lake behind him, George looked terribly human, noble even. Carrying his tools, whistling "Annie Laurie" under a sky threatening snow, ringed round by the trees which constantly watched us, George looked accomplished, and daring, to me.

George came in, put down saw, hammer, and the coffee can in which he had carried the nails. Then he took off his mackinaw and hung it on *its* peg beside the door. (*Its* peg because when you live in one room you have to be orderly; otherwise, socks turn up in the coffeepot, and the coffeepot turns up in bed. Such confusion may be exhilarating for the young, but at our age George and I find it ugly.) So the mackinaw went on *its* peg. Then George, like an Enoch Arden returning after a twenty-year absence, took a solemn searching around the room. Satisfied with his inspection, he went to the front window, folded his arms, and gazed out toward the lake.

"Agnes," he asked, "do you know what day this is?"

I knew. But I forestalled his saying the word I didn't want to hear. "Thursday, October 28, 1958," I told him.

George paid no attention to this. "Boxing in the spring was the last job I had in mind to do."

"Fine," I said, and hurried on. "Before I forget it, the Clasbys called. They want you to call back."

We have few neighbors, and the few are far away and mostly without phones. A phone call is an event.

George ignored the Clasbys' call. He turned away from the window and faced me; and he was bound, I knew then, to say the word I didn't want to hear.

"Agnes," George said, "what I set out to do two years ago is now done. I am now a retired man."

Now that's a simple word, and I suppose it occurs at least once in every issue of every newspaper and magazine published in the United States. And I know, too, that there are plenty of wives who don't, for various reasons, like the sound of that word. Some don't want to live on less money. Others don't want to be excluded from the social affairs that hinge upon their husband's jobs. And almost all, after being conditioned for forty years to their husband's absence, are made nervous by the prospect of having to live with him again. And this is perfectly natural. What would husbands think if *wives* suddenly announced that they were retiring from their housekeeping jobs and would, hereafter, spend the day with him in the office? The prospect would make a lot of husbands very uneasy, and nothing a wife could say about "greater companionship" or "time for her to let up a bit" would reassure him. Office routines, he'd feel sure, would just go to hell. Well, the home has its routines, too.

None of these fears bothered me about George's retirement. Since the death of George's mother, money has been no problem for us. The social affairs a school man's job open to him are duties for his wife rather than pleasures. A school man's wife is accustomed to having the P.-T.A. ladies, Junior Rally Committees, Citizens' Advisory Councils, members of the Tax-payers' League, the Scholastic Society, the Latin Forum, and winning basketball teams around the house; so she, unlike other wives, is no need of being rehabilitated for a life with others after forty years in solitary. She has been well prepared for togetherness. Retirement will simply cut down on the numbers.

What she isn't prepared for, or what I wasn't prepared for, when George announced at the age of fifty-eight that he intended to give up his job at the end of the year, was the picture this called up of George's past life. George didn't have to retire; his contract had three years to run; a committee of representative citizens had waited upon him asking him *not* to retire. Still he was determined to give up his job.

"I will finish out this year only," George told them, "and that ends it."

To me, it was as if he had said, "I will commit suicide in seven months." Not that life without work seems suicide to me. But to retire in your prime from your life's work? What does that say? It says that you haven't been with your life's work, that you've sold your life like a bag of groceries. Oh, it's the saddest thing in the world, I think, this desire men have to escape their jobs. Sadder than death or disease, because these come to us without our choosing; and our work, we have chosen. That's why I didn't want to hear George say the word. That word meant that George had suffered in his work. It meant that he'd made a bad bargain, underestimated his powers, or misunderstood them, miscalculated our needs. Forty years at the heart of his life gone by! George had traded his life for his living.

82

I suppose I should have been glad, this being so, to hear that George was escaping, that he was throwing off his chains. Instead, I couldn't bear to know that they had existed.

"Retirement," I said to George two years ago, "is death without burial."

"No," George said. "Retirement is resurrection after death."

Death! This gave me a sick feeling under the heart. George had complained on occasion. Who doesn't? I do, and I've loved my life as wife and housekeeper. But I had no idea that what he had been doing every day was something he longed to escape from.

I said, "George, wouldn't you feel downcast to discover that I've hated the housework, the cooking and cleaning and washing and bedmaking I've done all my life?"

"Yes," he said, "I would."

"It's the same for me with you."

"No, it isn't. Work's no curse for women."

"But it is for men?"

"Certainly. Didn't you ever read the Bible? Childbearing is woman's curse. And they've got a built-in retirement clause for that. Men have to decide for themselves when they're through."

"Women are *sad* to be through."

"Would you like to be pregnant now?"

"At my time of life . . ."

"Exactly the way I feel," George said, "at my time of life, still holding down a job."

We had had a vacation house on Lake McClintick for ten years and had spent at least a month there every summer. It was to this cabin George had planned to retire; and it was here, with the spring boxed in, that George had declared himself, on October 28, 1958, to be, in fact, and according to plan, retired.

Now this was certainly something for which I had been prepared. What George said was scarcely news; nevertheless, I felt shock, the same kind of shock I experienced when my mother, who had had a long sickness, finally died. I had expected her death for two years, but when she finally ceased to breathe I could not accept the change. Death, I knew all about; but not a world in which my own mother did not return me look for look. It was the same with George. After he said those words, though I was prepared for them, I felt as a woman might who sees her husband for the first time after he's entered a monastery. He looks the same, but he is not the same. He has renounced something. Now I don't want to romanticize the two of us, George and Agnes, into another Abelard and Héloïse. I hadn't lost George as Héloïse lost Abelard, but the man without a job was not the husband I had known.

I don't know what George felt that evening. I should have asked him. But the strangeness of his being without work embarrassed me. It didn't seem delicate to speak of it. Perhaps he expected a celebration of some kind, a ceremony even. He had refused the usual farewell retirement banquet at home. Perhaps this was the time for it. We had creamed chipped beef and hot soda biscuits that night for supper. Dessert was canned pears. Really a little less than I usually manage. We finished supper, did the usual chores, read a little, and went to bed. We forgot to call the Clasbys. That was the first night I imitated the hoot owls.

Since September these big downy birds, more silent in movement than snow, had begun, in the deepening cold of the autumn nights, to call each other from the treetops. Actually, I don't know whether they were in the tops of trees or not. I never saw one, except at dusk, when there is still as much green as black in the darkness, and then the owls were flying. You see them by chance when they glide overhead, noiseless as clouds. But in the night they make up for all this quiet evening gliding with a bombardment of hoots; and they *sound* then as if they were in the tops of trees. I don't know why they hoot; whether they are courting, or complaining of the cold, or simply conversing. They *are* conversing, whatever the subject. One owl calls, then waits for an answer before speaking again. The answer comes, and so the conversation goes on. The sound they make is deep and hollow. It seems mixed with feathers. They are doing, I suppose, what I had heard coyotes do in Southern California. But the coyote's voice is lean, filled with sand and dryness and the big stretch of the deserts. The owls sound northern and are hemmed in by the millions of trees, and their voices have the soft echoing roar that a sound-absorbent ceiling gives.

I knew George wasn't asleep on that first night of his official retirement. We sleep in a double bed, and he was too unmoving to be asleep. So I didn't have to worry about waking him. I hadn't known that I had been wanting to imitate a hoot owl; but surely I must have wanted to do so for a long, long time; otherwise it wouldn't have seemed so absolutely necessary and natural to shape my throat and make an accurate owl call. Nor such a relief to do so.

My success amazed me. Could I, if I had attempted it, have been doing this all my life? Had I, from the beginning, had this power? Not only was my imitation accurate, but it had carrying power; for after the same wait owl gives owl, I was, miracle of miracles, answered. I didn't press my luck, though. I was excited enough to have kept on hooting all night. But owls don't do that, I thought; and if I was going to imitate owls, I was determined to do it right.

Next morning, as if in recognition of all the night's other transformations, the earth itself was transformed. Snow had fallen, and yesterday's world had vanished. We were in the midst of something new. In any case, with the new snow, with my excitement over the discovery of my unexpected ability, I didn't think as much as I had expected to about George's altered state. Also, while we were still at the breakfast table, the Clasbys called again.

I answered, and Ed Clasby said they had intended running over to our place for a little advice, but since their car had broken down, could we come to their place? I wondered why we couldn't advise them on the phone, but Ed urged, "if it wasn't too much trouble," that we come over.

The Clasbys, Ed and Edie, were young people in their thirties with three stair-step children, one to five, and an older boy of nine. Ed worked at the motel at the other end of the lake, which put up sportsmen, mostly fishermen, during the season. The place closed the first of October, and I don't know what Ed had been accustomed to doing in the winter. It was about what he was going to do *this* winter that he wanted to see us.

I always had the feeling that the Clasbys should have lived someplace where it was warmer, where it mattered less if the glass fell out of a window or a shoe sole wore through. They needed some hounds under the porch and a jug of corn likker to pass round. The Clasbys themselves appeared to feel no lack of hounds, windowpanes, or jugs. No one could have been more hospitable. Everyone in Saskatchewan keeps a pot of coffee on the back of the stove all day long and puts a cup in your hand the minute you set a foot inside the door. But in no other home do you have to step across, around, and over such a welter of misplaced articles. (I take it that *anything* on the floor except rugs, furniture, and feet is misplaced.) And the Clasbys really welcome you.

There they stood in the midst of disaster, as any housekeeper judges disaster, able to concentrate on welcoming their guests.

I accord them the same admiration I would give to persons carrying on in spite of cyclone and hurricane.

Ed Clasby put a cup in my hands before I could get my mittens off. Maybe Ed really does hail from the Deep South. When I try to recall his voice, I hear the sweet prolonged relish for his own words that characterizes Southerners.

"It sure was good of you folks to make a trip on a morning like this. Don't think I don't appreciate it. Cletus, ram another stick of firewood in the cookstove." Cletus was the nine-year-old.

Ed and Edie looked alike; rather as if, not too far back in the pedigree of each, there had been a seal—the furred sea animal, I mean. The three stair steps were the same. Only Cletus showed a lack of seal blood. Some of his extra-human, washed-out appearance was no doubt the result of being surrounded by all those soft brown eyes, masses of soft brown hair, and plump softly sloping shoulders. Cletus was built like an icicle made of skimmed milk. He had broomstraw hair and wore it jagged, like an Italian actress. He was perfectly silent, but completely present. Cletus, as it turned out, was the reason we were there.

Ed came right to the point. He had the offer from a brother-in-law to go in with him in the air-taxi service the brother-in-law was setting up. Not only would this be to Ed's financial advantage, but Ed considered himself a natural mechanic. Being separated from engines had been for him, he said, the same as a musician's being separated from his violin or a jockey from his horse. I could see that this might be so, for, as Ed talked, he was tinkering with something out of his car. His fingers knew it so well he could work and talk at the same time, the way some women can knit and talk. What he was working on was the reason his car wouldn't run. Magneto, carburetor, distributor? I don't know. Anyway, something fair-sized and detachable. He had started working outside the night before and had had the car pretty well stripped down when dark came. Then, during the night, the snowstorm! He had left everything out there, as was his habit with engines, he said, in apple-pie order. It wasn't any trick locating his distributor, if that was what it was; but the smaller things were another story, to hell and gone under six inches of snow. He couldn't rake or sweep the snow away, he said (maybe he just didn't want to be bothered), because he'd send cotter pins and spark plugs flying. I'm making up the names of these small objects out there under the snow. I could write Ed; or, if I didn't intend to keep this away from George until I've finished, ask him, and get the proper names. But I don't think it matters. Engines probably have hundreds of namable small parts. So do human beings; but who bothers, in writing of men and women, with listing all of their bones, glands, and organs? This may be the machine age, but I don't feel inclined to do for an engine what I wouldn't do for a person.

In any case, the point is that most of those parts *were* still out there under the snow, and that when Ed wanted another he said, "Cletus, fetch me in a right-handed swivel bar." And Cletus would go out, and in a few minutes return with whatever it was Ed had asked for. Or at least I judge so, for never once did Ed say, "Cletus, didn't you hear me say a *right-handed* swivel bar?" Ed just took whatever Cletus handed him and went on with his knitting. I didn't give any thought to what Cletus did outside, because, while he was running and fetching, Edie was talking to me about their problems and telling me why it was they had asked us over.

But George interrupted our conversation. He was standing at a window, looking out into the yard. "Excuse me, Mrs. Clasby," he said, "but I want Agnes to see something."

88

I went to him, and George said, "Look at that boy out there, Agnes."

The thermometer stood at twenty and there was no sun. But out there in the snow, with no coat on, Cletus was fishing around in the snow as calm as a boy on the seashore in mid-summer. "Fish" is the wrong word. He wasn't fishing. First, he sized up the snow at his feet in a businesslike way, then he put his hand under it, made one or two delicate moves, and pulled up something. He never pulled up something and had a look at it. He looked, felt, pulled, and started for the house with what he had.

"He works like a surgeon, doesn't he?" George asked.

"More like a magician," I said, for I had my doubts, for all his boasting, that Ed had left the car's innards in any very predictable pattern, kidneys opposite each other, stomach in the middle, and so on.

"In any case," George said, as Cletus brought up something the size of a darning needle, "that's a remarkable performance we're watching."

In spite of the performance, when Ed and Edie got around to their reason for wanting to see us, George said he'd have to think it over. What they wanted was for us to take care of Cletus while Ed teamed up with his brother-in-law in the air-taxi business. The reasons they gave for wanting to leave Cletus with us were understandable and even humane. There were no schools at Lucknow, where they were going, and it seemed a pity to take Cletus out of school. And there was an even more understandable reason. Cletus was no child of theirs. He was not even a relation. Ed's brother had married a divorced woman with a child, Cletus. The mother had run away from Ed's brother; and Ed's brother, who didn't care after that whether he lived or died, died. And in a most unfortunate way.

He walked, whether on purpose or not, into a saw in the plywood factory where he worked. He was cut in two, Ed said, lengthwise.

I was horrified to hear this told before Cletus; but it was evidently an old story to him. Runaway mother. Runaway father, too, for all we knew. Stepfather cut in two lengthwise. Cletus never turned a hair. His nonchalance was remarkable. I suppose if you were to survive with the Clasbys, you'd have to learn to be nonchalant about a number of things.

"The reason we turned to you folks," Ed Clasby said, "is because George was a schoolteacher and is dedicated to learning. He wouldn't care to see a bright boy like Cletus done out of an education."

"George is retired," I said quickly. It surprised me how glib I could be with that word when I thought it was advantageous to use it.

There was no use trying to outglib Ed Clasby. "You ain't retired, Agnes," he said. "And at Cletus' age, most of the looking after him would fall on your shoulders."

This was, of course, God's truth. But it wasn't a very handy time to admit it. I didn't have to. George hasn't been an administrator for thirty years for nothing. He doesn't get maneuvered into a corner easily.

"We'll think it over, Ed, and let you know. When you planning on leaving?"

"A week, at the longest. Sooner if the weather moderates."

"Don't think we don't appreciate the confidence you've shown in us, Ed," George told him. "But this isn't anything to go into half-cocked."

So we left, leaving poor little Cletus like a parcel of goods put up for sale and not taken. I didn't feel any enthusiasm myself about taking on the care of a young magician who could find needles in snowdrifts. But he was human and so was I. I tried not to catch his eye.

Though I could've told him that if he wanted to live with us, not to worry. George had already decided to take him in. When George intends to say "no," he says it. When he intends to say "yes," he postpones. The consequences of any "yes" are usually greater than the consequences of any "no." George always wants to think his yeses over—even though he knows he's going to say them.

On the way home I said to George, "Where will he sleep?"

"The couch in the kitchen," George answered. "I'll fix up a screen to shut him off from us."

George didn't make the least pretense, with me, of needing time to think things over. "Clasby was right about one thing," he continued. "The bulk of the work will fall on you—or would, if I didn't do something about it. Which I will."

George began that very evening to do something about it. He washed the supper dishes. I couldn't have been more surprised if he had started knitting little bootees. I didn't know that George *could* wash dishes. It wasn't that George had had any theories about "man's work" and "woman's work." It was simply that in former times he hadn't been around at dishwashing time. George, at the sink, made me feel that I was living in a topsy-turvy world.

I went to bed thinking about the day's changes and wondering about the changes that were bound to come. I didn't hear any hoot owls, let alone *my* hoot owl. I was more asleep than awake when George, who had stayed up puttering around in his newly assumed role of housekeeper, said, "Agnes, why don't you answer?"

"Answer what?" I asked.

"Listen," he said.

91

I listened. Somewhere very near, on tree, or rooftree, an owl hooted.

"Your owl's come down for a little more talk," George said. "He's waiting for his nightly pillow talk."

As George said this, the owl on treetop, or rooftree, let loose with his long soft roll of sound. There was no reply from any other owl.

"He's talking to you, Agnes."

Now it's one thing, spontaneously and without forethought, to have imitated a hoot owl. It's another, to do it the second time, and at the bidding of a listening and waiting audience. You feel self-conscious. You feel you'll fail. You feel you'll make a laughing stock of yourself. It's one thing to call up spirits from the vasty deep; it's another to have them answer; and still another to be required to converse with them while your family listens. My voice stuck in my throat.

"Go on, Minerva," George said. "Hoot. You started this."

Minerva, goddess of wisdom, owl on her shoulder! That about silenced me. But then the owl, in the cold of the deep northern night, called again. No doubt I imagined it. Nevertheless, I thought there was a waiting note in the sound. And what waits can be disappointed. I answered, and there was, without the customary pause, an immediate answer. I was truly in touch with something. I forgot that George was listening. And to do him justice, he never made another sound to remind me that he was. I talked to that bird as I'd never talked to a human. If you say, "Naturally, you never hooted to a human being, did you?" you miss the point. Certainly I never hooted to a human being. And certainly "hoot" is the name given to the sound I made. Nevertheless, and whatever name you give that sound, I was speaking. I was speaking to what was roofless and wild, to what lived in the night and saw in the dark and fed on the living. I was able to say what I had never been able to say back at the bridge parties and P.-T.A.'s of Southern California. Nor to George himself, for that matter. George was listening now, but I wasn't speaking *to* him.

The conversation which I had started self-consciously ended naturally. When I had had my say, the owl had apparently had his. There was one distant call; then if he spoke again, his voice was indistinguishable from those of the other night criers.

Before I went to sleep again I had a moment's misgiving about Cletus. What was he going to think of living in a house with a woman who talked to hoot owls? Because I knew I would want to continue my conversation the next night. It was a moment's misgiving only. I was asleep in a wink, and the next thing I knew I was awake, smelling frying bacon and listening to the sough of cookstove and heater, both drawing briskly. George, who ordinarily never put a foot out of bed until he smelled coffee, *was* making himself over. And I needn't have worried about Cletus and hoot owls, as I learned later.

He came to stay with us at the end of the week. George had required less time than usual to think things over, and the weather had moderated, so that the Clasbys could be on their way earlier than they had anticipated. Cletus entered our lives like a daytime owl, blond, reflective, and outspoken. It was soon hard to believe that we had lived so much of our lives without him. He had only two disturbing habits. One, we could do nothing about. He was, as I said, outspoken. Well, he wasn't just outspoken. When he spoke out, he did so in words George and I never used. I don't mean that he was either saucy or dirty-minded. He said what he thought and he used the words he knew.

As an example of saying what he thought, one night when George was washing and Cletus was drying the dishes, Cletus said, "Who had this job before you got me?"

This might have sounded, if you didn't know Cletus, as if he

were saying, "How did you get along without me?" That wasn't
Cletus' intent. Information was all he wanted—and George
knew it.

"Agnes did the dishes before you came. Washed them *and*
dried them."

"And worked at her job, too?"

What Cletus called my "job" was a hobby I'd taken up after
George started doing the housework. Before I was married, I
had kept scrapbooks. Not the usual scrapbooks of a girl in her
teens: football programs, party invitations, hotel matchbooks. I
was never interested in things like that. Instead, I kept clip-
pings from magazines and newspapers, pictures of celebrities,
quotations from speeches, reproductions of famous pictures. I
know this sounds stuffy; and I probably was a stuffy girl. But
that's the kind of scrapbook I kept. I really thought of them as
providing a picture of my times, and myself as a kind of Sam-
uel Pepys with a paste pot. Colossal egoist! But what young
person isn't? Naturally, after I was married, I hadn't found
time for my hobby. But I hadn't been able to resist collecting
items either. I put these, loose, into cartons, and through all
our moving about, I hung onto the cartons. Now, with winter
shutting down, with the housework taken over by George, I
got out my scrapbooks again. Though I hadn't had time to fill
them, I had never been able to resist buying a fine scrapbook
when I saw one on sale; thus everything was at hand for the
resumption of my hobby. I had George move the large work-
bench he no longer needed, now that he had finished his car-
pentry work, inside. It was a fine big table, large enough to
hold two or three scrapbooks at a time. And to my surprise I
found that I now wanted to write captions for my pictures, as
well as paste them in the books. I wanted to say what I
thought about those pictures of people and past events. So

there I would be, when Cletus got home from school, seated at my big table, busy with pen, scissors, and paste pot.

I suppose it did *look* like a job.

"She didn't work at her job before you came," George explained to Cletus. "She did all the housework."

"What was *your* job then?" Cletus asked.

"I was the head of some schools."

"Like Mrs. Longnecker?"

Mrs. Longnecker was the principal of the two-room school Cletus attended.

"Yes. Except I had a couple of dozen schools under me."

"Why did they fire you?"

"They didn't. I retired."

"Retired?" Cletus asked.

"I stopped working—permanently."

"You're working now," Cletus said, "doing the dishes." And George was, grunting away as he scoured a baking dish in which the macaroni and cheese had burned. "And she's got the real job," Cletus said, nodding toward me, writing at my big table.

"That's one way of looking at it," George agreed.

Cletus concluded that conversation. "Looks like you got me just in time for the drying."

This is an example of Cletus' outspokenness, but not of his vocabulary. It's not easy to give an example of that, because words of that kind are only recently written down; but what follows illustrates it to some degree; also his outspokenness.

George drives Cletus three miles, morning and evening, to catch the bus which takes him to school, and back. One evening while Cletus was outside getting an armload of wood, George told me, "Mrs. Longnecker gave Cletus a whack across the hand with a ruler today. Left a considerable welt."

I was surprised. Cletus, according to his friends, was teacher's pet. "Why would she do a thing like that?"

George laughed a little. "She's nervous this week."

"Nervous this week?"

"Cletus says she's having the grannies this week."

"The grannies?" For a minute the word made no more sense than Chinese. Then I caught on, and I don't know whether I was the more surprised at the old-fashioned word or at Cletus' up-to-date knowledge.

"For heaven's sake," I said, "where did Cletus dig up a backwoodsy word like that?"

"He's a pretty backwoodsy boy," George said.

"Well, how does he happen to know so much about grannies and nervous, then?"

"They both happen in the backwoods."

We didn't try to do anything about Cletus' vocabulary or his outspokenness. He'd got his bad words by copying people who used them. We decided he would get his good words the same way. But his second habit, we did try to do something about. He had to get up every night. Now under ordinary circumstances that would have been of no consequence one way or another. But our bathroom was a privy back of the house a hundred feet; and the temperatures were sinking toward zero. Cletus didn't mind this nightly trip. He made it without a word of complaint. George was the one who complained.

George valued his sleep. What with hoot-owl conversations to listen to at bedtime, together with early-morning rising, he didn't like being awakened just as he had fallen soundly asleep. The noise wasn't Cletus' fault. Cletus naturally had to put on shoes for the trip. The floor wasn't carpeted. The door stuck, then squeaked, then had to be banged to get it to close tight. All this was repeated in reverse order on the return trip, squeak, bang, clop, clop; plus the rattling of the springs as Cletus, after his frosty journey, shook a while before getting warmed up.

On the night George decided that there had to be a change, I, the usually sound sleeper, was awakened by sounds I couldn't at first identify. They were outside the house, a muffled banging, an unending stomping and yelling.

I awakened George. "What's that noise?"

"Cletus," he said without a moment's pause. "It must be Cletus. I fell asleep before he came back." George leaped from the bed, raised the window, and shouted, "Cletus, Cletus, are you all right?"

The banging stopped. "Hell, no." The answer was faint, but firm.

"What's the trouble?"

"I'm locked in."

The privy had a wooden latch on the outside as well as the inside, and this had somehow fallen into place when Cletus entered. I don't know how long he had been out there. Thank God nothing was frostbitten.

But that decided George. "The boy has to have his own chamber pot," he said.

"There isn't much privacy," I reminded George.

"There's enough," George said. "Besides, we can sleep right through that. I'll drive you in to town today and you can buy one."

We bought one, or I did; though such a thing wasn't, even in that backwoods country, easy to locate. I might have been asking for a bustle for all the understanding I received. Maybe there's a more up-to-date word for it now. Maybe I just ran into some delicate-minded clerks. I got one, finally, at a second-hand store, by pointing.

Anyway, George thought we would have a good night's sleep

that night. No shoes, on or off. No floor boards squeaking. No bedsprings clattering. No doors banging. He had given Cletus a searchlight with a real lighthouse beam so that there would be no occasion for any stumbling about.

But I was wakened after a few hours' sleep by cold air flowing under the covers. George was sitting bolt upright, a hand over his eyes to shield them from the crisscrossing beams of that blinding searchlight of Cletus'.

"Cletus!" he called. "In God's name, what are you doing?"

"I'm hunting hoot owls."

"What?" George asked, louder than necessary, irritated because he believed he couldn't have heard aright.

"I'm hunting hoot owls," Cletus said again.

"There are no hoot owls in here."

"I'm hunting them outside, in the trees."

"You can't see them from inside," George told him.

"I can see their eyes," Cletus said. "They're looking down at us like tigers."

George, at that, lay down with a slap of his back against the mattress. He pulled the covers over his face, determined to sleep in spite of the searchlight. But Cletus turned it off at once and went back to bed himself.

Next morning he asked George if he should stop hunting hoot owls. "I was trying to be quiet," he said. "I didn't know the light would wake you up."

"No, you keep on," George said, sorry for the way he had yelled in the night. "I'll tie something over my eyes tonight."

That was three months ago. Since then George sent off for and received a "sleep mask," which shuts out every iota of light. Now he sleeps right through Cletus' nighttime hunts.

Soon after Cletus started this pastime of his (after all, he is only a little boy without parents, alone in the night), I got caught up with my scrapbooks—every loose item pasted in, every caption written. But by then I had the habit of sitting at this table working at my "job," as Cletus calls it. And since, with George taking over the household chores, there is no earthly reason why I shouldn't, here I sit from midmorning until midafternoon, indulging myself. I write all day; and when dusk comes, I have a chat with a hoot owl. And at night I'm wakened from my first sleep by a boy with elf locks, who sits on a chamber pot turning his flashlight hither and yon until the icicles on the eaves glitter like torches and he sees (he tells us) a circle of tiger eyes. What a life! Who on God's earth could have foreseen it? If I could have foreseen my life now, two years ago (not the reality, which is fine), but described in the words, "keep scrapbooks, talk to hoot owls, take in a boy with leaky kidneys," why, I would never have set foot out of Orange County.

And if George could have foreseen *his* life? He's growing herbs! Herbs! In a box in the kitchen window. Thyme, sweet marjoram, parsley, chives. Rue and rosemary, too, for all I know. He uses them in cooking. I never had patience, myself, in the old days, with women who took care of African violets—like mothers with nursing babies. Let alone *men* growing herbs. But why not? What I'm doing is queer enough.

Since I finished the scrapbooks, I've been writing this account of our life here. It's the last of March now. Often at noonday the icicles are dripping. George said there were signs of life in the spring he boxed over six months ago—on the day he said he had retired.

That's the name I gave this account when I finished it. "Retired." I wrote that word at the top of the first page and handed the document, pages stapled together, to George. "Read it," I said.

I was as uneasy as could be while he read. For all I knew,

what I'd said about him might make him mad. Or, worse still, might simply bore him. He took it all fine. He chuckled once or twice. Once he looked up to say, "I wouldn't care to be present when the Clasbys read this."

"Unless you mail this to them, then nail them to a chair while they read, there's not much danger of that, is there?"

"No," George said, "I reckon not."

When he finished he said, "I've got just one suggestion. You've got the wrong title."

"What should it be?" I asked.

"Semiretired," he said.

I confess to feeling a little asperity when George said I had the wrong title. It would be a funny thing, wouldn't it, if I didn't know the right title for my own piece of writing? But "Semiretired" was actually nearer the facts.

I was about to tell George so when Cletus spoke up. This all happened, I've forgotten to say, on a Saturday afternoon just after lunch. We were sitting around in the sunlight and drip, enjoying the letup school people feel, even after they're retired, on the weekend.

"I've got a better title," Cletus said.

I didn't know Cletus had read it. Obviously, there isn't much privacy around here, and I hadn't put my pages away as I wrote. I left them on my "desk" with an iron on top of them for a paperweight. There weren't any secrets in it, nothing to hurt anyone's feelings, except, as George noted, maybe the Clasbys. So I didn't care if Cletus had read it, but I didn't know he had. I never saw him at it.

But if I answered Cletus a little tartly, it wasn't because he'd read it; it was because he, like George, thought he could, with a snap of the fingers, produce the perfect title.

"What is your suggestion, Cletus?" I asked.

"Change of Life." Cletus said it fast, so proud of what he'd hit upon, he couldn't wait to have us hear it.

There was no use pretending Cletus didn't know that he was dealing in *double-entendre*. He did. That's why he was so proud of the title. Not just the change in our way of living: George at the sink instead of going to his office; me at my desk instead of at the sink; but the other, too. One stone used and two birds dead, with that title.

There was no more point in chiding Cletus for knowing about such things than there is in rebuking a third grader who happens to understand algebra. The third grader's caught on early to what he's bound (unless he's dimwitted) to learn in time, anyway. The same was true of Cletus.

So I spoke only of the practical aspects of such a title. "That might be a good title if I'd written only about George and me, Cletus. But you're in this story, too. What's changed for you? Going to school, studying; life hasn't changed much for you."

"Yes, it has," Cletus said without a minute's thought. "There's one big change. Every night I hunt hoot owls. Hunting hoot owls! Last night I saw fifteen eyes, and me in the middle of the circle. That's a change for me. Hunting hoot owls."

That hit a chord. It went too deep to talk about. I got up and started to clear the table, which George, unusual for him, had let stand while he read.

"You two go on up and have a look at the spring," I said. "I want a vacation from my job. I want to wash dishes."

That night when Cletus sent his beam from window to window, I thought, "Hunting for Hoot Owls." But doesn't that leave George out? George, with his sleep mask on, and his herbs on the kitchen window, and calling me "Minerva" when I answer that first call at dusk? No, I thought, everything you search for doesn't have to hoot.

I got out of bed silently, and went carefully across the icy floor to Cletus. I kneeled down so that I could follow the light as he flashed it from tree to tree. He was right. We were encircled. They were there, whether we hunted them or not; greater than stars, because they lived, because they looked back and had voices with which to answer us.

I tiptoed over to my desk, crossed out the old title, and wrote in the new. Naturally, in the dark, I made a big scrawl of it. But next morning the very size of the words seemed to be a part of their truth; and neither George nor Cletus, when they saw them, had any further suggestions to make.

Crimson
Ramblers
of the
World,
Farewell

The October morning, when thirteen-year-old Elizabeth Prescott opened her eyes, was sallow, like a faded sun tan. October mornings in Southern California can be many different ways, but this was the way Elizabeth liked best, sunshine remembered but not present. There had been just enough rain in the night to stir up all the scents locked in the dust by summer's heat and dryness. Hundreds of smells, at the very least, sailed into her nose. It made her feel a little crazy, so many smells she could not name: castor bean she recognized, eucalyptus, wild tobacco, licorice, off-bloom acacia, alfalfa, petunia, wet dirt, coffee perking for breakfast. But most of the scents she could not identify, sniff though she would.

Me, though, she thought triumphantly. I can smell me. I'm a real hound-nose. Though it was really no test, considering her hour-long lathering with rose-geranium soap before she had gone to bed. Her feet still felt withered from last night's soaking in the foot tub. She lifted the covers to look at them: wrinkled but lily white, like the feet of a dead knight.

She let the covers drop and thought, I wish I had somebody to smile at. Oh boy, I wish I could wake up and smile at somebody and not stop smiling all day long. I wish I could wake up and someone would look into smiling eyes and say, "Another beautiful day, darling." Someone who knew that she was willing to get up, eager to dedicate her whole day to silence, hard work, and smiling. I wish it would be Mother and she wouldn't yell "Get up," or even whisper it. I wish I could smile a message at Mother and have it recognized; if a smile collided with a smile, whammo, bango, there'd be a big crack-up. Splinters of smiles, first crashing, then sparkling in the air like an explosion in a diamond mine, or maybe in a bombed mirror factory.

Well, I know someone, she thought, to smile at. I know Crimson Rambler Rice. Though she'd have to wait for school to smile at Crimson Rambler, and maybe by school time she wouldn't feel like smiling. At home things happened to stop smiles.

"I never knew anyone by the name of Rice who was any account," her mother had said.

Her mother had known lots of Rices, all amounting to less than a hill of beans. "And no puns intended either." So it was too much to expect that the one Rice her daughter had run across would be an exception to the rule.

"What does this Clarence Rice's father do?"

Elizabeth didn't know. What did that have to do with Clarence? Clarence? No one called him that. He had red hair and ran fast. When he'd started school in September, the kids had wanted to call him Red. He wouldn't let them.

"That's not my name."

"What's your name, Red?"

"Crimson Rambler."

"Why, Red?"

"Because my hair's crimson and I can ramble."

"Your hair's sure crimson, Red, but can you ramble?"

"Ramble round anything here."

So they had a track meet. Crimson Rambler (he said) Rice

against the world. Everything on two feet he ran circles round. Dogs he kept up with (nobody had greyhounds at the Yorba Linda Grammar School). Ginny Todd's tomcat went past him like lightning past a hill. Then it climbed a tree.

"I'm no tree climber," Crimson Rambler said, "I never claimed that."

"How come you're a Crimson Rambler, then?" Elizabeth asked. "The crimson rambler is a climbing rose."

That decided the kids. If E. Prescott was against the Rambler, they were for him. She knew too much. No, that wasn't it. They didn't care how much she knew if only she'd keep it to herself. And she didn't, couldn't. Each morning on the way to school she rehearsed keeping it to herself. Then something like this would happen: Somebody who had *named* himself after a climber said he couldn't climb. So she had to point out the error.

"Crimson," the kids had said, just to show her, "you're a rambler, all right."

But Crimson Rambler didn't care how much she knew. He liked knowledge. He liked having his errors pointed out. He was a learner as well as a rambler. He liked her. He was the first boy who ever had—and shown it. He never said a loving word, but he didn't need to. He chose her first for every game; sat by her at lunchtime; when he passed the drawing paper he gave her more sheets than he gave anyone else; he never squirted anyone but her from the drinking fountain. And on Friday he had asked her to ride on Monday—this was Monday —on the handlebars of his bicycle. She had never ridden on any boy's handlebars, had never been asked before, had almost given up hoping.

Oh, Crimson Rambler! Thinking of his looks, she almost stopped smiling. They were too wonderful for smiles. Too ineluctable? Was that the word? Was it a *word!* Crimson Rambler's looks were one with all the stars and heavenly bodies and ancient gods. They were classical. When he smiled it was too sweet for the naked eye to endure. An expression at the corners of his mouth when he smiled said, All my strength and toughness and meanness (and he was strong and tough and mean) I am making sweet and gentle and quiet for you.

Oh Crimson Rambler Rice!

Who could she smile at now? Merv? Go smiling into Merv's room and say, "Brother, I forgive you everything?"

The trouble was she had nothing to forgive Merv. Mother was always saying, so that she and Howie could hear, "Merv is my favorite child." That was nothing to forgive Merv for. And there never *would* be anything to forgive Merv for and never any reason to smile at him either, because Merv wouldn't smile back. He wasn't mean or downcast, just too damn dead calm to smile.

Howie had something to forgive her for and she had something to forgive him for. "You'll never die of lockjaw," Howie had said to her.

That was something to forgive, and she was willing, but Howie was too mad at her to smile. She didn't blame Howie, though what she'd done had not been intended to hurt him. It had been intended to help him. The trouble was he didn't want help.

Mother had said, "Basil Cobb is teaching Howie dirty words." Howie was eight and Basil twelve.

"What kind of dirty words?"

"Never you mind. But you speak to him about it."

"Why can't Merv?"

"Merv wouldn't know what to say."

"I don't either."

"Something will come to you. It always does."

And it had. "Stop teaching my little brother dirty words."

"Like what, Movie Star Prescott?"

"Movie Star" was a thing she had to grin and bear. Because her name was Elizabeth and because she didn't look like a movie star, that's what mean kids called her.

"Like what?"

It was the first time in her life she'd been asked a question and had no answer. It was a humiliating thing to have to stand before a questioner wordless.

"Like what, Movie Star Prescott?"

She had no idea. She was ignorant as well as wordless.

"Like son of a bitch, Movie Star Prescott?"

So she slapped him. She knew it was a point of honor, when that was said, to fight. It was an aspersion cast upon your mother, and while you didn't have to fight for a brother, you had to fight for your mother. Otherwise you had a streak of yellow a yard wide. There were mothers, perhaps, you wouldn't want to fight for. But not hers.

Everywhere I look I see beauty, she thought; perhaps it was a defect of her eyes, like seeing double. Could both Crimson Rambler Rice and her mother be as beautiful as she thought them? Her mother had the two prettiest things in the world for a woman: little black curls at the back of her neck, falling down from the pulled-up knot of hair; and color in her face that swept back and forth from shell pink to deepest rose depending upon how glad or mad she was.

Her mother was very mad and very red when she heard of the slapping. "You have humiliated Howie," she said.

There was no disputing this.

"Here comes Sistie to button up your little pantsies, Howie baby," Basil would yell every time Howie came out of the boy's lavatory. There was no use denying that such talk was humiliating; just as there was no use expecting an early-morning smile from Howie either.

That left her father and her mother; and she knew she was already in bad with Father. Her hour-long bath in the kitchen last night had been, as much as anything, to wash away her troubles.

After supper her father had said, "Elizabeth, I'd like to have a little talk with you."

His voice, her full name, Mother's leaving the room had all told her that what Father had to say was serious. It was just dusk. He sat in his chair in the living room. His white shirt was visible but his dark trousers had disappeared into the big dark chair, and the big dark chair was disappearing in evening's shadow, going under like a sinking ship.

She stood before her father wanting to help him. It was not easy for her father to criticize her. She knew that. What came as natural as breathing to her mother hurt her father. She wanted to please her mother; but her father she wanted to help. She loved him, and almost the only way she had of showing it was being loving and dutiful with Mother. It was a wordless compact she and her father had. "If you love me, make your mother happy." That was what he said without words and what she without words agreed to. Father had recognized a fact: happiness, for him, was making Mother happy.

He gave everything to his wife, including his daughter and his daughter's love. She never kissed her father, hugged him, sat upon his knee as other daughters did. She never dared and he didn't want her to; not because he didn't like kissing and hugging *and* her, but because Mother would love him more if he sacrificed such pleasures—handed them over as a gift to her. So the way to show her father she loved him was to be cool to him and do loving things for Mother.

Only, time and again she failed: was cross, snappy, mean, selfish, critical, disobedient, and sometimes downright snarling-yelling mad. She loved her mother for the same reasons her father did, probably: for her funny jokes, her beautiful looks, her wonderful pies; and especially the excitement of living either in a cyclone or a storm cellar; one or the other all the time.

But what her father didn't see was that it was easier for him to be always calm and courteous, loving, in deed as in fact, to Mother than for her. Mother thought he was the most wonderful person in the world; she never slapped him, told him to shut up, asked him to do unreasonable things, or said to other people in his hearing, "He is not my favorite husband," the way she did with her when she said, "Liz is not my favorite child."

Her father asked a lot of his daughter. He asked her to be just as loving to her mother as he was to his wife. He asked her to forgo her love for him and present it as a gift to Mother. Since she really did love Mother, this required a love almost stronger than a human being could generate. And it made all her failures with Mother almost too heavy to bear. She failed two people when she failed Mother.

Last night her father had been resting his face in his hands. His eyes were out of sight. Only his Masonic ring caught lights and blinked a lodge greeting at her. In the silence, and knowing she had another double failure of some kind to face, her hands began to sweat and her stomach went slowly round and round, winding itself into a smaller and smaller knot to make room for a bigger and bigger sorrow.

"Elizabeth, don't answer me now. I want you to think about what I have to say for a while, then answer. Are you willing?"

Was she willing? She was willing to think until her brains steamed. Already the skin was tightening across her cheekbones and her mouth was widening and narrowing as she prepared herself to think. If thinking could undo the day before's yelling madness with Mother, she would think her eyeballs out of their sockets and break her eardrums with the pressure of cogitation.

"Tell me, Father," she said urgently. The engine of her brain was running hard, but it needed a direction in which to go.

"Elizabeth, you're such a fine girl, such a fine, bright, strong girl."

This was terrible: that her father thought he had to *say* these things.

"Your mother . . ." He couldn't go on.

"I love Mother."

"I know you do."

"But I argue, contradict, disobey, act scornful. . . ."

"Elizabeth, I think I'd be the happiest man on earth if you could get on better with your mother. I'd not ask for a thing more in life."

"I promise. I promise. . . ."

"Don't," her father urged. "Go think about it."

Thinking about it had been the whole trouble. If she could have spoken at once and without thinking, all she would have said was, "Oh, Father, I'll try to be better."

What she'd said later was the same thing exactly, only she'd had time while she was washing dishes to feel more and more. And the more she felt, the more impossible it was to come right out and say it. "Father, I'll try to be better." That's all it was, the same thing said in a fancy roundabout way. And, fool that she was, she'd even thought her father might enjoy the fanciness. She had wanted to bare her heart, make eternal promises, tell him of her steely resolutions; but not in so many words. Thinking had told her how to say it—and not say it. And how to spare them both tears by roundaboutness.

She did a wonderful job on the dishes, dried her hands, combed her hair, and went to stand again before her father. He had vanished from sight now except for the white shirt, an iceberg on the dark water.

"Father?"

"Yes, Elizabeth."

"Father, I want you to know that whereas in the past you have had in this house a big, rough, unmannerly Airedale dog, growling and showing his teeth, he is now about to be replaced. . . ."

Her father interrupted her. "Elizabeth, what's this long story about dogs? What's it got to do with your attitude toward your mother?"

"Why, everything." But the story would explain that.

"Whereas," she started over, "you have had this big unmannerly Airedale in the house, in the future you will have a small gentle lap dog, quiet, well-behaved, gentle. . . ."

Her father had sprung to his feet as if stabbed.

"Stop it," he ordered. "If what you're trying to do is to give me a demonstration of what your mother has to put up with day in and day out, you've succeeded."

"Father, please let me . . ."

Her father fell back into his chair. "Enough is enough. Go play. Go study. Whatever you want. You haven't the least idea of what I was asking you."

And all the time the shoe was on the other foot. She knew what he was asking and he didn't, but he wouldn't hear any more. All of him had gone from sight; the iceberg had sunk. Did they sink? No, melt. And Father was crying, she knew that; like something which thinks that because it is out of sight it can't be heard.

"Twenty-four hours a day of this," he said as she left. "No wonder your mother's nerves are frazzled."

"Frazzled?" her mother asked, coming from wherever she'd been listening to the conversation. "Who said anything about frazzled? And what's wrong with trying to make yourself clear by giving examples? The Bible does it all the time."

Elizabeth couldn't believe her ears. Mother saying that she was Biblical! And it was partly true. That was what was so astounding about Mother. She didn't skate around on the surface. She plunged in deep.

"The Bible's full of comparisons. Fig trees and lilies and houses built on sand. What's wrong with big dogs and little dogs, if they make the meaning clearer?"

Mother's arm around her was not a dead weight like other arms she'd had round her: uncles and aunts and such old worn-out huggers. Mother's arm was as alive as a king snake, warm and nonpoisonous, clasping her lovingly.

She snuggled into its curve. "Be this way forever," she prayed. Nine months ago, on the last day of the year, her mother sat up with her until the hikers came at midnight for the trip to Old Baldy. She hadn't asked her mother. Hadn't told her that the last hour of the old year, with snow on the mountain in the morning of the new year was important. Mother *knew*. Her mother read her like a book. And sometimes clapped her shut like a book. And there was no way to stop that. She could only love the times she was read and pondered and understood.

She had taken her long bath to help her wash away her father's scolding; and her knowledge that her mother's arm that had cradled could be raised as quickly against her.

Things like that couldn't be washed away of course, but she had awakened smelling the October morning, thinking of Crimson Rambler and the bicycle ride, and smiling. And no one to smile at but herself. So she jumped out of bed and did so, in the mirror. It will be a better face, she thought, with time and suffering; though it would never be the small-boned, black-haired, pink-petaled face (the best kind of face, in her opinion) of her mother. But it was hers, and this was a day in her life and no one else's, and the day of her first ride on the handlebars of a boy's bicycle. No old twerp's; though whoever had asked her, she'd have accepted. She knew that. But fate had spared her, had made the first the best. Oh, Crimson Rambler Rice. Had he shined it, tied a ribbon on, lived Friday, Saturday, and Sunday waiting for this day? Was he smiling, too, as he got up, happy to see that it had rained in the night so that they could have a sweet-smelling dust-free ride?

She went to the window and looked out in the direction of the foothills where Crimson Rambler lived. The sallow light was pinker now. In the barley field meadow larks were singing. A big unknown bird cleared the eucalyptus windbreak, then went up and up across the sky, straight and steady enough to be an airplane. No one had called her. From the kitchen, which was under her room—and which, as far as smells went, was practically in her room, her floor and the kitchen's ceiling being not only one and the same but with knotholes—the coffee smell came up stronger and stronger. Someone was up and cooking.

"The household is astir," she told herself. The words excited her. The smile went inward. She began her morning dance, which was mostly running and jumping; but the jumps were enormous flights that carried her half across the room. I'll invite Crimson Rambler for a ride on my wings in exchange for his bicycle courtesy.

Then she was suddenly tired as well as excited and lay down quickly on the floor and lifted the rug for a peek through the biggest knothole at life in the kitchen. Usually her father got up first and started things going: coffee, water for the oatmeal, oven heating for the toast. Sometimes he shaved at the kitchen sink. Every month or so she remembered to have a peek, and he had never known it, busy whistling, slicing bacon, having a trial cup of coffee. It was a secret she had, and the kitchen was her secret garden and the knothole her gate to enter.

On her stomach, comfortably full length, she lay quietly eye-spying her way into her secret garden. At first she saw no one, though there on the stove was the coffeepot perking and the griddle smoking. Somewhere she heard splashing and by getting a little way from the knothole she was able to see her father, stark naked, standing at the kitchen sink having a kind of sponge bath from the washbasin there. He was rinsing off his private parts, and though her every intention was to back away fast, her eye fitted itself to that knothole like a ball bearing to a socket; she gazed as if this were the sight she had been created to see. Her father sloshed and whistled. It was her mother, coming into the kitchen with her sixth sense of just where to look to catch her daughter at her worst, who looked up immediately through the knothole and deep into her daughter's eye. She didn't say a word. They stared at each other as if their eyes had fallen into a lock which someone else would have to break. Then, still without speaking a word, her mother left the room.

She was standing, with the rug back down, when her mother entered the room. Her mother still had on her nightgown. Her black hair was hanging down her shoulders; her cheeks were burning.

"Do you do this very often?"

"Do what?"

"Don't spar with me, Peeping Tom. Look down into the kitchen through your peephole?"

"I've looked before."

"Does your father know it?"

"I don't think so."

"Have you seen him naked before?"

"No."

"But you've been waiting for your chance?"

"No, I haven't."

"You weren't backing away very fast."

"I was going to. I was getting ready to."

"What do you have to do to get ready to stop looking at your naked father?"

"I don't know."

"What kind of a girl do you think you are, up to such tricks?"

"I don't know."

"Do you think Merv would do a thing like that?"

"No."

"You're right. He wouldn't. Merv is a clean, natural, decent boy. He wouldn't stoop to spying on his naked mother. Or father. That is an unnatural act. You have heard of unnatural acts, haven't you?"

"Yes."

"Do you know what they are?"

"No."

"Spying on your naked father. That's an unnatural act."

"I didn't intend to."

"Flat on your face, eye glued to a peephole? Did somebody push you there?"

"No."

"No, no, no. Well, since you don't know, I'll tell you what you are. You are perverted. You have an unnatural interest in sex. And your own father! Your father was awake half the night worrying about you and your story to him about being some kind of a dog. Even though I tried to explain it. What kind of a daughter tells her father she's a dog? Tell me."

"Crazy, I guess."

"Do you know what a female dog is called?"

"Yes."

"What?"

"A bitch."

"Don't be one. I'm not going to tell your father about this.

It would sicken him. But *I* know about it. And I am going to keep a close watch on you. Respect and obedience. That's all he wants from you. And with your tendencies, you'd better watch yourself when you get around *anything* with pants on."

At the bedroom door she said, "Wait until the rest of us have eaten. I don't think anyone would consider it a pleasure to eat with you this morning."

She didn't eat breakfast at all. She didn't go downstairs until her father had gone to work and her brothers had left for school.

When she came down the stairs her mother was waiting for her. "Elizabeth," she said, "I was upset, but what I said was for your own good. You're of an age now when you'll have to be careful. Guard yourself and your feelings."

Her mother put her arms around her and pressed her pink petal-cool cheek to hers, kissed her, as she sometimes did, on each eyelid, then stood in the door and waved until she went over the dip of the hill and out of sight.

The schoolyard was empty when she got there. She heard allegiance being pledged inside. Late was late, so she took an extra minute to inspect Crimson Rambler's bicycle; there it was on the rack, washed and polished and ready to go. Even the tires had been scrubbed. She tiptoed over to the bicycle and touched it. She felt daring. It was the next thing to touching Crimson Rambler himself. The bicycle was warm and smooth in the October sunlight, very bright, shining, and dust-free.

Even though Crimson Rambler Rice was two years older than she, over fifteen, actually, they were in the same room, and she had to walk in under his eyes. There was no use trying to smile. She wasn't happy that way any more, but she was excited, shaking even. She counted the steps to her desk and watched her feet to keep herself from staring at Crimson Rambler. But she saw him. She couldn't lower her eyelids far enough to hide even his clean sweat shirt or the comb marks in his freshly wet hair.

Arithmetic was first, and when Hank Simon passed the papers for this, he handed her a note, too. "Elizabeth" was printed on the outside in the big dashing way Crimson Rambler had. She opened it behind her arithmetic book.

It began "My sweetheart." That was all she read. "My sweetheart." That was really nauseating. She rose, surprising herself, and went with the note to the wastepaper basket at the front of the room. Then, looking straight at Crimson Rambler, she began to tear the note into tiny pieces. "Sweetheart"? Why, Crimson Rambler Rice, she thought, did you really think I could be anyone's sweetheart but mother's? I don't want a thing my mother doesn't give me, and anything anyone else gives me I'll give to her. Big old Crimson Rambler Rice, did you think you could win me away from my mother with your bicycle and silly notes? Did you think I'd fall for *anything* in pants? That shows how crazy you are, because people who've got any sense don't think much of girls like that. That shows you haven't got any standards to speak of, Crimson Rambler Rice, and I have.

The note, torn up, she let dribble in a little paper waterfall into the basket. Old silly Crimson Rambler and his "sweetheart"! Why, Mother, your merest loving glance means more to me than suggestive notes from boys.

Crimson Rambler stared at her, but she didn't care. By the time the last of his note had fallen into the basket, she'd stopped trembling. She walked back toward her desk feeling happy to have made it up to her mother for all her earlier wicked thoughts, feeling strong and calm. Feeling like her father, calm, helpful, and devoted.

She stopped at the desk of Fione Quigley, a sweet little girl who didn't understand decimals. "Slide over, Fione," she said. "I'll help you with your arithmetic."

She put her arm around Fione's shoulder and whispered, "It's the same as fractions, only another way of saying it."

She looked to see if Crimson Rambler was watching. He was. She gave him a long square look and with eyes said, Farewell, Crimson Rambler Rice. Never try to tempt me again.

Night
Piece for
Julia

To be alone in the night, to be cold, to be homeless, fleeing, perhaps: Julia had always feared these things.

Where was she? She couldn't be sure at first. Just outside Bentonville, perhaps. It was there she tried walking with her shoes off. Her pumps had cut into her heels until they were bleeding. But the icy gravel of the unpaved road hurt her feet more than the shoes. She stood still for a while without courage either to take another step forward or to force her cut feet back into her shoes. I always heard coldness numbed, she thought, but it doesn't; it hurts, too, and it makes the other hurt more. She could have walked in the half-frozen slush at the side of the road, but she still had a concern for her appearance that would not let her splash, stocking-footed, through the mud. Suddenly, almost spasmodically, she shoved her feet down into the shoes. The pain twisted her face. "I will think of them as outside myself," she said, "as if they were two animals, pets of mine that suffer." She laughed a little hysterically. My dogs, she thought. Why, other people have played this game. That's what soldiers say, and policemen, when they think they can't take another step. They say, "My dogs hurt," and walk right on. She looked down at her narrow feet in the rain-soaked, round-toed suède pumps, her ankles and insteps red through the gauzy stockings. "Poor dogs, *hundschen*," she said, "it is almost night. We'll rest soon."

She managed a few short stiff steps, then, with teeth grating, she swung into an approximation of her usual stride. The rain was turning to sleet, but the wind had veered so it was no longer in her face. She was so cold she could not tell whether the clothes under her coat were wet or not. She got her hand out of her glove and put it inside her coat, but it was so numb she couldn't tell wet from dry. Well, she thought, if I can't tell whether I'm wet or dry, what difference does it make?

It had been so dark all afternoon that the added darkness of nightfall was scarcely noticed. It only seemed to her that she could see less clearly than she had, as if her sight were tiring, too. She rubbed the back of her wet glove across her wet face, but still the sodden corn shocks that lined the road were gray and indistinct. In her effort to concentrate on something outside herself, she saw a bird perched on the snake fence beside the road. She was almost as surprised as if it had been a child. "What are you doing out in weather like this?" she said.

She thought she'd been through the town before, but always quickly, in an auto. Two or three sentences would be said, and then, while their dust still lingered in the single block of stores that made up the town, they would have passed beyond it, onto the road between the cornfields. But walking, limping, whipped (words she had no knowledge of before now had meaning so intense she thought their look alone would always in the future hurt her) by the wind-driven sleet, she measured out the short distance by a scale that added infinity to them. She limped from sign to sign, from gas station to gas station. Without these means of marking her progress she could never have gone on. "I will just walk to the next station," she would say, and when she had reached it she would hobble on to one more. The road was empty of cars, the service stations tight shut, their glass opaque with condensed moisture. Their swinging signs rattled in the wind with a sound of chains.

By the time she reached the town it was full night. Lights were on in most of the stores and houses. She skirted the main highway, taking a back street that paralleled it through town. She passed three or four shops, all closed; a dry-cleaning plant, a plumber's, a secondhand furniture store. The furniture store had one window set up as a bedroom, with a bird's-eye maple dresser, dressing table, and bed of a kind fashionable in the early nineteen hundreds. She leaned against the window, where she was somewhat protected from the sleet, and looked at the bed. It had a cheap factory-made patchwork quilt on it and two pillows in lavender slips. It looked like heaven to Julia, a bed, something she had taken for granted every night of her life before. I'll have to ask someplace, she thought. I can't go on in this cold. I'll have to risk it. I'll die if I don't. She held her hands against the glass. The yellow light behind it made it look warm, but to her icy hands it was only an extension of ice.

She saw herself in the mirror of the dressing table and instinctively tried to tidy herself. Her face looked as hard and white as a stone, like something already frozen. In the mirror her gray eyes were black, her wet yellow hair gray. Her fingers were almost too numb to push the fallen strands of her hair back under her dark cap. She got her lipstick out of her pocket and tried to put lips onto the blue scar the cold had made of her mouth, but her fingers were too stiff for that precise work. She thought she looked sick and water-soaked, but still neat. Now that she was ready to go on, she became aware again of her heels, throbbing with a pulse of pain that seemed to beat even in her eyes.

I'll stop at the first place, she thought. Everyone has to

sleep. No one would refuse me on a night like this. She walked on painfully, unable to joke any longer about her feet. The sleet bit into her face like fire.

She went up the steps of the first house where she saw a woman behind the undrawn blinds. From the street she had looked motherly, a plump, aproned woman with gray hair. She came to the door at once when Julia knocked.

"Well?" she asked in a harsh accusing voice.

"I haven't any money," Julia said. "I'm sick. I've been walking all afternoon. Will you let me have a bed for the night?"

"I'll call the authorities," the woman said. "There's a place for girls like you." She turned as if to go to a phone.

"No, no," Julia cried. "I won't bother you. I'll get to where I was going. Thank you."

The woman shut the door before she could turn around. "I didn't think she would," Julia said to console herself. "I didn't really expect it."

She got out of town as she had come into it, only more painfully, with more frequent stops. I always heard it was easy to freeze to death, she thought. She was shuddering all over, uncontrollably, so that the shuddering racked and hurt her. All of her body ached, as her hand had ached when, as a child, she had held a piece of ice as long as she could for a dare. "If there were only a snowbank, a bed of white snow where I could lie down and die. I would rest myself in it. I would pull it over me. I would press my cheek to it." But with this wet, ice-splintered ground, she would have to go on until she fell.

She was about to climb the curve of a small stone bridge when she saw the flicker of a red light beneath it, a fire, a windbreak, something to protect her from the sleet. She stumbled off the road and tried to run down the incline toward the fire. It was small, but really burning. She cupped her numb hands over it. Not until some of the heat had penetrated her skin did she look up, see the face of the man who sat with his back braced against the opposite side of the culvert. She would have screamed, but a tide of slow cold horror rose in her throat, choking her.

Julia stretched her legs out along the warm smooth sheets and opened her eyes, saw the silver lights on the green ruffled curtains, the acacia spilling over the round bowl. "You almost overdid it tonight," she told herself. "You almost screamed then." She put her warm hand on the soft satin over her heart. It was jarred by her heartbeat. She had almost overdone it, but it had worked again. Remembering that imagined suffering, that formless face, she was able to turn, once again, toward her husband, lying beside her in the warm sweet-smelling bed.

"So," he said in the tone of one who has been waiting. When he moved his hands slowly over her shallow breasts, she scarcely winced.

Live
Life
Deeply

At nine o'clock Friday morning, the Courtneys, then almost frantic over the disappearance of their fourteen-year-old daughter, Elspeth, received a phone call from a man who said his name was either Leighton D. or Creighton C. Hall. Ellie's father, who had answered the phone, was too upset to hear well, and the man at the other end of the wire was too upset, to judge by his voice, to speak clearly.

"I didn't quite catch your name," Mr. Courtney said.

"Creighton C. Hall," the man repeated.

The Courtneys had phoned everyone they thought might have any information concerning Ellie's whereabouts—friends, parents of friends, teachers; but they knew, and had called, no Halls. Mr. Courtney was going to tell Mr. Hall, who, he supposed, was calling on business, to please phone back later, when Mr. Hall once again repeated his name and added, "I'm calling from Merton Memorial Hospital."

Mr. Courtney knew at once, then, that Mr. Hall was calling about Ellie.

"Is she badly hurt?" he asked anxiously.

But before he would continue, Mr. Hall wanted to make

sure he was talking to the right person. "Is this Ellie's father?" he asked. "Is this John Courtney?"

"It is," Mr. Courtney answered, almost shouting in his impatience. "How's Ellie?"

"She's fine," Mr. Hall said, "now."

"Was she badly hurt?" Mr. Courtney asked again.

"She wasn't hurt at all."

"What's she doing at the hospital then?"

"She's here with me," Mr. Hall said.

"With you?" Mr. Courtney asked. "What's the matter with you?"

"There's nothing the matter with me," said Mr. Hall. "I'm here with my wife, who's having a baby."

At this minute Mrs. Courtney, who had been hanging onto her husband's arm trying to hear what was being said at the other end of the line and had caught little more than the word "hospital," could stand the suspense no longer.

"John," she asked, "is Ellie in the hospital?"

"Just a minute, please," Mr. Courtney told Mr. Hall.

Then he turned to his wife. "She's at the hospital. But she's all right. There's nothing wrong with her. She's with a man named Hall."

"What's she doing with him?" Mrs. Courtney asked, not feeling much reassured.

"His wife's having a baby," Mr. Courtney explained, and returned to his conversation with Mr. Hall.

Mrs. Courtney didn't feel that this information actually explained much and, while she waited impatiently for her husband to finish talking, she tried to imagine a chain of circumstances that would have landed Ellie at Merton Memorial Hospital in the company of an expectant father and mother.

Because her husband was in the midst of irrigating the lemons, he had been up earlier than usual that morning, about five-thirty. He had noticed that Ellie was not in her bed on the sleeping porch as he went out to work and, though she did not ordinarily get up any sooner than was necessary to catch the school bus, he hadn't thought much of her absence. The morning had been particularly nice, warm and shimmering, and Ellie might have risen romantically early to see the sun rise. Or hear the birds sing. Or, for that matter, to wash her face in the morning dew. Ellie had been subject to an unusual number of unexplainable fourteen-year-old vagaries during the past month, it seemed to him. Anyway, he had said nothing about Ellie's absence to his wife until he returned to the house for breakfast. "Ellie back yet?" he had asked as he sat down at the table in the kitchen.

It was only then that Mrs. Courtney learned that Ellie had been gone since five-thirty—or at least since five-thirty. How much earlier, they had no way of knowing. Mrs. Courtney had walked down to the arroyo at the back of the ranch, one of Ellie's favorite spots; Mr. Courtney had tramped up the first slopes of the foothills north of the ranch; they had both shouted and called. There had been no response. Ellie missed her breakfast, then missed the bus. At eight o'clock the Courtneys began to phone, and were beginning, when Mr. Hall called at nine, to think of the police.

Mrs. Courtney had felt particularly uneasy because Ellie had put on at that hour of the morning (or earlier) not her school clothes or a pair of shorts, but her very best outfit, her white Easter suit. This was Ellie's first suit, and she was unusually proud of it. Ellie didn't care whether her other clothes were on hangers or on the floor, but her suit she kept not only on a hanger, but in a clothes bag with two old, faded, but still faintly sweet sachets dangling across its shoulders. The fact that Ellie had worn her suit convinced Mrs. Courtney that her daughter's absence was something planned—not merely a spontaneous morning ramble that had somehow extended itself. But, spontaneous or planned, she didn't understand the Halls' connection with it.

The minute her husband hung up, she wanted to know everything and all at once.

"Take it easy, Gloria," Mr. Courtney said. "Ellie is there. She's not hurt in any way or sick. And she's with this Hall. That's all I know. We're going over to the hospital right away. To get her."

"Didn't this Hall explain anything to you?" Mrs. Courtney asked. "How he happened to have picked up a fourteen-year-old girl in the first place? I should think he'd feel duty-bound to make some explanation."

"I don't know that he did pick her up. Besides, Ellie didn't want him to call us at all. He was calling without her knowing it."

"That's what *he* said," Mrs. Courtney reminded her husband.

Mr. Courtney admitted that all he had heard was Mr. Hall's version of the affair. "Hall wasn't in any mood to talk at all," he defended him, "with his wife having a baby."

"You mean—she's in labor now?"

"That's what I gathered." Mr. Courtney, who was wearing a sleeveless undershirt, went into his bedroom, brought out a shirt, and began to unbutton it. "You going to wear what you've got on into the hospital?" he asked. What Mrs. Courtney had on was a faded-denim slack suit.

"I don't suppose I should go at all," she said worriedly. "This call could be a hoax. It might be just a plan of Hall's to get us away from the house. I think I should stay here."

"Maybe you're right," Mr. Courtney said. "I'll call you the minute I get there. And you call me if anything happens here."

Mrs. Courtney, noticing her husband's mud-spattered khaki pants and heavy irrigation boots, had a momentary impulse to call him back to change. She was too anxious to have word at once from Ellie to really care how he looked, however, and she let him leave without a word about his appearance.

Merton Memorial Hospital was only six miles from the Courtney ranch, two miles outside the town of Tenant, where Ellie went to school. Mr. Courtney was there in ten minutes. Feeling as worried as any expectant father, he asked the way to the maternity ward of the first person he encountered inside the building.

"Third floor," he was told. "Waiting room's at the end of the hall. You can't miss it."

The waiting room had a door with a glass inset, and Mr. Courtney saw, before he entered it, that Ellie was not there. Its occupants were three men. The three men looked as if they might be members of three separate generations: a battered-looking, unshaven young man; a forty-year-old, pink and fresh-faced; an old fellow with his grizzled, shovel-shaped beard half hidden behind a copy of the *Rotarian.*

Mr. Courtney entered the little room, which was forbiddingly cheerful, with maple tavern chairs and bright hunting prints, and glanced doubtfully about.

"I'm looking for a Mr. Hall," he said. "Creighton C. Hall."

"That'd be me," the young fellow answered, stubbing out his half-smoked cigarette in a mound of other half-smoked cigarettes.

"Where's Ellie?" Mr. Courtney asked at once.

"She went out to get something to eat. She . . ."

"I told you I'd be right over," Mr. Courtney said, interrupting him.

"She'd already gone when I called."

Mr. Courtney, anxious to discover what kind of a fellow his daughter was mixed up with, sat down beside Mr. Hall. Hall was young, twenty-two or -three, blond, with a smudge of darker whiskers and a manner half truculent, half worried.

"I wish you could have kept my daughter here until I came," Mr. Courtney said.

"Well, she hadn't had any breakfast or any supper or any sleep," Hall explained. "It was about time she ate."

This lack of supper and sleep was news to Mr. Courtney. "Where'd she go? I'll pick her up."

Mr. Hall shrugged. "I don't know where she went. She went with his wife. Ask him." He nodded across the room to where the middle-aged man sat facing them.

"Excuse me," Mr. Courtney said, "I believe my daughter went out with your wife to get something to eat. Do you happen to know where they went?"

"Haven't any more idea than a jack rabbit," the pink-faced man answered, obviously happy to relieve the tedium of waiting with talk. "We left home so early this morning my wife didn't get her coffee, so she was going to drive back into town for it. But I don't know where she'd go. We're just here because our daughter's having a baby. We don't know the town. Was that your little girl that went with my wife?"

"Well, I think so," Mr. Courtney said.

"She's a nice little girl. Looked kind of peaked, though, and when my wife said she was going out for coffee, Mr. Hall suggested the little girl go along. They'll be right back, I can assure you. My wife could hardly bear to tear herself away and, except for the coffee, wouldn't've. If my wife don't have her coffee by ten o'clock, she's atremble in every limb. You might say she's a coffee addict."

Creighton Hall gave Mr. Courtney a sardonic look and lit another cigarette. Mr. Courtney said, "It was kind of your wife to take my daughter with her," then quickly turned his chair so that he faced Mr. Hall. This put his back to the other man.

"Do you know Ellie?" he asked.

"Never saw her before this morning."

"Where was she then?"

"Reservoir Hill."

Reservoir Hill, besides being a hill and the location of the town of Tenant's water supply, was a kind of semipark, with a grove of eucalyptus trees, numerous shrubs, oleanders, red-berries, Carpenteria, Matalija poppies, and the like. There were, in addition, a few tables for picnickers and a couple of grills where steaks could be broiled and coffee made. Since the Hill was not more than four miles from their ranch, the Court-neys had eaten supper there more than once.

"What time was this? When you first saw her?"

"I didn't notice. Six, maybe, or maybe a little before."

"How'd *you* happen to be there at that hour?" Mr. Courtney asked, feeling suddenly suspicious.

"I was up there trying to make up my mind whether my wife should have this Caesarean or not."

Mr. Courtney felt a sudden pricking of conscience. Here he was, interested only in Ellie, while this young fellow's wife was perhaps in a bad way.

"How *is* your wife?" he asked.

"I don't know. You can't find out anything around here. She's having it now."

"The Caesarean?"

Hall nodded somberly.

"They say that's the easiest way." Mr. Courtney tried to re-assure him. "No danger at all."

"Not when you've already been in labor thirty-six hours," Hall said. "Not when your heart's not any too good anyway.

But God, it was just as bad the other way. Worse, it looked like to me, because it might last longer."

"What'd your wife want?"

"She wasn't in any condition to know what she wanted. All she *said* was, do whatever's cheapest."

"Didn't the doctors advise you?"

"You know doctors. They're not sticking their necks out. On the one hand, this seems our best course; on the other hand, it don't seem so good. It was all up to me."

"Well, it's hard lines," Mr. Courtney said. "I know."

"Ellie your only kid?"

Mr. Courtney nodded.

"I sure don't blame you. This is my last. My wife's never going through this again. Look at that old fellow down there," he said.

Mr. Courtney looked cautiously over his shoulder. The grizzled beard was now hidden behind a University of California bulletin. "These grandfathers take it pretty calm," he said.

"He's no grandfather," Hall said. "Well, he may be a grandfather, but he's not getting this kid secondhand. It's his own. His ninth."

Mr. Courtney could not refrain from another look.

"Took him three wives to do it, though," Hall said bitterly. Then, as a nurse came to the door, he leaped to his feet.

"Mr. Beamish," the nurse said, "your daughter's just presented you with a fine seven-pound granddaughter. Would you like to have a little peek at her?"

Mr. Beamish bustled up and out. At the door he turned back to say, "If my wife comes, tell her where I am."

Mr. Hall, still on his feet, called, "Nurse, nurse, how's my wife?" But the nurse either didn't hear him or didn't want to answer.

"Damned machines," he said, sitting down. "They got no more feeling than a tombstone." Then, as if he didn't like the sound of his final word, he hurried on. "Your wife have any trouble when your daughter was born?"

Mr. Courtney was glad to get back to Ellie. He sympathized with Hall but, actually, he scarcely knew any more about Ellie than he had when he left home.

"A little," he said, "but it turned out all right. It usually does. About Ellie, now—what was she doing up on Reservoir Hill at that hour of the morning? Did she tell you?"

Hall gave him a sharp, tough look. "Yeah, she told me."

Mr. Courtney waited.

"She was figuring out how she could do away with herself."

When he took his next breath, Mr. Courtney was aware of it. "Do away with herself?"

Hall paused as if he would give Mr. Courtney a chance to say once more that everything usually turned out all right; but Mr. Courtney said nothing. "Don't tell her I told you, though," Hall said. "She don't want you to know anything about it."

"But she told *you?*"

"Sure. I was feeling like hell and she was feeling like hell, so we told each other our troubles. She was walking around up there crying and I was sitting there darned near it. 'Sis,' I said, 'I don't know whether my wife's going to live or die. What's your trouble?' So she told me."

"I didn't know Ellie had any real troubles, not any real troubles."

"This isn't any real trouble," Hall said, "except to a kid. But right at present she thinks that her life's ruined. That she can't ever go back to school and so forth. So she wishes she were dead."

Mr. Courtney had been seeing the Reservoir. It was a deep

gray-green pool with steep, concrete-lined sides. In the early morning a milky mist sometimes hung over it.

"But why?" he asked. "Why does she feel this way?"

"Because she thinks she's a laughingstock, and that's a thing a kid can't stand. And because a person she loved, and about worshiped, I guess, went and did this to her."

Mr. Courtney supposed he must have looked pretty stricken, for Hall said quickly, "It was one of her teachers. You know a Miss Fisher?"

Mr. Courtney nodded. Love and worship were the proper words, all right, for what Ellie felt for Miss Fisher. They lived, at home, on an everlasting diet of the remarkable Miss Fisher. They knew all about her wonderful voice (she read poetry aloud to her classes), her vast knowledge, her sensitive perceptions (shadows by moonlight are much more beautiful than shadows by sunlight), her glorious hair (red), her fastidiousness (she always wore gloves and a hat, even when she went for the shortest stroll). Insofar as it was possible for a fourteen-year-old to model herself upon a thirty-five-year-old, Ellie had done so. And Ellie believed, her father thought, that Miss Fisher had, in return, some special regard for her.

"Yes," Mr. Courtney said. "I know she has a teacher named Fisher. And you're right. Ellie thinks she's wonderful."

"Well," Hall said, "that wonderful old bastard ought to have her neck wrung a couple of times."

"Why?" Mr. Courtney asked. "What's she done?"

"The kids hand these compositions in to her. Little short ones. Snapshots or something, they call them."

"Impressions."

"Yeah, impressions. Well, your kid wrote one that she was proud of. She really believed in this one. And when she walks into class, this Fisher has it all written out on the board. Then in a few well-chosen, witty words, she takes the skin right off your daughter, peels her right down naked before all those kids. Has everybody laughing their heads off to think anybody'd be such a damn fool as to write such stuff. Fisher doesn't say your daughter wrote it, but a couple of the kids know it, and they tell everyone, so now everybody's guying her and kidding her. She can't take two steps without being yelled at by somebody, and she thinks the great Fisher thinks she's a fool. So life's not worth living any more. See?"

Mr. Courtney saw, all right. "What was the piece about? Something kind of funny?"

"No, sir, it wasn't. I believe it myself and I think it's darned good. It's called 'Live Life Deeply.' That's what they yell at her now, she says. 'Come on and live life deeply,' they yell every time she sticks her head out a door. You want to read it?" Hall asked. "I got it here."

He took a much-folded piece of binder paper from his wallet. "I told Ellie I'd like to keep it. I wasn't kidding her either. I really would. It kind of fit my case this morning."

Mr. Courtney unfolded the single sheet of paper. It was pretty dirty and pretty tear-stained. At the top in Ellie's large sturdy letters were the words, "Live Life Deeply. An Impression."

"Life," it began, "may be compared to a glorious sea and human beings to bathers. Some wade in ankle deep, some to their waists, and some all over. Let us not hesitate in the shallows of life, wet only to the ankles, but plunge bravely in. Let us live life deeply. Out where the breakers crash—"

Suddenly Mr. Courtney did not want to read any more of it. He refolded the sheet and handed it back to Hall. Hall put it in his wallet. "You see anything wrong with it?" he asked.

Mr. Courtney shook his head. "Not for fourteen."

"This Fisher made her stand up and try to tell what she

meant by living life deeply and how it was different from living on the heights. All that crap."

Mr. Courtney groaned.

"Here they are now," Hall said.

Mr. Courtney turned around. It was a surprise to him to see Ellie looking, except that her suit was dirty and grass-stained and she herself somewhat pale, about as usual. He had been so recently up at the Reservoir and in that classroom that he felt that he, at least, had changed. He got to his feet and started toward Ellie, but as he did so, a nurse, coming in behind her, called, "Mr. Hall, you're a papa," and Mr. Hall shot out in front of him.

"How's my wife?" he demanded.

"She's fine, just fine," the nurse said; then seeing the woman with Ellie added, "And you've got a sweet little granddaughter, Mrs. Beamish."

"What's mine?" Hall wanted to know.

"Daughter," the nurse said. "Eight pounds. Takes after Papa."

"Wowie!" Hall cried. "Come on, everybody. Meet Miss Hall."

"You know you just get a little peep at her through the glass," the nurse told him. "Just a wee little peep!"

"Sure, sure," Hall said. "I go to the movies. Come on, Ellie," he said, taking her hand. "Let's get the hell out of here." Hall and Ellie, half running, led the way down the corridor. Behind them, more sedately, followed Mrs. Beamish, Mr. Courtney, and the nurse.

Hall admired his daughter immensely. "She sure does look better than that little old red grandfather's kid, don't she?" he exulted.

The nurse explained that babies born by Caesarean section were always whiter than others.

"Don't start belittling my daughter," Hall advised.

While Hall was peering and praising, Mr. Courtney remembered that he hadn't called his wife. "I'll be right back," he told Ellie, and hurried off to find a phone booth.

As soon as Mr. Courtney left, Hall said to Ellie, "I called your father. I told him all about it. I had to. I let him read that piece, too."

During the excitement of seeing the new baby, Ellie had had a little respite from her troubles. Now she felt their full weight returning to her.

"Look here," Hall said, "there was nothing wrong with that piece, if you meant it."

Ellie looked up at him inquiringly.

"I mean, were you a show-off? Just blowing your top to get a little attention? Just saying, live life deep, but not meaning it?"

"Oh, no," Ellie said sadly. "I meant it. That's the trouble."

"Trouble? What the hell!" Hall exclaimed. "You're just where you wanted to be."

"Am I?" Ellie asked, struggling to see what Hall meant.

"Why, sure. You got your folks half nuts worrying about you, you've ruined your best dress, you're cutting school, the kids all yell at you, and the great Miss Fisher thinks you write tripe. What more do you want?"

Ellie was speechless.

"Well, maybe you didn't mean it," Hall said. "Maybe what you really want to do is wallow around all your life in a big chocolate sundae. Is that it?"

"Oh, no!" Ellie said.

"Well, okay then." Hall made a motion as if to give Ellie a friendly spank, evidently decided that she was not a big-enough girl for that, and ended up with a half-slap, half-pat to the cheek.

"Keep your chin up, kid," he said. "That's what I'm going to tell my daughter."

As soon as they were out of the hospital grounds, Ellie asked her father if she had to go back to school that afternoon.

"No," Mr. Courtney told her, "you don't. I finish irrigating tomorrow, and the next day we can leave. For a week, as far as I'm concerned. Go up to Yosemite. It'd be nice up there this time of the year. How'd you like that?"

"I'd like it," Ellie said, "but I couldn't do it. I couldn't miss that much school. You know," she added, "I've got a good idea for an Impression for next week. I'm going to call it, 'A Morning in a Maternity Ward.' I don't see how anybody can yell that at me, do you?"

Ellie's father made a sudden, unintelligible sound, and Ellie turned to look at him. She couldn't bear to think that he was doing what it seemed he might be, and she looked quickly away—at the familiar countryside, which, because she was unaccustomed to seeing it in the middle of a school morning, was strange and exciting to her.

Mother's
Day

Alban, my husband, and I had come down to
spend the Mother's Day weekend with my widowed mother on
her ranch south of Los Angeles. We found her too concerned
over my Aunt El-Dora, however, to participate very whole-
headedly in any celebration in honor of her day. What my
Aunt El-Dora was doing was neither illegal nor, as far as I
could see, immoral. Still, it didn't sit well with Mother.

"Where is her pride?" she asked me.

I didn't know. And I didn't feel responsible in the way
Mother did. Although I'm only five years younger than Aunt
El-Dora, the pride of the aunt is not the concern of the niece.

Mother and I were in the dining room of the house that has
been my mother's home since the death of her father-in-law.
The afternoon was warm and we sat resting, cooling our arms
on the dark walnut of the big pseudo-Spanish table, Mother at
one end, I at the other. We had paused, for a minute or two
we thought, in the dining room after washing the lunch dishes,
on our way to more comfortable chairs in the living room, but
after the custom of women we had lingered there. In the living
room, the electric clock with the cathedral chimes sounded half
past something.

138

Mother looked at her wristwatch. "Half past three," she said. "It's getting late." But neither of us moved.

Behind Mother were the French doors that open onto what is called in Southern California "an outdoor living room"— really, a greenhouse made of lathes and covered, in this case, with an enormous wisteria vine. Through the doors I could see Alban stretched full length in the canopied glider, reading the *Post* about Botts, the Earthworm Tractor fellow, and keeping time to the glider's creak with his stockinged toes. The *Post*, as he leafed through it, rustled gently, echoing the clatter of the palms along the driveway. Mockingbirds sang from habit. Their hearts were not in it. Only at dusk do they really lift their voices. The air was heavy with the scent of the wisteria vine, which was in full bloom, and of the Valencia groves, which were in bloom, too, and added their fragrance to that of the wisteria. Strong though they were, heavy and musky and sweet, these scents did not enter Mother's thickly curtained, heavily carpeted room very freely. Mother wants to be indoors or out; she likes definite boundaries. That's one reason she was troubled about El-Dora. The boundaries about El-Dora seemed wavering and uncertain.

"Right here in the shadow of the church, too," she lamented.

"It would have to be a pretty long shadow," I told her. "El-Dora being a mile and a half down the road from the church." I meant it for a joke; my intention was to lighten the talk.

"You know what I mean," Mother said, unsmiling.

I did indeed. The churches of the Temple Brethren cast longer, darker shadows than those of any other denomination. I know. I, too, am a Temple Brother, like Mother, like El-Dora. Or at least as El-Dora *was*.

Outside the creak of the glider had ceased.

"Why don't you take Alban a glass of lemonade?" Mother asked.

Mother is always alert to find ways in which I can please Alban. She was happy when Alban came courting. I think she was afraid I might be an old maid. I know she didn't think me very attractive as a girl. It hurt me then, but I understand it better now. She didn't like her own looks and I was her spit and image. If you don't like your own looks, it is irritating, I suppose, to see them popping out at you on unexpected occasions and from unexpected angles. Mirrors you can avoid, but a young daughter has to be with you at least part of the time. Who made Mother think she was unattractive? Not my father. Father and Mother never came home from any place, church, or party that he didn't say, "Ethel, you were far and away the best-looking woman there." He would stand off, cocking his head as if to truly assess her, then repeat after this deliberate scanning, "Far and away. Far and away."

And it was the truth. He wasn't simply reassuring her, or flattering her. What she thinks now of the face we have in common I don't know. Someday I'm going to ask her. I looked at her against the light of the French windows: head, with its puff of gunmetal hair, not gray but ash blond darkened, held to one side as she listened for the sound of the glider to announce that Alban was once more at ease. Her pink lips were full and pleasant over her teeth, which have a slight outward slant; her eyes, big and shining, are sea-blue and flecked as that blue always is with green. And all of her, from the gunmetal hair to the finger mangled in a corn chopper when she was a girl, alive and shining in spite of her sixty years. I don't know how the Temple Brethren ever caught her. They didn't, of course. She was born one, just as I was.

Anyway, that's my face, too, minus twenty-five years. And while I admit, as I read recently, that no woman with a long upper lip can be *pretty*, still we're not as plain as Mother thinks. But the habit, early formed, of compensating to Alban for my lack of beauty still persists. I got the pitcher of lemonade from the refrigerator, poured a glass, and took it to him.

The lathe house under its canopy of blossoming wisteria was a big purple cave. So beautiful! I felt loving toward the whole human race simply to think that it was capable of developing a vine like the wisteria and of training it over a support like a lathe house so that for a week or two in spring there would exist a room lined with amethysts and scented like honey. The light was lavender-colored. Bees seemed to be hanging in the air. And over all the dry, homesick rustle of palms along the driveway.

"It's like being in a big, sweet purple cave," I told Alban.

He was deep in his story and didn't hear me. He drained the glass, put it down, and said, "Your mother's never happy unless she's feeding someone, is she?"

"I wouldn't say never."

He shook the seeds in the bottom of the glass. "Got any more?"

"Lots more," I said, and fetched the pitcher.

"I knew he'd like it," my mother told me as I went out with it.

When I had reseated myself at my end of the table, she began to speak again of Aunt El-Dora. "Go down to see her, Merlin. You're of El-Dora's generation. She'll listen to you."

El-Dora . . . Merlin . . . Those names tell you something—a good deal, perhaps—about the women of my generation. We are the El-Doras, Merlins, La Fays, Valoes, Vernices, Lu Renes. And we are the daughters of the Ethels, the Rachels, the Hannahs, the Graces. They made their gestures of protest in naming us. Gave us the burden of their unrealized dreams.

El-Dora's mother, Rachel, was my grandfather's sister. Great-aunt Rachel ˌhad had seven children before moving at the age of forty-five to Southern California. The youngest of that pre-California group was ten. No one, probably not Aunt Rachel herself, had expected any more. Then in three years, three more: Royal, Carmencita, and El-Dora. Thus an aunt so near my own age.

"What do you want me to say, Mother?"

"Her pride . . ." Mother began again.

"After all," I reminded Mother, "he *is* her husband. It's her legal and moral—"

"Legal, perhaps," my mother interrupted me, "but not moral."

There was no use arguing. Instead, I listened to the tu-rooing of the doves that had once belonged to my grandfather but that on his death had been freed and now lived, such as had escaped boys and hawks and cats, in the eucalyptus trees at the back of the grove. Mother listened, too, and in remembering Grandfather thought, I suppose, of his sister, El-Dora's mother.

"I'm glad Aunt Rachel isn't here to see El-Dora now."

"Would she make El-Dora punish her, I wonder, the way she used to?"

My mother put her hand to her eyes as if to shut out an unpleasant sight. "I never liked that. I'm sure it was wrong."

"The first time I saw it was at the mock wedding."

"Mock wedding? I don't remember any mock wedding."

"Remember" is always a magic word, but especially when mother and daughter use it. Years ago they saw the same thing —or, rather, the same event happened before their eyes—and now, twenty years later, they discover that each saw something entirely different from the other. The mother tells her story; the daughter tells. What each saw is unbelievable. What each missed is unbelievable. Put the two stories together, and there, perhaps, is the real event. But who can say what the real event is?

Mother remembered the mock wedding after I had described it. But she hadn't been there; she had only heard about it. It happened while Caprice—Caprice is my younger sister—and I were visiting Grandfather Webster in this very house. One afternoon we walked down the oiled road between the orange groves to play with Aunt Rachel's children.

"Do you remember," I asked my mother, "that we used to have the second story of Aunt Rachel's tank house for a playhouse?"

My mother nodded. "I do remember. El-Dora is living there now."

"Living there? How can she?"

"She's renting the front house. And the tank house has been fixed up. The pump and tank were taken out years ago. It's really very attractive. The only place hereabouts where you can see over the groves now they've grown so high."

Usually, because of the engine for the pump and the smell of whatever it was they burned in it—distillate or kerosene—we played ship in the tank house when I was a child. Crew below with the pump and engine, passengers upstairs. But that day El-Dora told us the minute we arrived that we were going to play bride and groom.

"The trouble was," I told Mother, "there wasn't a suitable groom."

"There still isn't," my mother said, her face in a twinkle grown flinty and condemning.

"Oh, Mother!" I exclaimed. I hated to see her like this, and in a flash her face had changed once more. Back was the pink-mouthed, loving mother, and I longed to make amends for my unfair thoughts of a minute before. Happy to have her back and loving, I said, my voice soft with the pleasant thing I had remembered, "I remember I wore that natural linen dress you had embroidered so beautifully for me."

"Oh, pshaw," Mother said.

"I remember how proud I was of it, starting out for El-Dora's that afternoon."

Mother was beginning to remember, too. "I can see you and Caprice starting out for Aunt Rachel's that afternoon. I can see you both now, plain as day, and I remember thinking Caprice looked awfully wispy and washed-out beside you."

"Oh, Mother!" I said. Twenty-five years and still pleased by that. And not a word of truth in it. Caprice is and was a real beauty, about as wispy and washed-out as a cherry tree in full bloom. But I loved remembering that dress. I had felt good in it. I was a chubby girl, and the skirt had been full enough for me to move comfortably. And it had smelled good, that linen fabric, like freshly mowed lawns or newly baled hay.

"Mother, has linen changed in the way it smells?"

"I think it has. I think it's something they do to pre-shrink it—or make it wrinkle-resistant."

"I used to think that dress smelled like Ireland."

"Perhaps it did, dear."

I was remembering more and more: the roses with which El-Dora had decorated the playroom—Gold of Ophir, opal-colored and cinnamon-sweet. She had made a wedding veil of a lace curtain, and a wedding dress from one of Aunt Rachel's white nightgowns. There was a wedding bouquet of nasturtiums made spray-style, and even a big bowl of pink champagne.

"Champagne!" Mother exclaimed when I told her this. "Why, that's impossible."

I had thought of it as champagne for so long that I had almost forgotten it *was* impossible. It was actually lemonade colored with beet juice and frothed with bicarbonate of soda.

I don't know why it didn't make us sick. What it did was make us drunk—beautifully, beautifully drunk, at first; then fighting drunk later on.

"We got drunk as lords on it."

"Drunk as lords! Why, Merlin!"

"Except for that there would never have been a fight."

We were drunk on pink lemonade, and from drunkenness we went easily to blows. El-Dora had tried to make me be the groom. It was ridiculous to have a bride twice as big as the groom, I thought, but El-Dora was set on being a bride. She had an old suit of Royal's for me to wear, with a fancy vest and a boutonniere, and though I wanted to be the bride myself, to please El-Dora I began to put on the groom's suit. But it was too tight for me. I wasn't built for boy's clothes. It hurt me and I could see how silly I looked in it.

"I'm not going to be any old groom," I told El-Dora.

"Oh, yes, you are," she said, and began rebuttoning the button I was unbuttoning.

"I won't!" I yelled.

"You will!" she yelled, pushing me back into the suit I was tearing myself out of. The end of that was blows, of course. El-Dora slapped me and I cried. Bellowed, I suppose. Anyway, Aunt Rachel heard and came running.

When she was told what had happened, she said, "El-Dora, you have done wrong. You have made me suffer. Now I want you to show all your friends just how you make your mother suffer when you do wrong." So she forced El-Dora to hit her over and over again.

My mother groaned when I told her this. Then after a few minutes' silence she asked in a voice I could scarcely hear, "Did she have El-Dora use a switch—or something?"

"No. Her hand."

"Where?" Mother whispered.

"The face."

"Slapping?"

"Yes. El-Dora had slapped me, you know."

Mother rubbed her hands over her own face. After a while she said, "How could Aunt Rachel *make* a big fifteen-year-old girl do that . . . if she didn't want to? I couldn't have forced you—under any circumstances—to do such a thing, could I?"

"I don't know. If you had trained me to do that since I was little—perhaps."

"But at fifteen . . . couldn't El-Dora have revolted?"

"Maybe at fifteen she didn't want to."

"You mean she enjoyed hitting her own mother?"

"She hit her pretty hard."

This was such a terrible thought to my mother she propped her elbows on the table and rested her face in her hands as if something had given way inside her. So we sat in silence for some time, she with her face in her hands, I looking beyond her to where Alban lay in the glider. Whether it was our silence or the fact that he had finished both his story and the lemonade I don't know. Anyway, Alban came in then, carrying the empty pitcher. He put it on the table, looked at me, looked at Mother, then said, "Something bothering you ladies on this fine afternoon?"

"We were talking about Aunt El-Dora."

Alban pulled out a chair and sat down. "She in trouble again?"

"Mother thinks so."

"Well, my conscience is clear. I tried to keep her on the straight and narrow the one chance I had."

Mother lifted her face from her hands. "When was this, Alban?"

"I told you about it at the time, Mother," I said.

But *Alban* had never told her about it.

146

"When El-Dora decided to leave her first husband—what was his name?" Alban asked.

"Vergil," Mother supplied.

"When she decided to leave Vergil, she came to see me at my office. They were living up north then, and El-Dora offered to sell me a lot of her personal belongings, cheap. She wanted to raise some quick money."

"Did you buy them?" Mother asked, out of courtesy, for now that she had been reminded she surely remembered my telling her of El-Dora's call on Alban.

"Not I. In the first place, they were not things we had any use for. In the second place, I wasn't going to have any part in encouraging her to leave a respectable hard-working man like Vergil to take up with an unknown quantity like that tramp printer. And how right I was."

Mother nodded. "I know. El-Dora came home after that broke up. She used to come down here and cry on my shoulder until she found Walt."

"Well, what's wrong now? Does she want to divorce Walt now?"

"Oh, no. The shoe's on the other foot . . . now."

"Walt wants to divorce her?"

"No, I mean the shoe's on the other foot because she *ought* to want to divorce him. Or at least she ought not to want to live with him. She *couldn't* live with him if she had any pride."

Alban pursed his lips and cocked his head. "Walt stepping out on her?"

"Worse than that, much worse."

I could see Alban wondering what Mother would consider worse than that. He started to say something, then changed his mind and waited for Mother to explain.

"Walt's living with another woman."

"You mean he's left El-Dora?"

147

"He's left her for five days of the week. He lives with this woman down at Indio, where his job is five days of the week. Then he comes up here on Friday nights and lives with El-Dora."

"Maybe she doesn't know anything about it," Alban said. "The wife's always the last one to know anything about it, they say."

"She knows about it, all right."

"Well, maybe she likes it," Alban suggested. "Maybe two days of Walt is enough."

"She does not like it," Mother said with dignity. "She is eating her heart out. She begins crying the minute he leaves her Sunday evening and she doesn't stop crying until Thursday when she starts planning for his return. It's disgusting. But she won't listen to a word of criticism of Walt. She says she loves him and he's her husband and if she can't be with him seven days a week then she is happy to be with him two days a week. Is it legal to live that way, Alban? You know something about the law."

"El-Dora certainly isn't doing anything illegal. Walt's her husband and she's got every legal right to live with him when she can."

"But that woman in Indio? Isn't El-Dora helping her break the law? Isn't that collusion or something?"

Alban smiled. "I don't think you could prove very easily that living with your husband is encouraging him to take up with another woman. It could work out that way, of course, but legally you wouldn't have much of a case."

"Anyway, it's immoral," Mother repeated. "Oh, something has just broken in El-Dora. Something has just given way. She's too soft. If she'd put her foot down and tell Walt he either had to stay home or get out, he'd stay home. But she won't do it. 'Walt has to do whatever he wants to,' she says. 'Joie's a lot younger than I am. I can't blame Walt for being attracted to her.' "

"Joie this Indio dame?" Alban asked.

Mother nodded. " 'Joie's got a beautiful voice,' El-Dora says, 'and Walt's always loved music.' Where's her spunk? Why doesn't she have some faith in herself?"

"El-Dora's a good-looking woman," Alban admitted.

"Well, why doesn't she stand up for her rights, then?"

"Oh, Mother, there aren't any rights in love."

My mother turned on me impatiently. "I know your views, Merlin. Just now I'm talking to Alban. She ought to say to Walt, 'Leave that woman or leave me!' Oughtn't she, Alban?"

"She's afraid he might do it, Mother."

Mother threw her hands in the air. "Oh, I give up. In your own way, Merlin, you're as bad as El-Dora. But I do think you ought to go down and call on her anyway. Even if you won't back me up."

Alban said, "No reason why we can't do that, is there, Merlin?"

"Thank God, Alban," Mother exclaimed, "that in you we have a man who has never given us a moment's worry."

Alban made some slight sound—laugh, snort, sigh. I couldn't say which. Then he repeated his invitation. "It's a nice hour for a walk. Let's go down to see El-Dora, Merlin."

Mother decided it. She got up from the table. "Good," she said. "Bring El-Dora back with you. Sunday evening's the mournful time for her. I'll fry a chicken for supper—we'll stir up a little merriment."

"This is your day, Mother Webster," Alban said. "You're supposed to be taking it easy, not cooking up meals for love-sick relatives."

"A mother is never more happy than when looking after the welfare of her brood," Mother said.

This was unusually unctuous talk for Mother, though a kind she often falls into with Alban. As if embarrassed by it, she hurried at once to the kitchen and was already bustling about with supper preparations when Alban and I started out for El-Dora's.

The evening couldn't have been prettier. There was just enough duskiness to soften all outlines: orange trees were big green tents and the verbena that covered the ground between the road and the groves was a Persian carpet. It was a road I'd known all my life, the very one I'd walked down to attend the mock wedding. Then, of course, time had been forever and I hadn't bothered to look at things like trees and flowers. Now time was half used up for me and I knew it and I took in what I could while I could. And it was all so beautiful. I wanted Alban and me to do something about it together. What, I don't know, since Alban certainly wasn't going to talk about it, and would only listen grudgingly if I began to speak about what he called "Merlin's beauties of nature."

But a man and a woman shouldn't walk separated through such things, should they? Walk down a road at evening not touching? I wanted to put my hand out to Alban. Take hold of him, touch him, tell him.

I don't suppose it can be a fact that Alban has sharper elbows, knees, Adam's apple, finger tips, and so on, than other men? That there is something harsh, dry, twiglike, and painful about all these projections, members of the body, whatever is the proper name for them? It cannot be, in fact, true, yet the truth is I've often been hurt by them, and my impression on reaching out to Alban is of running into some kind of thorny growth. But the evening's beauty was too much to endure alone, so I put my arm through his. Though I didn't risk saying anything. Just lifted my head in a motion that included and commented.

So thus thornily linked and without a word we walked down the road to Aunt Rachel's house, and past it, down the driveway to the tank house where El-Dora now lived. The tank house stood in the center of a half-dozen pepper trees, and its big shingled tower rose through and above the lacy fronds of the pepper trees like a lighthouse tower above waves. Lights were already on, and the top section of the Dutch door was open to let in the evening's sweetness and coolness. And Walt was still there. At the far side of the room he sat in a rocking chair, reading. El-Dora was a foot or two from him, stirring something on the stove. Between stirs she would come over, lean against Walt's shoulder, and read with him. Once she brought a spoonful of whatever she was cooking for him to taste. Once he laughed, then read aloud to her the passage that had made him laugh. When she went back to the stove, she held onto his hand and he let his arm stretch full length so the link wouldn't be broken. Both were smiling. I don't mean a grin; their expressions hadn't much to do with their mouths being open or their teeth showing. But what lies behind a smile, the feeling that curves the mouth and bares the teeth, that look was on—or perhaps the word is "behind"—their faces.

Alban and I stood staring through the screen of pepper-tree branches like any peeping Toms, convinced that this was no time to come calling but unable or unwilling to tear ourselves away from what we saw. I can't speak for what Alban thought. What I thought was, So this is marriage. I'd been *in* it for sixteen years, but I'd never seen it before; never seen before "the matrimonial state" as apart from two married people together, which is just a quantity, not a quality.

But the surface we were looking at wasn't all. The moment of parting was near when the clasping hand would unclasp and Walt would go back to Joie and her sweet songs. The touching was real for itself, but for El-Dora, anyway, there was desperation in it. She hovered, she touched, fed, listened, in agony. I could feel it. Her heart was breaking. And *your* heart, I reminded myself, is not breaking. It was some consolation.

Alban brought me to my senses. He touched my arm with his sharp-ended fingers and we went tiptoeing out of that yard like people leaving a church service. Once onto the road, we walked along silently. I didn't try to take Alban's arm again. My thoughts were given over to El-Dora's situation, with losing Walt, and I didn't hear Alban when he spoke.

"What did you say?" I asked.

Alban replied in a harsh voice. "What I said was, 'All that and Joie, too.'"

I was startled. I had thought only of El-Dora's misery and I had taken for granted that that was what Alban had been thinking of. The fact that Alban had not been concerned about El-Dora at all, had just thought how well off Walt was, stopped me in my tracks.

Alban stopped also and faced me. "Why did you do it?" he asked.

I didn't know what he was talking about.

"Why were you and your mother so set on catching me? Two big, good-looking women closing in on one poor puny nineteen-year-old-? Why did you do it?"

I said, "I was only nineteen, too." But I thought, Good-looking? Then, all so unnecessary.

"I didn't intend to close in on you, Alban."

"I know it. I scarcely figured in the plan."

We stood facing each other under the darkening sky. Alban reached out a hand to me, patted me two or three times, very gently for Alban. "Forget it, Merlin. It was a long time ago."

We walked home, serenaded by the mockingbirds, which are night singers, as I've said.

Mother had decked the table as if for a party. In the center was an angel-food cake decorated with sweet peas. Candles in mother's best cut-glass holders were already lit. The room was filled with the smell of frying chicken.

Mother's face fell when she came out of the kitchen and saw that we were alone. "Where's El-Dora?"

When I told her that Walt was still there and that we hadn't wanted to disturb them, she was silent for a while, then said, "I blame El-Dora's mother for all this. I place the blame squarely on Aunt Rachel for the unnatural life her daughter is leading. She broke the girl's spirit."

She stopped abruptly. It is one of Mother's rules not to bore Alban with troubles—hers or mine. She hurried into the kitchen and came back at once with some pretty, fruity drink —non-alcoholic, of course.

"Alban," she cried, "I've made something better for you than you had this afternoon."

"It will have to be good then," Alban answered very politely, taking a glass.

When each had his glass, Mother said, "Let's drink to Alban."

But Alban wouldn't have it that way. "This is your day, Mother Webster, not mine. Let's drink to Mother's Day."

Mother, who knew nothing about the etiquette of toasts, drained her glass with us. As we put our empty glasses back on the tray, the palms were clattering again with what I suppose is their true sound—a sound of the desert, of dryness and loneliness and vast infertile wastes of sand. But here amidst our irrigated groves and in our stucco bungalows we have long since learned to associate that sound with home.

The
Heavy
Stone

When Frances Redmond returned from the florist with the lilies, the choir was just leaving the church. Their final practice before Easter was over. All had gone well, and the singers, now homeward bound, were content with themselves, Mr. Donner, their director, and the holy season. They were preparing to celebrate. Two or three of the choir members stopped to admire the lilies, which Frances had in the back of the station wagon, but only Mr. Donner volunteered to help her carry them into the church. Frances was a little amazed to see him clasp his fine white hands about the rough clay pots, for she had heard it said that Mr. Donner was so proud of his hands, which he displayed conspicuously when directing the choir, that he would use them for no rough work whatsoever, and that for even ordinary chores he protected them with cotton gloves.

After Mr. Donner left and before she began placing the lilies along the edge of the choir loft, Frances brought them all together in a gardenlike clump in front of the altar. They had cost much more than she had expected, forty-eight dollars for the twelve, and what she would use for money during the next weeks at school she didn't know. Still, because they were so beautiful and because Joel had been so fond of lilies, she didn't regret buying them. They were a wonderfully stately flower, proud and mysterious. Like the church itself, she thought.

With a delicate stroke she touched the pin-point diamond frosting of one of the lilies. She thought of herself as a lover of flowers, but she knew she was not; not in any such way, certainly, as her brother Joel had been. At ten, Joel had been growing lilies from seed, a difficult accomplishment even for a grown gardener. On his eighteenth birthday he had sent her yellow violets picked on the green hills back of Fort Ord. And on the day he had been killed his friend had written them that Joel had in his breast pocket a handful of native wild cyclamen, the shooting stars of California's early spring.

It was this love of Joel's for flowers that had first suggested to Frances that she decorate the church in his memory at Eastertime. It was not by any means her sole reason for the undertaking, but it was the easiest to explain and the one she mentioned first to her mother.

Her mother had been pleased, but matter-of-fact. "Dear," she had said, "this isn't anything you'll be able to do just hit or miss, you know. It will have to be done properly and be ready on time. And it will be a great deal of work."

"Nobody asked Joel what he wanted to do in the army," she had replied. "He had to do whatever he was told to do, and no questions asked. I'm no better than Joel. I can do what needs to be done."

"I know," her mother told her, "but someone has always taken care of the church decorations before. It's nothing you really must do."

"That's the trouble," Frances said. "I've always let someone else do the work and I've just enjoyed and admired. This time I want to do the work."

155

This time, though she had not been able to say so to her mother, she hoped to feel herself close to Joel in doing, as he had done, work to which she wasn't accustomed. And because it would be work with flowers, which Joel had loved, and for an occasion that celebrated the triumph of life over death, she hoped, too, that she might be able to lighten the pain that, since Joel's death, had rested like a heavy stone upon her heart.

"And Frances," her mother had said finally, "decorating the church for Easter isn't a thing to do with set teeth. A grim duty to undertake because it needs to be done and somebody has to do it."

"Oh, Mother!" she had exclaimed. "Do you think you have to tell me that!"

How could anything connected with Joel be done in any way except with love? Since his death she had been trying very hard to be more like him—and that meant being more loving. In decorating the church, she wanted to express her growing likeness to her brother. And though she had not been able to make all this clear to her mother, for neither of them was yet able to speak of Joel at any length without breaking down, her mother understood her purposes sufficiently to arrange with Dr. Emmons, their pastor, for her to undertake the work.

Leaning over the lilies, taking deep breaths of their fragrance, which seemed somehow golden to Frances, like the powder in their throats, she was very happy she *had* undertaken it. Everything was going well. She had been working all day and was bone tired, but there wasn't much left to do. The worst had been putting the yellow Spanish broom, which she had gathered in the hills back of town, on the ledges under the high, arched windows. That had been a job for a monkey, not a human being. To do this she had had to balance dangerously and uncertainly on top of a wobbling stepladder, and now in the small of her back she could feel her muscles trembling like frayed ropes. Placing the cheese-cloth, which she had dyed purple and bordered with fleurs-de-lis cut from gilt paper, over the expanse of gray cold plaster behind the choir loft had taken acrobatics which were almost beyond her, too.

Her plan had been to frame the choir loft, which was above and behind the altar and pulpit, with a foot-high hedge of lily-studded greenery. The greenery part had been simple: man-zanita branches brought down from the hills. What had not been simple, what in any other circumstances she would have called absolutely hellish, was putting the chicken wire, which was to provide the framework for the branches, in place. She did, finally, get it in place, but only because she had been willing to struggle on, in spite of a torn dress and bleeding hands. But the wire was firmly attached now, and it held up the gray-green manzanita, so that the choir would appear to rise for its singing from a formal garden of clipped hedges and nodding lilies. Still touching the lilies, still bending over them, Frances reviewed what was yet to be done. Almost nothing: place the lilies behind the choir-loft hedge so that they would nod over it; put the tall candles in the two gold and crystal candelabra she had brought from home; tie the great floral cross, sheathed with creamy stock and banded with golden lilies, to the railing in front of the choir loft. That was all.

All her exasperation and weariness began to leave her. She could see the church as it would be when every frond and flower was in place, the candles lighted, and the lilies, spray-ing outward from the arms of the cross, promised Easter joy to all. She felt very happy, very loving, and very near Joel. This was how Joel would feel if he were here working, she thought.

Contentedly she began to sing the song the choir had been practicing. "Halleluiah, Christ is risen. Gone is now the heavy stone."

"Those are the words," somebody said, and Frances whirled about to see Mrs. Askew, the choir's first soprano, walking noiselessly down the aisle.

"Oh! Mrs. Askew," she exclaimed. "I didn't hear you."

"As I was saying," Mrs. Askew continued, "those are the words, all right, but I've never heard that tune before. I should think that melody would have been dinned into you after all the practices you've listened to, Frances. Halleluiah, Christ is risen. Gone is now the heavy stone," Mrs. Askew sang in her high flawless voice, so that Frances felt as if she were having a private Easter service of her own. "It's a perfectly simple, easy melody."

"I know," Frances said, humbly. "I can't sing."

Then, to hide her embarrassment at having been overheard, she said, "I love lilies, don't you, Mrs. Askew? Don't you think they look just like the spirit of Easter?"

"They'd look like the spirit of Christmas or the spirit of the Fourth of July, I guess, if we used them then," said Mrs. Askew. She bent over one of the lilies, shaking her head at what she saw. "Look at this! Turning brown on the edges already. Where'd you get these, Frances?"

"Rossi's," said Frances proudly. Rossi's was the "right" place to buy flowers.

"That explains it," said Mrs. Askew with conviction. "Here's one about to drop its head already." The head of the lily Mrs. Askew was pointing to looked perfectly secure and fresh to Frances, but Mrs. Askew was evidently right. She had only to bend it back and forth a few times before it fell off, dropped to the floor, spraying some of its golden powder onto Mrs. Askew's black pumps. She bent to flick it off with her handkerchief.

"That Rossi's," she said irritably.

Frances felt humiliated. She had gone to the best and most expensive florist and had bought the most expensive lilies. This was something on which she could not possibly have tried to economize. "I thought Rossi's was good," she faltered. "And I particularly reminded them that the lilies were for the church."

"Frances Redmond," Mrs. Askew exclaimed, "you didn't go and do that!"

"Why, yes," said Frances, "I did. I was proud that they were for the church."

"You didn't tell them *what* church?"

"Of course," said Frances.

"Well, that *does* explain it."

"Explain what?" Frances asked, bewildered.

"These poor, fading, second-rate lilies."

"Are . . . are Rossi's known for poor lilies?"

Mrs. Askew snorted. "Rossi's is known for very fine lilies, and they all go to Mr. Rossi's own church. I bet he's laughing his head off right now at wishing this sorry bunch of stuff on us while *his* church will have lilies four feet high and six to a stem." Mrs. Askew loosened another petal and let it fall to the floor. "Falling to pieces already! You poor child. You were certainly taken in."

Frances could not believe such a thing, not of Mr. Rossi, who was round and fat and had seemed kind. He had given her a daphne cluster for her coat when she left, and had wished her success with her decorating and a happy Easter. "Mr. Rossi would never think of such a thing," she declared warmly. "He helped me pick out the lilies himself."

Mrs. Askew laughed dryly. "I can well believe it."

"Not for Easter," protested Frances, "not for a church, he wouldn't do such a thing. Nobody could."

"Why, that's nothing," Mrs. Askew assured her. "Our church always gets its flowers of Eby's. The Ebys belong here, and I for one would be good and sore at Charley Eby if he didn't send his second-rate stuff to some other church and save his first-rate stuff for us. That's nothing more than sound merchandising and sticking by those who stick by you. It's the way businesses are run!"

"But Easter isn't a business!" Frances protested.

"Selling lilies is a business," said Mrs. Askew with finality, "and Pete Rossi did a good stroke of business when he got rid of these. You weren't figuring on just leaving them huddled together here, were you, Frances?"

"No," said Frances, though she was almost ashamed to admit she had any plans at all for the lilies, so much diminished were they in her eyes by Mrs. Askew's disparagement. "I had planned to put them on the edge of the choir loft back of the hedge. The idea was," she explained doubtfully, "to make it look as if the choir were singing in a garden."

"Garden!" said Mrs. Askew shortly. "If it were a garden, you wouldn't catch me singing in it. Bugs, drafts, poor accoustics, and any Tom, Dick, or Harry who wanted, listening! But looking like a garden is something else. I'll carry a couple of pots up for you, if you like. My gloves are either up there or I've lost them."

Frances carried two pots herself, and when these, with Mrs. Askew's two, were placed behind the manzanita hedge some of the pleasure she had first felt in the lilies, and had lost while listening to Mrs. Askew, returned. "What do you think?" she asked shyly. "Will they do?"

Mrs. Askew pursed her lips thoughtfully. "Well, since

you've asked my honest opinion, Frances, I think the hedge is a little too high. I've heard many a member of this congregation say that they liked to see, as well as hear, the choir. They don't care about disembodied voices. If that was all they were after, they'd stay home and listen to their record players. They want to see as well as hear. Of course, nothing would suit any of *us* better than to be absolutely out of sight. But I don't think, in a case like this, we have a right to consult our own selfish wishes. So for that reason I'd try to find some way to lower these lilies. Here're my gloves," she said, spying them under the chair she had occupied at practice.

"Lower them or maybe bank 'em around the pulpit," she advised from the back of the church, on her way out. "That's my advice."

There wasn't any way to lower the lilies. They had either to rest on the ledge where they were or be done away with altogether. Frances placed them all as she had planned. Perhaps now and then a lily would obscure someone's view of a singer, but, she thought irritably, I don't believe people are as crazy about seeing the choir sing as Mrs. Askew thinks. I know I'd far rather look at a lily than Mrs. Askew, and I bet other people would, too. She walked to the back of the church. From there the choir loft looked truly gardenlike, with the lilies lifting their creamy trumpets above the bank of green, and she decided they should stay.

She did not know how to get the large flowered cross attached to the railing of the choir loft without the janitor Mr. Leggett's help. But since he had been so cross about the extra work she had already caused him, she attempted it herself. By seven o'clock it was firmly in place, and there wasn't a leaf or flower petal left on the floor or a pew cushion out of place. She seated herelf in the back row for a final check on her handiwork. In the peaceful orderly room, much of the pleasure she had had in planning the decorations returned. She wished she could light the candles, but was afraid to do so.

There was nothing whatever that still needed doing, she decided, unless she righted one of the sprays of larkspur which was hanging unevenly from the shallow, tripod-supported bowl in front of the pulpit.

I wish I hadn't seen that, she thought, but she got up and put the spray back in place. "There," she said, "stay put, now."

As she talked to the flowers, or to Joel, or perhaps to herself because she was so tired, she heard a gentle thudding on the swinging doors which opened out of the main vestibule into church.

"Come in," she called, and two old ladies whose faces she had often seen in church, but whose names she could not remember, came hesitantly through the doors.

"We wouldn't interrupt you for anything," one said, "but we do want to see what you've done."

"You're not interrupting at all," Frances told them. "I've finished."

"We meant the conversation."

Frances laughed. "I was talking to the flowers. Telling them not to go slipping and sliding about."

"Yes," they agreed. "They are hard to manage sometimes. In that shallow bowl, especially."

Frances walked to the back of the church and stood close to the two women, one square and rather tall, the other short and round. Both were gray and spectacled and both wore blue-and-white print dresses buttoning down the front. She remembered that they were sisters, the tall one a Mrs. Something, and the short round one a Miss Something, but Miss or Mrs. what, she simply could not think.

"I'm Frances Redmond," she told them, hoping they would

say who they were, but they continued to gaze about, wordlessly. "I've been decorating the church."

"Yes, we heard you were."

"How do you think it looks?" Frances asked, hoping for a morsel of praise.

"It looks lovely, dear. Lovely and up-to-date," the short sister said.

"Up-to-date?" Frances repeated, wondering what was up-to-date about lilies and crosses and armloads of Spanish broom.

"Nothing old-fashioned," the tall sister explained. "And all those lilies! Lilies are so dear this Easter. How did you ever persuade the Finance Committee to let you spend so much money?"

Frances didn't quite know how to answer. "I bought them myself," she said finally.

The two sisters looked at each other. "Well, that explains a good deal," the tall one said. She turned to Frances. "That was sweet of you, dear, very unselfish of you to share your bounty with us. You mustn't forget, though, that the Bible says that it is harder for a camel to pass through a needle's eye than for a rich man to enter Heaven!"

Frances was not quite sure what was being said to her, though she felt uneasy about its import. And all possible answers seemed awkward to her. If she said, "I pauperized myself to buy them, practically," it would sound as if she were asking praise for her sacrifice. And if she didn't say that, it would sound as if she were admitting that she was rich, which was certainly not true. She did not even like to use the word "rich" in church, where other things were so much more important. With a sudden inspiration as to how the truth might be told and the word avoided, she said, "I guess I won't have any trouble getting through the needle's eye."

The sisters gave each other another look, and the plump

one said gently, "None of us can speak with any certainty of such matters, dear. Though we may all hope."

"Oh, I didn't mean that," Frances said intensely. "I could never mean that." This was the worst that had yet happened to her, that anyone should think her so smug and stupid. "That was the furthest thing from my mind. What I meant was . . ." But the sisters were uninterested in what she meant. They were interested only in the decorations, and when they had inspected these closely they were ready to go.

"Thank you, dear," the round sister said. "It was very sweet of you to let a couple of old ladies have a close peek at what you've done."

And the tall one added, "Yes, we're on the shelf now, Clara and I. But we're still interested in what the younger generation has to offer, even if we can't keep up with them. Everything you have done, dear, has the modern touch. I think your cross is especially modern. We would never have thought of that, would we, Clara?"

"Modern?" faltered Frances. "How do you mean, modern?"

"Oh, I don't know. Just modern. That band of gold lilies, for instance. And the flowers spraying out that way. Not like the poor old rugged cross of our day. But then, our day has passed. Thank you, dear, for giving us a little preview."

After the sisters left, Frances tried to see the cross through their eyes, but it was impossible. In the empty, quiet church it looked timeless to her, simple and beautiful, frothed over with the foam of its white flowers, splashed with the gold lilies.

When she got home she told her mother about the two old ladies. " 'So modern, so modern,' they kept saying," she said, between bites of the cold chicken and hot cocoa which her mother had insisted she eat.

164

"Well, there's nothing wrong with modern, is there?" her mother asked.

"There is when you say it the way Emma said it. 'It's very modern, isn't it, Clara?'"

"Oh," said her mother. "Clara and Emma!"

"Do you know them, Mother?"

"Yes."

"Well, they don't think much of your daughter or her decorations. Why're they so interested in decorations, anyway?"

But her mother, instead of answering, suddenly noticed her empty cocoa cup. "Have some more cocoa, Frances," she urged.

"I'll take it upstairs with me," Frances said, lifting the filled cup. "I feel damaged. I bet I climbed up and down that stepladder a thousand times."

"Do you want me to call you in the morning?" her mother asked. "With the first service at nine, you'd better be there at eight-thirty, hadn't you?"

Frances yawned, wanted to stretch, but couldn't with the cup in her hand. "Better call me at seven-thirty. I want to get there in time to see if anything's fallen to pieces during the night." She gave her mother's shoulder a squeeze with her free hand. "It looks nice, Mama. You'll be proud of it."

Next morning she blinked sleepily up at her mother. "It can't be seven-thirty already," she said.

"It isn't," her mother said, "but Dr. Emmons wants to talk to you."

"Here?" she said, sitting up, half awake.

"Oh, no, not here. On the phone."

Frances ran out into the hall in her pajamas. "Darn! I bet something's gone to pieces."

"Dr. Emmons?" she said.

"Good morning, Frances," Dr. Emmons said. "First of all, Frances, I want to thank you for the beautiful piece of work you've done. It's given me much pleasure. I've just returned from a little tour of inspection with Mrs. Askew and Mr. Donner, and I can't tell you how the sight of your beautiful flowers has heartened me."

Frances relaxed. Nothing had collapsed, no one had stepped on a forgotten thumbtack, Mr. Leggett hadn't complained of extra leaves to sweep up. It was Easter morning. Through the open door she could see the sun, yellow as lily pollen on her bedroom floor. Already, from those churches with early services, the Easter bells were beginning to peal.

"Thank you, Dr. Emmons," she said happily. "I loved doing it."

"There is one little thing, Frances," Dr. Emmons went on, "or, rather, to be strictly truthful, two. Mrs. Askew feels the choir is somewhat hidden by your decorations. Mrs. Askew has been our soloist for ten years, and I'm sure you want her to be happy as much as I do."

"Oh, yes, Dr. Emmons!" said Frances.

"I've told Mrs. Askew that, if you agreed, four or five inches might be clipped from the top of the hedge. The choir has worked hard, and it is quite understandable that they want to convey their Easter message face to face with their neighbors. But only you, my dear Frances, can do any cutting, and then only if you really want to. What do you think?"

"I'll be right over and do it," Frances said.

"Well, if you think best, Frances. It's a matter wholly for you to decide. The other little thing is this. Mr. Donner says a goodly number of our nonmusical members follow the music by watching him direct rather than by listening. And he hates particularly to disappoint them this morning when so much of the service will be musical. Can you hear me, Frances?"

"Yes," said Frances, "I can."

"Mr. Donner thinks that the removal of just a few of the more exuberant sprays from the cross, Frances, would be all that was necessary."

"Yes," said Frances.

"You quite understand, don't you, Frances, that all this is absolutely up to you? You've created a beautiful effect, and no one but you is to touch it. In case you do want to make any changes, however, Mr. Donner will wait at the church for a half hour so that he can tell you which are the sprays that need cutting."

"Tell him I'll be there," said Frances.

She repeated the conversation to her mother as she hurriedly washed and dressed. Mrs. Redmond brought a cup of coffee up to her, and Frances tried to hold it with one hand and comb her hair with the other.

"You understand, don't you, Frances," her mother said solicitously, "that this sort of thing is bound to happen where a number of people are involved? No matter how perfect the result is, it's bound to disappoint someone."

"Of course," said Frances, giving up the hair combing. "I wasn't born yesterday."

"You've worked so hard," her mother said. "I don't want you to be hurt by someone who thinks the arrangements could be better."

Frances put down her cup. "Mother," she said, "I'm not the least hurt. I don't care a whoop about what you call my arrangements. I really don't."

She jumped up from the bench in front of the dressing table. She really didn't give a whoop about the arrangements.

If someone, if anyone, had suggested other flowers, other plans, she would not have cared in the least. Sunflowers instead of lilies, crowns instead of fleurs-de-lis, anchors instead of crosses. What did hurt, what hurt so hard that she could not speak of it, could not really look at it, but must work fast enough to keep it out of sight, was the reason . . . the reason . . . back of every objection, of every need for change . . . of . . . But she would not let the reason emerge, she would not let it come between her and Easter, between her and Joel, between her and love.

"Hurt," she told her mother. "It's nothing more than a few little mechanical things. What kind of a daughter do you think you've got, anyway, not to be able to take a little criticism? Me, I'm sensible."

She clapped her hat on her uncombed hair, stuffed bobby pins, necklace, stockings, and make-up into her bag, laid her cheek against her mother's, and said, "Look, Ma, I'm strong stuff."

Her mother leaned over the banister as she ran downstairs. "Frances, you're not thinking of going in to church on Easter morning barelegged and with your hair streaming down your back, are you?"

Frances paused at the front door. "I'll finish up in the ladies' rest room after I've done the clipping and changing. Don't worry, I'll look fine in the Easter parade."

The clipping and changing were not much. Mrs. Askew had the hedge marked like a lady's skirt for shortening. Clip off the tops of the manzanita bushes, sweep up the resultant mess, and that job was finished. The hedge, in her opinion, lost its natural look by this operation, but the choir would now be able to sing in utmost visibility. And anyway, what did it matter how high an artificial hedge was? Not at all, of course.

Mr. Donner was there to point out the changes he wanted made on the cross. Most of the band of golden lilies would have to go, and much of that froth of white she had so admired. This work required more delicacy and precision than trimming the hedge, and Frances, in her nervous hurry to be done in time, was not able to do it well. Meaning to take only one spray of stock, she loosened others. Trying to get at one lily, she broke off two or three, until finally, when she had finished, the cross had become ragged and partial: sagging where it should have been upright, pocked with losses where it should have been complete and firm. But Mr. Donner was content. He was not now obscured in his directing by the cross, and he clasped Frances' hand heartily with both his fine white ones.

"Good girl," he said. "Nice co-operative child! Now run and put yourself in order."

Francis did run, because the church was already beginning to fill with people. She had left her handbag in the ladies' room, which opened out of the main vestibule. Now she hurried in, locked the door behind her, rinsed her face and hands, put on her stockings, and started on her hair. She finally got it up, and her hat on, but she looked so frightful she took her hat off and started all over again. Then, just as she was in the middle of this second attempt, she remembered the candles. They were unlighted! They must be lit, and she hadn't spoken to a soul about them. It would be too pitiful for them to stand there shedding no light amidst the flowers and music, while the beautiful words were sung and spoken.

In spite of her half-combed hair, she ran out into the vestibule, now filled with people. She searched for someone she knew and finally caught the eye of Mr. Sewell, one of the ushers. She beckoned frantically to him, and Mr. Sewell abandoned, with apologies, the couple he had been ready to guide to a pew, and came to her.

"Oh! Mr. Sewell," Frances said, "I forgot the candles. They went completely out of my mind. They must be lit. Have you any matches?"

Mr. Sewell looked at her half-combed hair dubiously, as if he were afraid she wanted to run, hatless, through the congregation to light the candles herself. But she didn't. She didn't care who lit them. Just so they were lit.

"That's all been taken care of," Mr. Sewell assured her briskly. "At the beginning of the choral prelude, two ushers in blue suits are going to march down and light them. One down either aisle. Make a nice little ceremony of it."

"Oh! Fine," said Frances, "fine! I had forgotten it completely."

"It's all taken care of," Mr. Sewell assured her. "I planned it myself."

Frances stepped back into the ladies' room and started once more on her hair. It went up better, now that all her responsibilities were taken care of. She got her hat on just right, with the ribbons falling over her collar in back as they should, and, thank goodness, she hadn't forgotten her gloves.

She was ready to leave, had her hand on the doorknob even, when from the organ there came the first strong triumphant notes, followed by a silence in which she could hear, in the vestibule, the slight shuffling sound of the two ushers in blue suits getting into step before proceeding down their separate aisles for the candle lighting.

Then the organ became triumphant, the choir lifted its voice in the hymn of joy, the very doorknob in Frances' hand trembled with the force of the music. This was the hour for which she had waited, for which she had worked, the hour of love that would restore and reunite, the hour of the resurrection. "Halleluiah, Christ is risen," sang the choir. "Gone is now the heavy stone."

She stepped out into the vestibule. Mrs. Askew was singing. Mr. Donner, hands white as lilies, was not obscured by the cross as he conducted. The two sisters had been given a back seat. The cross, less modern than it had been, still did not make them smile. Were Mr. Rossi's lilies really beginning to brown? Dr. Emmons' glasses sparkled in the morning light. The two ushers stately and square in suits that seemed to match trod in time to the music toward the candles.

Frances ran back into the ladies' room, the music following her. "Gone is now the heavy stone."

She dropped to her knees and laid her cheek against the cool enamel pedestal of the washbasin. When she was able to stop crying, she tiptoed back into the vestibule and out of the church. Outside the church she heard the last of the singing: "Christ is risen."

99.6

Nurse Williams came for the lunch tray. She was cheerful and crackling. "A fine lunch," she said. "I always say there is no one who can equal Graham in making a pudding! And you have eaten everything. That is fine."

The woman in bed did not trouble to tell her that the taste of food meant nothing to her. The doctors had told her that she must eat to get well. Then she would eat: no matter what the food was, no matter how it tasted, she would never send a crumb back. She was determined to get well. She was determined to live. So long as there remained a single word she had never read, a single tree she had never seen, she would live. But she knew better than to attempt to convey any of this to the nurse. Instead, she asked her, and waited for the answer with breath barely sliding out of her lungs before she called it back, "It's going to be warm today, isn't it?"

The nurse considered. There had been a high fog that morning, and shreds of it were still caught in the eucalyptus on the hills. But the sun had come through, and a pale and watery light fell on the administration building below them.

"Oh, no," she said, shaking her head. "It won't warm up this

172

afternoon. Too much fog this morning. Well, have a good rest, Mrs. Kent." And off she went with the tray, limber-legged and bustling.

Mrs. Kent thought bitterly: If I were a nurse, I would learn the answers people wanted and give them to them. It is going to be hot, and if my temperature's up a little it will be the heat. It is folly for doctors to say that bodily temperature doesn't vary with the weather. If you put a kettle over the fire it gets hot, doesn't it? I shall expect a little rise this afternoon, because of the heat.

No reading or writing was permitted for a half hour after lunch. For that half hour one merely digested—and thought. And when that half hour was over, rest period began, and for two hours one rested—and thought. Then at three, temperatures were taken and faces washed. It was for three Mrs. Kent waited. It was for that hour she awakened in the morning. Yet, in the morning she had other interests: could read her paper, open her mail. But the thought of three o'clock was there behind all, distorting and embittering all, though not until now, after lunch, did it begin to displace all else. Each morning she entered an open space, a space in which there was room for many things, but as the day wore on, it narrowed like a funnel. Now, after lunch, there was yet room for her to move upright, though she was cramped; but, from that time on, the funnel contracted very rapidly until she was lying flat, writhing toward the opening, burning, burning, encompassed by the hot bright metal of the funnel's spout. At three she emerged; sad, despairing perhaps, but not bound.

Mrs. Kent half sat up in bed. Thus raised, she could see herself in the mirror on the wall opposite. Behind her cheekbones, behind her eyes, she could feel a tide of warmth. But her face, reflected in the mirror, looked white and cool.

If only it would stay that way. Perhaps it would. She put

her hand to her cheek, but the cheek was hot. Not so hot, however, as some days, she thought. She lay back with a stir of hope; perhaps there would be no flush today. Three months ago that word had only pleasant connotations for her: "the flush of hope," "the flush of youth." Now it meant but one thing: "the hectic flush of the dying consumptive." Sometime, years ago, she had read that phrase, and it had meant nothing to her; six words in some story. How had she been able to read with no horrible start, no coagulation of blood, no premonition of doom, these terrible words? Yet, premonitions there may have been, for the words had stayed with her. She could even remember the book in which she had first read them, a book called *English Orphans*; a silly book she had gulped down when she was ten or eleven years old. There was a girl in the book named Rose, a headstrong girl who would not obey her mother. She was a vain girl, too, and she went to a party in a snowstorm with only a scarf about her shoulders and light dancing slippers on her feet. But she was punished for her wayward ways. She began to cough, she had a hectic flush, she died.

Mrs. Kent turned her top pillow over so that she might have the cool side against her shoulders. She carefully pushed her hair back so that it did not touch her cheeks, keep from her whatever air was stirring. At the top of each cheek, she could feel a round spot burning, burning. She could feel waves of heat given off by those discs of fire. She could feel the spots growing in circumference, until they would cover her entire face. But she reminded herself that this had little to do with temperature, for one day when her flush had been deepest and most painful, her temperature had been almost normal. This was unpleasant, it was hateful, but it meant nothing.

All footsteps had ceased. It was after one. Rest period. She made an effort to direct her mind to matters beyond her sickness. But what else matters, she thought. My temperature tells me how I progress. It tells me whether I am living or dying. It is the only real thing. What is past is mine no more and my temperature will tell me whether or not I have a future. Why do people say to me, "But you have always done so many things. Your memories must be a great comfort." In books, authors who have never known a sick day have their heroines, sick to death, luxuriate in their memories. My memories burn and scald me. Had I never known any other life, then I would never have known the bitterness of renunciation. Blot out my memory! Let me forget that I have a husband, a child, work. Let my body forget that it ever sprung into the air, cleft a wave, or clambered up a rock. Clean my mind of torturing memories—then this routine of death may be bearable.

We all overdramatize our ills, I suppose. Or do we? Even Keats: "That is arterial blood. It is my death warrant." Ah, but it was! Katherine Mansfield leaped from her bed to say, "Hark, hark, the lark at heaven's gate sings," and, with the consumptive's beautiful feeling for contrast, had a hemorrhage, and all of her beautiful words were blotted out forever.

Mrs. Kent raised herself in bed that she might look at her face again. The flush spread to ear and jawbone, a satiny purplish mask. Her eyes were bright and large; bright and large like a bunny's eyes when it is lifted by its long soft ears, and the stick that is to crush the delicate bones of its head is poised above it. And yet people cried, "How well you look, Marianne. Anyone can tell that with that fine color there's little wrong with you." Anyone who knows anything can tell a block away I'm consumptive.

The handbook said, "Many nervous girls and women may have a temperature for months after all activity has stopped." I'm nervous. This temperature probably means nothing. I may not even have any today. Ninety-nine and six-tenths yesterday. That's nothing, really nothing. It doesn't go on the doctor's chart until it's over 99.6. That's only a degree. Many a child goes to school with that temperature. And it's so hot today. The heat really accounts for four-tenths of a degree. If it weren't for the heat, my temperature would probably be only 99.2. And for many people, for sensitive, emotional people, 99 is normal. That only gives me two-tenths of a degree of fever. And what's two-tenths of a degree? Many thermometers have more than that much error! They incline to err with age. Oh, if I only had a new thermometer; this old one has the habit of rising; the mercury mounts before I get it near my mouth. If I were to lift it now and look at it, I would see that it had already risen. This is the hour it triumphs. It waits for three o'clock so that it can see me tremble. When I hold it in my mouth, my heart beats so that it is jarred by every thud. It shan't have that satisfaction today. I don't care if it reads 99.6; that's just the heat and my nervousness.

Why do I delude myself so? It is fever, fever. My eyelids are hot against my eyes. My armpits are dry; the back of my neck burns. It is fever. "You must fight, Marianne," they say. How fight fever? What cool thought can quench a fire? Let green waves with their heavy, cool weight fall upon me, bathe me with the foam of many waves, and still, deep in me, this coal would burn. Let snow fall upon me, let it be blown against my body by a bleak, icy wind, let all earth be held in a black frost, rigid as iron, and still my body would pulse with heat. Let me lie naked, face down, upon an iceberg floating in a frozen sea, and my hot breast would melt the ice beneath me.

"You must fight, Marianne!" I cannot fight this flame. I am fevered and I must die. I shall be consumed. They say

truly, "She has consumption," for I am being consumed.
Cranmer offered his hand to the flame first because it was
a traitor. My whole body has betrayed me. I offer it to the
flames. Burn and blacken, lick flesh from bones and turn bones
to powder, and then at last a wind will blow through the
powder and I shall be cool.

Oh, God, forgive my thoughts. Let me not burn. Give me
a normal temperature for just a day, and tomorrow I shall not
mind the fever again. Just today, just as a sign I make some
progress. That is not much to ask, God. Most people have it
and never thank you, and, oh! God, I will thank you forever.
I will praise your blessed name through eternity. I will be an
ever-vocal witness of your loving kindness. If it couldn't be
98.6, then 99. I do not ask the impossible, God. I do not ask
that I have no fever, only that it will be a little better than
yesterday, as a sign that this will pass away. Oh, I do not fear.
I have asked in faith. I shall be better today. This is perhaps
the turning point, I shall remember that from this day, all
went better.

"It's not bad today, is it, Miss Williams?"

"Not bad at all, Mrs. Kent. The same as yesterday, 99.6."

The Day
of the
Hawk

Thursday, February 16

The doctor said that if I could watch "something die, without flinching," I could consider myself well again. Something, he said, that "needed to die, that had to be killed in the course of events."

I told him I didn't think that made much difference. The "needing to die" part. The agony of salt isn't any easier for the silvery slug because the gardener says it needs to die, and kerosene and flame aren't any more soothing to ants because their death is a good riddance. Oh, God, in what agony will they wave their little hands! No, if I'm to watch something die, it won't matter whether it needs to die or not; what we feel doesn't affect an animal's feelings. The lamb isn't reassured when it sees the knife at its throat by the thought that it is needed for chops. No, I think more clearly about this than does Uncle Doc, for all that I'm the patient and he's the doctor. He could learn some things from me.

I think I can do it, though. I've accepted death—it has to be. But if I am to look at something die, it had as well be a lark as a pig. It's all one to them whether they die for our sport or our good. I know I can do it. I've made progress in the last six months, I'm sure, and I shall take the first opportunity to prove it to Uncle Doc. Jim will be so glad if I can, for things couldn't have gone on much longer as they were. That I can admit this shows that I *have* made progress. Jim is so strong and reasonable that my weakness has been harder for him to bear than it would be for most men.

Friday, February 17

The weather has been stormy, so I have stayed in my room all day, reading and writing. Jim says that if he were the doctor, he'd take pen and paper from me. He says that I write, write, write, brooding over old and past things, and that this makes me more neurotic. But he's wrong. Really, it's just the other way around. I *am* young, and, as Jim says, my life is before me; but there have been sad happenings in the past, and though I do make an effort, my mind goes over and over them, and I think, If only I had done this or that, how different everything might be.

And as I think I'm back again to the moment when the decision had to be made, without knowing it my fingernails go into my palms, and all my body is rigid with effort. But when I write down these speculations and remorses, it eases my mind; it's out of my mind then, down here, and I need not think just how it all came about; and if I want to justify myself for saying "yes," I can look back here and see how then it seemed the only thing to do. I can read it here, as if it had happened to some other woman; and I can understand how it happened to me.

Nothing I planned as a girl have I been able to carry out; except that I still write in my journal each day—and have for ten years. I like to look at the journals; there are twenty of them, quite a long row. Well, I've produced something.

Sunday, February 19

And still it rains. Not heavily, but there have been gusts all day. Jim has been playing golf even so. He is not fond of golf, but he says it helps him meet the right men, and there's nothing he wouldn't do to advance himself. He told me that when he married me, and it's been true.

Before he left he wanted to know when I was going to get out and put the doctor's advice to the test. I'm willing to any time. I want to, really want to; but Jim agreed it might be foolish venturing out into this rain.

Though it isn't a cold rain. California rains in February aren't cold, ever. Elinor was in this afternoon with a great bunch of yellow violets she had picked on Hunter's Hill. They were wet from the rain, and so sweet; sweeter and richer than blue violets, because yellow is a richer color than blue. Smelling them didn't seem enough; there was no depth of satisfaction in that! I wanted to bite them, to taste spring in them, to press them hard against my breast.

But when I did this, and rocked in delight to feel them so cool and fresh against my skin, Elinor said, "Stop that."

Once you've been ill, everyone wants you to be calm and repressed. Jim is always telling me to walk more slowly, for instance; but then, he did this even before we were married. But the violets were lovely, and I put them in a brown jug Mother used for cream when Elinor and I were girls at home. I put the jug on the window sill, and it was almost as if the rain outside were falling on the violets. A green-and-yellow ladybug, shaped like a raindrop, crawled up the pane from the flowers. I raised the window and put it outside, for it's of use somewhere for pollinization. It made sense to put it outside.

Elinor and I talked of old times: how poor we were then and how happy, too. Elinor is happy now, for she is getting ahead with her painting. She looked beautiful, with her pale cool cheeks and black hair.

She said, "Do you remember how we used to plan to make a name together? You writing books, I illustrating them? The first one was going to be 'Thimble Farm.' Do you remember you said you were going to know all there was to know in this world?"

I told her I remembered, but that then I thought I could know all things in my mind from books and from observation. I didn't know of a knowledge to be got through veins and nerves and muscles. I didn't know anything about a knowledge that could thicken one's blood with sorrow.

Elinor cried out, "Oh, let's not talk of now, Sylvia. You've been sick. Let's think about our days at home. You were loud and cheerful then. Always clowning. Do you remember the dance you used to do to the 'Blue Danube'? Newspapers for wings, footstools for hedges? Then you would be a spring-intoxicated butterfly, you said, and fly about. How Mother used to laugh. You were fat, then, you know, and not at all graceful. When I would tell you you were fat, you'd say you were a 'pinguid pismire,' and when I said you were loud, you'd say you were a 'cachinnating cockalorum.' You did love big words."

So she talked on and on, laughing and smoking and putting her ashes in her pocket like a boy. I knew what she was trying to do, for she kept glancing at me out of the corner of her eye, and she looked pleased when I smiled. But there is no need for that sort of thing with me any more. I'm quite reconciled and content.

I enjoyed the talk of our days at home with Mother for its own sake, not because it was distracting. I hadn't remembered for a long time that I used to be able to milk; or that I could squirt a stream right into Tabby's mouth. And how once, when Elinor and I were delivering milk at night, we got frightened and sang "God will take care of you, o'er all the way, through all the day" all the way home. It was Sunday night, and they heard us at church and thought we were sacrilegious, but we were really earnest and prayerful.

We were laughing and admiring the colors of the afterglow through the eucalyptus, a beautiful wintry green flecked with burnished gold and rose, when Jim came in. We had forgotten to turn on the lights, and only Elinor's cigarette gleamed from where she sat in the window seat.

Jim switched on the light and said, "No moping in the dark, girls." Though it wasn't dark yet. Then he said to me, "How's my pet? Haven't been smoking, have you?"

Jim thinks smoking is unwomanly, as well as dangerous in other ways. I hadn't, so Jim began to tell us about his golf. He had played with Mr. Nathan. He could have beaten him, but he said Nathan would enjoy playing with him more next time if he let him win. Elinor left before he had time to finish. Jim called her a "little devil," and she says she hates diminutives.

Monday, February 20

"My room really has for me a touch of fairy. Is there anything better than my room. Anything outside?" Katherine Mansfield said that, and I feel it, too. My room isn't beautiful, but it holds so many things I love: my books, my pictures, my little ticking clock. My candles waiting to burn for me. And, sitting here on my window seat, I can see old Skytop, with its head in the clouds this morning, and the Santa Ana looks as if it had a fair stream of water in it after last night's rain. The sky is clearing now, though, and I think I'll go out this afternoon. I've been inside for months, and there's no longer any need of it. Uncle Doc is right. I'm ready to live an unsheltered life.

The Day of the Hawk

The talk with Elinor yesterday afternoon has made me think again of how this all came about. All would have been different, I suppose, if I had never met Jim—or never married him. But once I had met him I think I never considered anything else. Oh! I cannot analyze my actions. Though I ask myself a thousand times, "Why?" I can never answer. I can only see myself doing what I did as if compelled.

I suppose Elinor's yellow violets brought it all to mind again. I was picking violets on Hunter's Hill when I first met Jim. I had gone up on a Sunday afternoon late. After reading and writing all day, I wanted fresh air more than I wanted violets, but the hill was covered, and they were so beautiful I couldn't resist picking them.

When I had my hands full I went to the little round palm-covered summerhouse on top of the hill to rest and watch the valley lights come on. Jim was there. He had been there all afternoon studying. I had seen him before, of course, and had even spoken to him in the newspaper office. He was the new man in Meyer Feldstrom's office. I thought he was—I still think he is—the most beautiful man I've ever seen. I have often tried to describe him in order to discover why this particular face is, for me, so compelling. What it has—not just a beauty of line and coloring, of black hair and eyes, and clean fine jaw line, and a nose not blurred with flesh—is a definite promise of compassionate intelligence. It moved me then, as it does now, and then I had no reason in the world not to be happy that he liked me.

We talked in the summerhouse for some time that evening. He said, I remember, that the social notes I wrote for the paper were the best social notes he had ever read. He knew my Uncle Horace, the editor. He knew my Uncle Doc.

I don't know whether it was then, or later, he told me of his life. He was almost thirty then. He had been poor, not as Elinor and I were poor, but living in squalor and misery, with a lazy, unambitious family about him. He had rid himself of them, and by denial and hard work and absolutely ruthless determination had finished college and passed his bar examinations. And every step since then had been toward an advancement. Belleview isn't a large place, but Feldstrom's is known all over the state, and next year Jim takes Meyer's place when he goes to Washington. All this is only the beginning, Jim says, and I know he's right.

I suspect it was partly because of his ambition and determination that he appealed to me. I dream so much, and carry so little through myself. I don't know why he wanted to marry me. I didn't, even then, do the things he likes a woman to. I wasn't pretty. Or not very. Of course my being related to everyone for miles about was some help to him. Anyway, we did marry. I was wild to marry him, hating the delay of getting clothes and household things together.

Elinor cried all through the ceremony, and when she took my flowers she said, "You damned idiot," but the minister thought she said, "God bless you," and smiled on her.

Tuesday, February 21

The rain is over, I'm sure. The fragrance of the lilies under my window determines me to go out this afternoon. I haven't set my foot on earth for six months, and then before that I was in bed for three months. Uncle Doc was here this morning to see if I had been out yet and had followed his advice. I told him no, but that I was going this afternoon.

Then he said, "Remember, Sylvia, avoid nothing. You cannot change anything. You must either accept life as it is or continue to hide here in your room as you have done for six months. That isn't living: to sit here on the window seat and peer out at life like some old, half-blind owl, and write in your book that the sun shines, or it doesn't."

Oh! Uncle Doc is good for me, and what he says is true.

Then he said, "Sylvia, you've never talked to me of what lay behind your trouble. I know the outlines, of course, and it isn't out of any curiosity I ask you, but for your own sake. Until you can talk of this thing, put it away from you in words, the seeds of it are still deep in you, and though you think you give it no nourishment, it will grow in spite of you."

I told him I could not talk of it, not to him even; not even though I knew he was right; I knew he was a thousand times right.

"Well, Sylvia," he said, "you know what you can do, though I know what's best for you to do. Could you write it in your book, Sylvia? Write it all out for me? Then when I've read it, perhaps we can talk."

I didn't tell him I would, I couldn't promise. But I think I can and that it will help. To write here has helped with everything else; and I hope that when I see the words written out, saying that this I did, and this, it will be as if another woman, and not I, had been responsible for those actions. But even if for Uncle Doc I'm able to write the facts, they won't be true. Not in all the lines of every book in the world can the truth of what I felt night after night after night, and day after day, be recorded.

When I told Jim, he said, "In God's name, why didn't you take care?" Just that, nothing else. I shall never forget these words. I said, "What difference can two months make?" He said, "It makes all the difference in the world to my image and to the way your family is going to think of me." I said, "We're married. No one's going to pay any attention to a baby a

185

month or two early." He said, "There's no need to take a chance on that. I'll arrange things."

Jim respected you so much, Uncle Doc, he didn't want me to breathe a word of it to you. "There's no use dragging him into it. I'll make the arrangements, and no one will be the wiser." He made the arrangements, and I did as he said; and we were all wiser and sadder.

I don't need to tell you the rest, Uncle Doc. I was sick then, and you came. As long as I was sick, everything was all right. I could think of nothing but the pain. And I believed I would die, too. Oh, I longed to die. But you know that I got better, and finally you brought me home, and soon I was as strong as ever.

It wasn't until the day of the hawk, was it, Uncle Doc, that you knew, about the other? I had known for a long time, but until then I had kept it hidden from everyone. At first I myself did not understand what compelled me to act as I did. And then I knew and justified my actions to myself. I had to do what I did. It was the only retribution I could make—I must help all living things to stay alive. Now nothing more must die because of me, and perhaps many things that would have died, except for me, would live.

I was busy all those early days after I came home from the hospital, busy and happy and crafty, that Jim might not know. Oh, it took time and patience. There were the bees caught in the gum of a diseased tree, alive and fighting, but doomed to die. I saved them all. I gave them hours of life they would not otherwise have had.

When the water ran low in the reservoir, carp and catfish were left half exposed to the air, floundering and dying. I saved them, too. It was backbreaking work carrying them in a bucket of water to put in a ditch that hadn't gone dry. But I did it, and all the thanks I wanted was in the eyes of those fish, as they looked at me with gratitude when I dropped them in the water. They blessed me with their eyes and forgave me my sin.

But it wasn't only animals: it was plants as well, for they are tender and living, and they can suffer and die even as we. If ivy was choking out a violet, I must dig it up and plant it where it might live. A strand of honeysuckle vine had worked under the telephone wire where it ran around the corner of the house, and was growing yellow and pinched. It would soon have died, but I saved it, and it bloomed with heavier blossom than it ever had before. Pale new grass pushed itself from beneath heavy boards that were holding it down. I lifted the boards to give the grass a taste of the sun. But when the boards were lifted, clay-colored sow bugs ran about in dismay. The sun which brought life to the grass brought death to them, so I carried them to a damp darkness where they might live.

I know now that I cannot do as I did then, but I cannot but believe that what I did then was right; that a virtue bloomed in me then that I do not now have; that if all were made as I was then, this world would know a happiness it has long forgotten.

Yes, Uncle Doc, I am reconciled, though I cannot say that those days were wrong. I was very close to all living things then, and though it meant agony to me whenever they suffered, I rejoiced when they triumphed and lived. I helped thousands of animals and plants. I kept a record; each night I wrote down what I had been able to do during the day, for it seemed to me then as if there were a scale and on one side was my sin, heavy, black, horrible, and on the other were all the soft, velvet-throated flowers and the animals with their wary, tolerant eyes, which except for me would be dead, sunk into formless pulp. Each night I added to the living side of the scales what I had saved during the day: perhaps only a hairy spider, or a big-eyed wasp, but always the other side weighed heavier and sometimes I feared I could never balance it. And I never have, for a thousand lives saved cannot replace one life taken.

All this time, though, you, and Jim, too, knew I was unwell and strange. You didn't know until the day of the hawk, did you, that I was "unbalanced," as Jim said. You remember that I cried out that that was just the word, "unbalanced," and that I must work day and night until the scales balanced again. When Jim said that, I believed the scales I saw were visible to all, and all saw that my sin was so heavy and black that the scales kicked the beam.

Do you remember the day of the hawk, Uncle Doc? You and Elinor and Jim and I had driven over the hills through the barley fields east of town. The barley was waist-high and bearded, but blue-green yet, and not ready for the bailer. I asked Jim to stop so that we could watch the wind waves in the barley, and the cloud shadows that swept like ships across it. While we sat watching, a hawk flew low, and there was a movement, not of the wind in the barley. I knew the hawk was hanging over a rabbit or a squirrel that had run into the barley to hide. But there were patches of thin barley, and all at once the hawk swooped down, and I knew that the next minute it would have its talons in soft flesh and fur. So, before any of you could stop me, I was through the barbed-wire fence, and into the barley, screaming and waving my arms. But I had hesitated a minute too long, and the hawk dropped on the bunny. Can you forget that rabbit's cry as it felt the hawk's talons enter its flesh, a thin, clear, childlike cry of anguish and surprise?

Then I was overwhelmed to think that once more I had failed, and that death had come again through me, and I forgot to be crafty and secret, and cried and screamed. I was determined not to go home, but to sit there on the little hill that overlooked the barley field and save whatever else came there for shelter. I lay on my face and clung to the rocks, for Jim tried by force to make me leave. It was then that Jim called me unbalanced. That was the day you knew at last, and the day you finally took me away.

I never told you the reason for the day of the hawk until now; and now you will understand that it was right for me to do as I did, and that only in that way could I expiate my sin. But in the hospital where you took me, and in these months here at home, I have seen that I cannot go on as I was. I am reconciled to bearing the burden of what I did. I accept death. I tried to be a god and to give life. Now that is past, and I shall do as you say, Uncle Doc. I shall go outside. I shall have Jim's friends here again. I want his smile and praise. Uncle Doc, you will not for my sake show to Jim any of that hostility for him I feel you sometimes have? Oh, do not, for I want his kindness; more, much more than that, more than I can easily write.

Now I have told you everything, and I am glad, glad you asked it of me. You share the heaviness now, and my heart is much lighter for that sharing. The rain is over, Uncle Doc. I shall call Elinor and ask her to walk with me this afternoon. You shall have this tomorrow to read; then let us never speak of it again. It will still be a dark thing, but behind me.

Tuesday, 4:00 p.m.

Elinor has just left: she wouldn't go with me. But Jim is home now changing his clothes. We're going to walk through the orchard; see if the rain caused much washing. I think the cover crop held the soil, though; there's little mud on the road.

There should be some tangerines left on the two trees at the far end of the ranch. I think no one has been back there for weeks.

I have on my brown boots and pants and my green sweater and cap. I've admired myself in the mirror for ten minutes. I look so strong and hearty. I look a very mountaineer whose boots cover miles every day. My face looked back at me from the mirror like anybody's face, friendly, and even, yes, good.

Oh! I am happy, happy! In spite of Elinor and what she said this afternoon. I told her I was going out; that Uncle Doc thought I was able to and should. She was glad about that, but she wanted me to leave Jim and live with her and Mother. She has never liked or appreciated Jim, never. I do not know why, for he has always been kind and gallant to her. She was bitter and urgent, walking about the room, rearranging my books and pictures and not knowing what she did. Her mouth got thin and straight, as it does when she's in earnest, and her cheeks burned.

She said, "Sylvia, remember the old days. We can bring them back." I wouldn't listen to her. She said, "Sylvia, you can't bring it off without help. You won't get it. Forgive me, Sylvia, but come home with me."

I told her I couldn't leave Jim. She was angry when she left, not even "Good-by," and her gloves and books forgotten on the table.

I hear Jim's door close and his heavy steps; he, too, has changed into his boots. So, we leave the house, and it's darkness, and we go out into the orchard.

September

So long since I have written here. Uncle Doc brought me my book weeks ago, but I could not bear to open it. I boasted of my happiness and virtue. Oh, God, I claimed them for my own. One must never do that. Perhaps if I had not, I wouldn't have lost them. But I lost them, I lost them in a minute, in less than a minute, between dusk and dark. The sun went down, with the heel of my boot I put out the light, and its scream was red, red on the black clouds. Red, red on the windows. Red in Jim's eyes, red on the heel of my boot. Red and shrill, pain screamed red and shrill, and then was quiet. Gray, nasty pulpy death. I put out the light. I brought gray, pulpy death again. I killed. I killed.

Jim said, "Kill it."

It came out of its hole, half drowned, and its fur was streaked with mud and it shivered with the cold.

It cried, "Save me." It cried, "Give me life."

Jim kicked it with his boot, and he called to me, "Step on that damned gopher!"

I longed to please him. This was my test. I stepped, and its bones crackled like thunder and its cry was like lightning through the thunder.

My boot was the end of the world for it. It lifted its eyes to my face and asked for life. I trod it down to the dust, down to join my son. I sent him a playmate.

My son will say to him, "Do you know my mother?"

And he will answer, "Death is your mother. Murder is her name. And she is red, red and dripping in heavy boots."

Oh, murder is my name, murder is my name, and I am red that all shall know.

Like
Visitant
of Air

The great equinoctial storms were past, but heavy rain still fell. The greasy swells of the Atlantic were indented by multitudinous wind-driven drops. In England, as far north as Yorkshire rain was sprayed down the mouths of wide chimneys and hissed for a second on well-fed fires.

Through all of October the New England coast was pelted with the loose, not very cold rain of early fall. In Boston, in Cambridge, the cobblestones were drenched and lumbering cart horses put down their feet warily; gutters were fluid and eaves musical. There was so much rain that what the ear noticed was not the constant gurgle and splash, but its cessation.

Moss was especially green in the northern niches of the stone walls about Concord. Emerson, in his study, harkened with pleasure to the cheerful drumming; Minott got out his fishing tackle and came home in the evening, wet, but with a goodly string of pickerel.

Thoreau, at Walden, leaned back in his hard chair and listened attentively. He left the page before him on his little slant-topped desk half-filled. His ear, attuned to the music of the telegraph wire and the owl's cry, to the dry rustle of scrub-oak leaves and the surflike sound of the draft in his stove, heard much in the rain others missed.

It was water, it was wet, it was rain. The sounds said more than that to Thoreau. He knew the pools and ponds, the creeks and rills and marshes it was filling now; he knew the roots that sucked thirstily, the summer-dried nests that swelled as if with life beneath the day-long downpour.

He noted the wind's veering, its increase in velocity. His big nose picked up through the cabin's unplastered walls the spicy scent of wet and wind-bruised sassafras.

He walked to the door, and, opening it, looked out into the dark wet night. It was late. In Concord all lights were out. In Emerson's home, in Channing's, in Cyrus Hubbard's, all slept, or lay unsleeping listening to the constant long liquid chuckle of the rain. He thrust a hand out into the stormy night in order to come at the rain more nakedly.

He had a sudden longing to step out into the rain, to walk toward someone, to walk to someone, come bone-drenched to someone and enter; to be known and dried, and say without preamble what the rain, its sound and meaning, were to him. His muscled and adroit hand closed about the water his palm held.

Where go? To whom speak? In Concord no one listened for his footsteps. He closed the door. In the light of his well-trimmed lamp rain water glistened on his brown hand. He looked down at his half-written page . . . and yet, there was someone to whom he spoke. He wrote for someone, his words were for some ear.

He pulled out his chair, picked up his pen and held it poised, listening, then laid it down.

On the table lay the books. On the hearth burned the fire,

meager but ruddy, not less alive for being small. It was after-noon if you looked at the clock, night if darkness counted.

In the doorway of the room Anne stood, twilight and order laced together like a poem for her reading. An ordered beauty. To know, oh! not to know, that was to presume, but to believe, that for one evening, at least, they were safe, that nothing could take the books, the small fire, the windows neatly set away from them; to believe that for one evening nothing could interrupt their words; no screaming, no stumbling, no sobbing. And that there would be no dying away into silence until a suitable ending had been reached. The framed, the metered, the musical, the self-contained: these they would make and these would endure beyond flesh.

Anne was the poet; the room, that night, was poetry to her of a kind her soft and well-intentioned words could never make real. She stood on the poem's threshold; it was pain not to en-ter.

The room was taut with perfection; a pin-point tension lay across it like the film with which a brimming glass protects its flood. It seemed, perhaps, as if she would never enter, but stand, always outside, regarding.

Yet the hand as well as the eye loves order, and she walked down into the room and touched the three stacks of books that waited on the table: Charlotte's the highest; Emily's a single book and writing block; her own, which made her smile, books and papers, needles and folded cloth, and thimble atop it all like a dome or minaret. "My little writing housewife," Emily had called her.

She paced from hearth to window the way the three were used to pace together. She straightened the hearthrug, which, angled by inches from the horizontal, was setting the room awry. Now the room was perfect, nothing lacking, spare and warm and clean; shining like holiness, and twice as reassuring. This was what Emily had said.

She pressed her hand against the window. Glass could not stop the wind's cold force; what her hand felt was, beyond the glass, buffeting Emily's whole body as she tramped the moors.

"Anne," said Charlotte, coming into the room with her quick unquiet steps, her hurried household rustle which echoed the wind, "stand away from those draughts. Or put on a shawl."

"Emily's walking in the wind," said Anne.

"She's dressed for it," said Charlotte. And then with her implacable rectitude, "At least I hope she is."

"It's so late," said Anne. "I'd be afraid out this time of night. I'd think she'd come in when night comes."

"Oh, Emily . . . Emily," said Charlotte, her dark solicitous face both loving and chagrined. "She'll stay out later, I don't doubt. I've gone and angered her."

"Angered?" asked Anne.

"Come," said Charlotte, "let's poke up the fire. Let's not be so cautious. Let's send a few sparks up the chimney."

She laid her arms across Anne's shoulders. Together they paced the stretch from window to fire. Charlotte rattled the grate with energy. "Throw on another chunk, Anne. Let's have a blaze . . . let's remember tonight. Emily's got her wind. Let's us have a fire. If I choose fire and Emily the wind, what do you choose, Anne?"

"The sea," said Anne softly. "I've always loved it. And flowers, too," she said. "May I choose two, Charlotte?"

"Throw on another piece," said Charlotte, poking fiercely. "Yes, I give you flowers and the sea. I keep fire," she said.

"Emily'll want rain, too," said Anne. "And some place to see the wind and rain from. She'll want the moors to go with them."

"All right." Charlotte stood with her back to the blazing fire. "Wind, rain, the moors. That makes three for Emily. You take three now."

"The sea. Flowers." Anne thought. "Love," she added.

"That's not the same," Charlotte objected. "You changed the category. That's noumenon, not phenomenon."

"All the same," said Anne, "I take it. Flowers, the sea, love."

"Oh, Anne, Anne," said Charlotte. "Here we stand talking. Here we stand choosing. As if we could choose. Do you ever think where we are, Anne? The moors hanging over us, the graveyard below. Lost between them. No one knows we live or breathe. No one ever will know. And you choose love. Who is there to love? Have you seen a face? Heard a voice?"

"I didn't mean it that way, not just that way."

"Why not?" asked Charlotte, leaning forward, so that her thin sallow face was rosy in the light. "Why not? We have a right to. We have talent here. We have great talent here, worthy to be loved and great enough for honor."

"Loving-kindness," said Anne, "was what . . ."

"Loving-kindness," said Charlotte scornfully. "That's due to all. That's duty." She stood away from the table where she was leaning. She trod the few steps before the fireplace as if the fire she had chosen burned in her heart. "I think of something beyond loving-kindness. I think of Emily," she said. "Do you think loving-kindness her just dessert?"

"She never spoke," said Anne, "of wanting . . ."

"She never will speak," said Charlotte. "The hills can molder, these tombstones rot"—Charlotte's dark head flashed hillward and graveward—"before she'll speak. But she will write . . . she does write."

"Charlotte," said Anne, "you didn't . . ."

"I did," said Charlotte somberly. "I did, and she is angry . . . and if she should stay out all night . . . if she should catch her death out there . . . and I suffer because of it . . . forever—still, what I did was right."

"Right," said Anne. "It was her private book."

"You knew about it?"

"Yes" was the only answer, but Anne would only nod her head.

"Why?" asked Charlotte. "Why would she not tell me? Why only you?"

"You would do something about it," Anne said. "You would talk about it."

"I will," said Charlotte. "I will do something about it. I will talk about it. Emily is a genius."

Anne started up from her stool. Genius—that was a solemn word, and Charlotte used words carefully.

"Did you read them all, Charlotte?"

"Every one."

"What did she say to you?"

"About six words . . . thief . . . peeping Tom."

"They were hers, her soul."

"It is a great soul. It has no right to hide. Here in this house, by this fire, even, lines no other woman could have written." Charlotte was rigidly quiet when she became excited. "She can imagine greatly, write lines so wild and melancholy, so terse and vigorous, no man alive can equal them. But she's a woman . . . she will write in a private book . . . walk on the moor, and all will be lost."

Anne said, "You write, too, Charlotte."

"I do," said Charlotte. "I mean to make it known. But I cannot do what Emily does. I see this world. Emily sees beyond. I can tell you how the wind sounds round the corner of this house. Emily hears how it sounded before there was ever a house for it to touch. She shall be known, too."

"Charlotte," asked Anne, "even if she does not want it?"

"She does want it," said Charlotte fiercely. "Why did she not destroy them? Why did she copy them carefully? Writing's not just the hand moving. It's speaking to someone, somewhere. Emily shall have her chance to see to whom she's speaking."

Anne went to Charlotte. She pressed her hand against the two veins that sharply throbbed on Charlotte's forehead. "I have a book of poems, too," she said. "Will you read them, Charlotte?"

Charlotte, trusted, was fierce no longer. "See, Anne, I told you this is a night to remember."

"They aren't like Emily's," said Anne.

"Oh, no," said Charlotte. "How could they be? You aren't like Emily. They'll be good and sweet."

"But not great."

"Goodness and sweetness are great," said Charlotte. "They'll be in a book all together." She leaned toward the fire as if reading them there. "Think of it, Anne. The three of us together."

The wind had died away from its steady blowing, but sudden explosive gusts still rattled the shutters. "It's coming on to rain again," said Charlotte. "Listen."

"Emily'll be in now," said Anne. "She won't leave us worrying."

Keeper growled in the entryway. "Emily," called Charlotte.

Anne's eyes waited for Emily. She came in quietly. There were drops of rain on her brown hair. She closed the door quickly behind her so that no wind could have entered the room; still there was something like wind and like autumn in the room now that she was there. Anne gazed at her sister. When she is on the moors, she is the wind. She does not just listen to it; she cries with it, she swoops with it . . . she can't be expected to stop all of a sudden.

Perfection in a room. Polished, with curtains and chairs; a wooden wall with glass set in it; a hole bricked up in one wall for a fire; dishes to eat from; and a needle to pull thread through a cloth . . . But the wind will blow it all away. Let all housewifely things vanish! While she watched Emily, the walls irked Anne; they fretted her. Let them blow away; perhaps then she, too, could hear the wind, as it had sounded before it ever blew near the dusted and neatly kept corners of a house.

Emily leaned against the mantel, tall and supple, one hand extended toward the fire. "It's warming up outside," she said, "now that it's begun to rain."

We'll talk of the weather now, Anne thought; but no, Charlotte would not.

"Emily," she said, "I'm sorry if I pained you. I'm not sorry I read your poems. It was my duty, and I'm thankful every hour that I chanced on that book. I think it was put in my way. I think there was Providence in it."

Emily inclined her head toward the hand that rested on the mantel and sniffed at a piece of gorse she'd brought in with her. She seemed still to be where it had been.

"Emily," said Charlotte, "you must work at them. They must be copied. I have plans. They don't belong to you. They belong to the world."

"The world," said Emily, and threw her piece of gorse into the fire. Anne watched it curl there. It was almost as if Emily herself were burning. "They belong to me. They did belong to me," she said. She picked up her book and writing block from the table.

"Where are you going?" Charlotte asked.

"To my room," said Emily.

Charlotte sprang from her chair. "You've just come in, you're cold. I must go read to Papa, anyway. Stay, stay. I won't be here to annoy you." She took her own stack of belongings under her arm. At the door she turned back. "Bonnie love," Charlotte said; but Anne saw no change in Emily's face as the door closed behind Charlotte.

Emily replaced her things, then whistled Keeper in from the hall. She sat before the fire, one arm about his neck.

"She said," said Anne, explaining Charlotte, "you were a genius."

Emily stroked Keeper's knobby ears, and when she stopped, Keeper's nose nudged her into stroking again.

"She said," Anne went on, "you had a right to find the person for whom those words were written." She hesitated before Emily's indifference. She said, "The one to whom your heart spoke had a right to hear your words."

"How could poems be written," asked Emily, "to someone unknown?"

"You know someone?" asked Anne.

Emily laughed. She has a better laugh, Anne thought, than anyone else in this house; neither thin, nor sharp, nor wild. "Which curate?" Emily asked. "Perhaps the little man who sells us writing paper? Or that schoolmaster Charlotte reveres? Annie, Annie."

"She said it isn't only the *hand* that writes."

"It isn't, it isn't," said Emily.

" 'The heart speaking'—those were Charlotte's words."

"That's fanciful," Emily said.

"We chose three things while you were out."

"For me, too?" asked Emily.

"For you," Anne told her. "The wind, the moors, rain."

Emily was silent.

"For me, flowers, the sea, love. I meant loving-kindness, but Charlotte thought not."

Emily looked up from the fire and said nothing.

Like Visitant of Air

"She said there was in this house that which was worthy of love and honor."

"Let it stay here," said Emily violently, clutching Keeper's scruff so sharply he growled. "Let it stay here. There is one who hears. I shall never find him. There is one in whose ear my words would be like his own. I shall never know him. Every syllable I say he would say yes to. He exists. He is not fancy. He lives. This wind blows to him, this rain sounds to him as it does to me. His step would match mine. These walls would mean as little to him as they do to me. Listen," she said.

The rain was being slapped against the house; there was no sound any longer of drops, but of water heavy as a wave against the side of a ship.

"That is real. He is real. Charlotte is mistaken. There is no one else to hear or who cares to hear. Love and honor," she said, "I have nothing to sell for them. They are a gift."

Anne watched her sister. She spoke as if she saw; she looked as if she communed, as if behind the wind, beyond the rain, there was a voice that answered, an ear that heard.

Anne waited a long time before she spoke again. "Charlotte said this would be a night to remember."

Emily, half reclining on Keeper, lay back, her eyes on the fire that had begun to burn low.

"Who will remember?" she asked.

At Walden, Thoreau, who had for a long time sat motionless, listening to the ceaseless autumnal drumming, glanced back over what he had been writing: *"this afternoon . . . shall I go down this long hill in the rain? . . . I ask myself. And I say to myself, Yes, roam far . . . you are really free. The noble life is continuous and unremitting . . . live with a longer radius . . . Dismiss prudence. . . ."*

He picked up his pen, dipped it in ink and wrote again. *"Remember only what is promised. Make the day light you and night hold a candle."*

He remembered the night outside, unlit and candleless; he heard the wind and rain. Alone he listened, alone he spoke. He opened his door once more, once more thrust his hand out into the darkness, and spoke with great urgency. "Where are you?" he said. "Where are you?"

The
Condemned
Librarian

Louise McKay, M.D., the librarian at Beaumont High School, sent me another card today. It was on the wickerwork table, where Mother puts my snack, when I got home from teaching. This afternoon the snack was orange juice and graham crackers, the orange juice in a plain glass, so that the deepness, the thickness of the color was almost like a flame inside a hurricane lamp. The graham crackers were on a blue willowware plate, and it just so happened that Dr. McKay's card was Van Gogh's "Sunflowers." It was a perfect still life, the colors increasing in intensity through the pale sand of the wickerwork table to the great bong (I want to say), for I swear I could hear it, of Van Gogh's flaming sunflowers. I looked at the picture Mother had composed for me (I don't doubt) for some time before I read Dr. McKay's card.

Dr. McKay sends me about four cards a year—not at any particular season, Christmas, Easter, or the like. Her sentiments are not suited to such festivals. Usually her message is only a line or two: "Why did you do it?" or "Condemned, condemned, condemned." Something very dramatic and always on a post card, so that the world at large can read it if it chooses. Mother shows her perfect tact by saying nothing if she does read. Perhaps she doesn't; though a single sentence in a big masculine hand is hard to miss. Except for her choice of the Van Gogh print, which showed her malice, Dr. McKay's message this afternoon was very mild—for her. "I am still here, which will no doubt make you happy."

Apart from the fact that anyone interested in the welfare of human beings generally would want her there (or at least not practicing in a hospital), it does make me happy. This evening when I pulled down the flag, I was somehow reassured, standing there in the schoolyard with the cold north wind blowing the dust in my face, to think that over there on the other side of the mountains Louise McKay was ending her day, too. Take away the mountains and fields and we might be gazing into each other's eyes.

I sat down in my room with the juice my mother had squeezed—we hate substitutes—and looked at the card and remembered when I had first seen that marching handwriting. Everything else about her has changed, but not that. I saw it first on the card she gave me telling me of my next date with her. From the moment I arrived at Oakland State, I started hearing about Dr. Louise McKay. She was a real campus heroine, though for no real reason. Except that at a teachers college, with no football heroes, no faculty members with off-campus reputations, the craving for superiority must satisfy itself on the material at hand, however skimpy. And for a student body made up of kids and middle-aged teachers come to Oakland from the lost little towns of mountain and desert, I suppose it was easy to think of Dr. McKay as heroic or fascinating or accomplished.

I was different, though. I was neither middle-aged nor a kid. I was twenty-six years old and I had come to Oakland expecting something. I had had choices. I had made sacrifices to get there, sacrifices for which no "heroic" lady doctor, however "fascinating," "well dressed" (I can't remember all the phrases used about her now), could be a substitute.

I had a very difficult time deciding to go to Oakland State. I had taught at Liberty School for six years and I loved that place. It was "beautiful for situation," as the Bible says, located ten miles out of town in the rolling semi-dry upland country where the crop was grain, not apricots and peaches. It was a one-room school, and I was its only teacher. It stood in the midst of this sea of barley and oats like an island. In winter and spring this big green sea of ripening grain rolled and tossed about us—all but crested and broke—all but, though never quite. In a way, this was irritating.

For half the year at Liberty there were no barley waves to watch, only the close-cut stubble of reaped fields and the enormous upthrust of the San Jacinto Mountains beyond. Color was my delight then. I used to sit out in the schoolyard at noon or recess and paint. A former teacher had discarded an old sleigh-back sofa, had it put out in the yard halfway between the school and the woodshed. It stood amidst the volunteer oats and mustard like a larger growth. It seemed planted in earth. In the fall when Santa Anas blew, tumbleweeds piled up about it. I don't know how long it had been there when I arrived, but it had taken well to its life in the fields; its legs balanced, its springs stayed inside the upholstery, and the upholstery itself still kept some of its original cherry tones. There I sat—when I wasn't playing ball with the kids—like a hunter, hidden in a game blind; only my game wasn't lions and tigers, it was the whole world, so to speak: the mountains, the grain fields, the kids, the schoolhouse itself. I sat there and painted.

Oh, not well. I've never said that, ever. Never claimed that for a minute. And it's easy to impress children and country people who think it's uncanny if you can draw an apple that looks like an apple. And I could do much more than that. I could make mountains that looked like mountains, children who looked like children. How that impressed the parents! So I had gotten in the habit of being praised, though from no one who counted, no one who knew. I had been sensibly brought up by my mother, taught to evaluate these plaudits rightly. I understood that my schoolyard talent didn't make me a Bonheur or Cassatt. Even so, there was nothing else I had ever wanted to do. This schoolteaching was just a way of making money, of helping my mother, who was a widow.

So, because of the time I had for painting and because of the gifts Liberty School had for my eyes, I had six happy years. I sat like a queen on that sofa in the grass while the meadowlarks sang and the butcherbirds first caught their lunches, then impaled their suppers, still kicking, on the barbed-wire fence. I didn't paint all the time, of course. Kids learned to read there. At the end of the sixth year there was only one eighth grader who could beat me in mental arithmetic. I was the acknowledged champion at skin-the-cat and could play adequately any position on the softball team.

There was not much left to learn at Liberty, and I began, I don't know how, to feel that learning, not teaching, was my business.

In the middle of my sixth year I had to put a tarpaulin over the sofa. A spring broke through the upholstery, a leg crumbled. After that I had to prop it on a piece of stove wood. That spring I noticed for the first time that the babies of age six I had taught my first year were developing Adam's apples or busts. Girls who had been thirteen and fourteen my first year came back to visit Liberty School, married and with babies in their arms.

"You haven't changed," they would tell me. "Oh, it's a real anchor to find you here, just the same."

Their husbands, who were often boys my own age, twenty-four or twenty-five, treated me like an older woman. I might have been their mother, or mother-in-law. I was the woman who had taught their wives. I don't think I looked so much old then as ageless. I've taken out some of the snaps of that year, pictures taken at school. My face, in a way, looks as young as my pupils'; in other ways, as old as Mt. Tahquitz. It looks back at me with the real stony innocence of a face in a coffin —or a cradle.

At Thanksgiving time I was to be out of school three days before the holiday, so that I could have a minor operation. When I left school on Friday, Mary Elizabeth Ross, one of my fourth graders, clasped me fondly and said, "May I be the first to hold your baby when you get back from the hospital?"

She wouldn't believe it when I told her I was going to the hospital because I was sick, not to get a baby, and she cried when I came back to school empty-armed.

That I noticed these things showed my restlessness. It might have passed, I might have settled in to a lifetime on that is-land, except that at Christmas I hung some of my paintings with my pupils' pictures at the annual Teachers' Institute ex-hibit. They caused a stir, and I began foolishly to dream of painting full time, of going to a big city, Los Angeles or San Francisco, where I would take a studio and have lessons. I didn't mention the idea to anyone, scarcely to myself. When anyone else suggested such a thing to me, I pooh-poohed it. "Me, paint? Don't be funny."

But I dreamed of it; the less I said, the more I dreamed; and the more I dreamed, the less possible talking became. I didn't paint much that winter, but I moved through those months with the feel of a paintbrush in my hand. I could feel, way up in my arm, the strokes I would need to make to put Tahquitz, dead white against the green winter sky on canvas, put it there so people could see how it really floated, that great

207

peak, was hung aloft there like a giant ship against the sky. But I didn't say a word to anyone about my plans, not even to the School Board when I handed in my resignation at Easter. I hadn't lost my head entirely. I told them I was going to "study." I didn't say what. They thought education, of course.

The minute I had resigned, I was filled with fear. I sat on my three-legged sofa amidst the waves of grain that never crested and shivered until school was out. I had undoubtedly been a fool; not only was I without money, but where would I find anything as good as what I had? Everything began to say "stay." I would enter my room at night (the one in which I now write), which my mother kept so exquisitely, books ranged according to size and color, the white bedspread at once taut and velvety, the blue iris in a fan-shaped arc in a brown bowl— and I was a part of that composition. If I walked out, the composition collapsed. And outside, I, too, was a fragment. I would stand there asking myself, "Where will you find anything better?"

There was never any answer.

I could only find something different, and possibly worse. So why go? I had seen myself as a lady Sherwood Anderson, locking the factory door behind me and walking down the tracks toward freedom and self-expression. I could dream that dream but I was afraid to act it. I would stand in my perfectly neat bedroom and frighten myself with pictures of my next room, far away, sordid, with strangers on each side. Fear was in my chest like a stone that whole spring. I had no talent, I was gambling everything on an egotistical attention-seeking whim. It was perfectly natural to have done so, but my misery finally drove me to talking with my mother. It was perfectly natural, she assured me, to want a change of scene and occupation. Who didn't occasionally? But why run away to big cities and studios? Why wouldn't the perfectly natural, perfectly logical thing (since I'd already resigned) be to go to Oakland State and study for my Secondary Credential? The minute I, or Mother—I don't remember which of us—thought of this way out, I was filled with bliss, real bliss. I would get away, go to a real city, be surrounded with people devoted to learning, but not risk everything.

I heard about Dr. Louise McKay from the minute I arrived on the campus. She was, as I've said, a kind of college heroine, though it was hard to understand why. What had she done that was so remarkable? She had been a high-school librarian, and had become a doctor. What's so extraordinary about that? The girls, and by that I mean the women students—for many of them were teachers themselves, well along in their thirties and forties, or even fifties—the girls always spoke about Louise McKay's change of profession as if it were a Lazaruslike feat; as if she had practically risen from the dead. People are always so romantic about doctors, and it's understandable, I suppose, dealing as they do with life and death. But Louise McKay! The girls talked about her as if what she'd done had been not only romantic, but also heroic.

In the first place, they emphasized her age. Forty-two! To me at twenty-six that didn't, of course, seem young. Still, it was silly to go on about her as if she were a Grandma Moses of medicine—and as if medicine itself were not, quite simply, anything more than doctoring people; saying, "This ails you" and "I think this pill will help you." They spoke of doctoring as if it were as hazardous as piloting a jet plane. And they spoke of Louise McKay's size, "that tiny, tiny thing," as if she'd been a six-year-old, praising her for her age and her youth at one and the same time. Her size, they said, made it seem as if the child-examining-doll game were reversed; as if doll took out stethoscope and examined child. She was that tiny and dainty, they said, that long-lashed and pink-cheeked. They exclaimed over

her clothes, too. They were delightful in themselves, but particularly so because they emphasized the contrast between her
profession and her person. She was a scientist and might have
been expected to wear something manly and practical—or
something dowdy. She did neither. They'd all been to her for
their physical examinations—somehow I'd never been scheduled
for that—and could give a complete inventory of her chic
wardrobe. I saw her only once before I called on her profes-
sionally in December. I didn't see many people, as a matter of
fact, at Oakland State, in any capacity, except professional.

True, I was studying. Not that the work was difficult—or
interesting either. History of Education, Principles of Secondary Education, Classroom Management, Curriculum Development. But the books were better than the people. Had I lived
out there on my three-legged sofa with children and nature too
long? Or was there something really wrong with the people in
teachers colleges? Anyway, I had no friends, and the nearer I
got to a Secondary Credential, the less I wanted it. But I
wanted something—miserably, achingly, wretchedly, I wanted
something. Whether or not this longing, this sense of something lost, had anything to do with the illness that came upon
me toward the end of December, I don't know. I attributed
this illness at first to the raw damp bay weather after my lifetime in the warmth and dryness of the inland foothills; I
thought that my lack of routine, after days of orderly teaching,
might be responsible, and, finally, after I had adopted a routine
and had stayed indoors out of the mists and fogs and the dis-
comfort persisted, I told myself that everyone as he grew older
lost some of his early exuberant health. I was no longer in my
first youth, and thus, "when my health began to fail"—I
thought of it in that way rather than as having any specific
ailment—accounted for my miseries. I had always been impatient with the shufflings and snufflings, the caution on stairs

and at the table of the no-longer-young. I thought they could do better if they tried. Now I began to understand that they couldn't do better and that they probably were trying. I was trying. I couldn't do better. I panted on the hills and puffed on the library steps. I leaned against handrails, I hawked and spat and harrumphed like any oldster past his prime. I did what I could to regain the well-being of my youth. I took long walks to get back my lost wind, ate sparingly, plunged under tingling showers.

By the end of December I felt so miserable I decided to see Dr. McKay at the infirmary. So many new things had been discovered about glands and vitamins, about toxins and anti-toxins, that one pill a day was possibly all that stood between me and perfect health. I had the feeling, as people do who have always been well, that a doctor commands a kind of magic—can heal with a glance. Even Dr. McKay, this little ex-librarian, a doll of a woman, with her big splashy earrings and high-heeled shoes and expensive perfumes, could cast a spell of health upon me.

That was the first time I'd ever seen Louise McKay close. My first thought was, She looks every inch her age. She had dark hair considerably grayed, there were lines about her eyes, and her throat muscles were somewhat slack. My second thought was, Why doesn't she admit it? I was dressed more like a middle-aged woman than she. Of course, since she had on a white surgeon's coat, all that could be seen of her "personal attire" was the three or four inches of brown tweed skirt beneath it. But she wore red, very high-heeled shell pumps. Her hair was set in a modified page boy, ends turned under in a soft roll, with a thick, rather tangly fringe across her forehead. It was a somewhat advanced hair style for that year—certainly for a middle-aged doctor. Her eyebrows, which were thick and dark, had been obviously shaped by plucking, and her fingernails were painted coral. She was smiling when I came in. She had considerable color in her face for a dark-haired woman, and she sat at a desk with flowers and pictures on it—not family pictures, but little prints of famous paintings.

She said, looking at her appointment calendar, which had my name on it, "Miss McCullars?"

I said, "Yes."

Then she said, "I see we have something in common." She meant our Scotch names of course, but out of some contrariness which I find hard to explain now, I pretended not to understand, so that she had to explain her little joke to me. But then, it wasn't very funny. She discovered, in looking through her files, that I hadn't had the usual physical examination on entering college.

"Why not?" she asked.

"I didn't get a notice to come," I said, "so I just skipped it."

"It would've helped," she told me, "to have that record now to check against. Just what seems to be the trouble?"

"It's probably nothing. I'm probably just the campus hypochondriac."

"That role's already filled."

I didn't feel well even then, though the stimulation of the talk and of seeing the famous Dr. McKay did make me forget some of my miseries. So I began that afternoon what I always continued in her office—an impersonation of high-spirited, head-tossing health. I don't know why. It wasn't a planned or analyzed action. It just happened that the minute I opened her office door I began to act the part of a person bursting with vitality and health. There I was, practically dying on my feet, as it was later proved, but hiding the fact by every device I could command. What did I think I was doing? The truth is, I wasn't thinking at all.

"I must say you don't look sick," she admitted. Then she began to ask me about my medical history.

"I don't have any medical history. Except measles at fifteen."

"Was there some specific question you wanted to ask me? Some problem?"

So she thought I was one of those girls? Or one of her worshipers just come in to marvel.

"I don't feel well."

"What specifically?"

"Oh—aches and pains."

"Where?"

"Oh—here, there, and everywhere."

"We'll run a few tests, and I'll examine you. The nurse will help you get undressed."

When it was over, she said, "Is your temperature ordinarily a little high?"

"I don't know. I never take it."

"You have a couple of degrees now."

"Above or below normal?"

A little of her school-librarian manner came out. "Are you trying to be funny?"

I wasn't in the least.

"A fever is always above normal."

"What does it mean to have a fever?"

"An infection of some sort."

"It could be a tooth? A tonsil?"

"Yes, it could be. I want to see you tomorrow at ten."

I remember my visit next morning very well. The acacia trees were in bloom, and Dr. McKay's office was filled with their dusty honeybee scent. Dr. McKay was still in street clothes—a blouse, white, high-necked, but frothy with lace and semitransparent, so that you saw more lace beneath. As if she were determined to have everything, I thought: age and youth, practicality and ornamentation, science and femininity. You hero of the campus, I thought, ironically. But she rebuked us schoolteachers by the way she dressed and held herself—and lived, I expected; she really did. And I, I rebuked her in turn, for our hurt honor.

"How do you feel this morning?" she asked.

What did she think to uncover in me? A crybaby and complainer, she standing there in her lovely clothes and I in my dress sun-faded from the Liberty schoolyard?

"Fine," I told her, "I feel fine."

How I felt was her business to discover, wasn't it, not mine to tell? If I knew exactly how I felt, and why, what would've been the use of seeing a doctor? Besides, once again in her office I was stimulated by her presence so that my miseries when not there seemed quite possibly something I had imagined.

"I wanted to check your temperature this morning," she told me.

She sat me down on a white stool, put a thermometer in my mouth, then, while we waited, asked me questions which she thought I could answer with a nod of the head.

"You like teaching? You want to go on with it? You have made friends here?"

She was surprised when she took the thermometer from my mouth. After looking at it thoughtfully, she shook it down and said, "Morning temperature, too."

"You didn't expect that?"

"No, frankly, I didn't."

"Why not?"

"In the kind of infection I suspected you had, a morning temperature isn't usual."

I didn't ask what infection she suspected. I had come to her office willing to be thumped, X-rayed, tested in any way she thought best. I was willing to give her samples of sputum or urine, to cough when told to cough, say ahhh or hold my breath while she counted ten. Whatever she told me to do I would do. But she had turned doctor, not I. If she was a doctor, not a librarian, now was her chance to prove it. Here I was with my fever, come willingly to her office. Let her tell me its cause.

For the next month, Dr. McKay lived, so far as I was concerned, the life of a medical detective, trying to find the villain behind the temperature. The trouble was that the villain's habits differed from day to day. It was as if a murderer had a half-dozen different thumbprints, and left now one, now another, behind him. One day much temperature, the next day none. Dr. McKay eliminated villain after villain: malaria, tonsillitis, rheumatic fever, infected teeth. And while she found disease after disease which I did not have, I grew steadily worse. By May about the only time I ever felt well was while I was in Dr. McKay's office. Entering it was like going onto a stage. However near I might have been to collapse before that oak door opened, once inside it I was able to play with perfect ease my role of health. I was unable, actually, to do anything else. I assumed health when I entered her office, as they say Dickens, unable to stand without support, assumed health when he walked out before an audience.

It was nothing I planned. I couldn't by an act of will have feigned exuberance and well-being, gone to her office day after day consciously to play the role of Miss Good Health of 1940, could I? No, something unconscious happened the minute I crossed that threshold, something electric—and ironic. I stood, sat, stooped, reclined, breathed soft, breathed hard, answered questions, flexed my muscles, exposed my reflexes for Dr. McKay with vigor and pleasure—and irony. Especially irony. I was sick, sick, falling apart, crumbling dying on my feet, and I knew it. And this woman, this campus hero whose province it was to know it, was ignorant of the fact. I didn't know what ailed me and wasn't supposed to. She was. It was her business to know.

In the beginning, tuberculosis had been included among the other suspected diseases. But the nontubercular fever pattern, the absence of positive sputum, the identical sounds of the lungs when percussed all had persuaded Dr. McKay that the trouble lay elsewhere. I did not speculate at all about my sickness. I had never been sick before, or even, for that matter, known a sick person. For all I knew, I might have elephantiasis or leprosy, and when Dr. McKay began once again to suspect tuberculosis, I was co-operative and untroubled. She was going to give me what she called a "patch test." Whether this is still used, I don't know. The test then consisted of the introduction of a small number of tubercle bacilli to a patch of scraped skin. If, after a day or two, there was no "positive" reaction, no inflammation of the skin, one was thought to have no tubercular infection.

On the day Dr. McKay began this test she used the word "tuberculosis" for the first time. I had experienced when I entered her office that afternoon my usual heightening of well-being, what amounted to a real gaiety.

"So you still don't give up?" I asked when she announced her plan for the new test. "Still won't admit that what you have on your hands is a hypochondriac?"

It was a beautiful afternoon in late May. School was almost over for the year. Students drifted past the window walking slowly homeward, relishing the sunshine and the blossoming hawthorn, their faces lifted to the light. Cubberly and Thorndyke and Dewey given the go-by for an hour or two. Some of this end-of-the-year, lovely-day quiet came into my interview with Dr. McKay. Though it had started with my usual high-spirited banter, I stopped that. It seemed inappropriate. I experienced my usual unusual well-being, but there was added to it that strange, quiet, listening tenderness which marks the attainment of a pinnacle of some kind.

Dr. McKay stood before her window, her surgeon's jacket off—I was her last patient for the day—in her usual frothy blouse, very snow-white against the rose-red of the hawthorn trees.

She turned away from the window and said to me, "You aren't a hypochondriac."

She shook her head. "I don't know." Then she explained the patch test to me.

"Tuberculosis?" I asked. "And no hectic flush, no graveyard cough, no skin and bones?"

The words were still bantering, possibly, but the tone had changed, tender, tender, humorous, and fondling; the battle—if there had been one—over; and the issue, whatever it was, settled. "In spite of all that, this test?"

"In spite of all that," she said.

She did the scraping deftly. I watched her hands, and while I doubt that there is any such thing as a "surgeon's hands," Dr. McKay's didn't look like a librarian's either, marked by fifteen years of mucilage pots, library stamps, and ten-cent fines. I could smell her perfume and note at close range the degree to which she defied time and the expected categories.

"Come back Monday at the same time," she told me when she had finished.

"What do you expect Monday?" I asked.

"I'm no prophet," she answered. "If I were . . ." She didn't finish her sentence.

We parted like comrades who have been together on a long and dangerous expedition. I don't know what she felt or thought—that she had really discovered, at last, the cause of my illness, perhaps. What I felt is difficult to describe. Certainly my feelings were not those of the usual patient threatened with tuberculosis. Instead, I experienced a tranquillity I hadn't known for a long time. I felt like a lover and a winner, triumphant but tranquil. I knew there would be no positive reaction to the skin test. Beyond that I didn't think.

I was quite right about the reaction. Dr. McKay was completely professional Monday afternoon; buttoned up in her jacket, stethoscope hanging about her neck. I entered her office feeling well, but strange. My veins seemed bursting with blood or triumph. I looked out the window and remembered where I had been a year ago. Breathing was difficult, but in the past months I had learned to live without breathing. I wore a special dress that afternoon because I thought the occasion special. I wouldn't be seeing Dr. McKay again. It was made of white men's-shirting Madras and had a deep scooped neckline, bordered with a ruffle.

"How do you feel?" Dr. McKay asked, as she always did, when I entered.

"Out of this world," I told her.

"Don't joke," she said.

"I wasn't. It's the truth. I feel wonderful."

"Let's have a look at the arm."

"You won't find anything."

"How do you know? Did you peek?"

"No, I didn't, but you won't find anything."

"I'll have a look anyway."

There was nothing, just as I'd known. Not a streak of pink even. Nothing but the marks of the adhesive tape to distinguish one arm from the other. Dr. McKay looked and looked. She touched the skin and pinched it.

"Okay," she said, "you win."

"What do you mean I win? You didn't want me to be infected, did you?"

"Of course not."

"I told you all along I was a hypochondriac."

"Okay, Miss McCullars," she said again, "you win." She sat down at her desk and wrote something on my record sheet.

"What's the final verdict?" I asked.

She handed the sheet to me. What she had written was "TB patch test negative. Fluctuating temperature due to neurotic causes."

"So I won't need to come back?"

"No."

"Nor worry about my lungs?"

"No."

Then with precise timing, as if that were the cue for which for almost six months I had been waiting, I had, there in Dr. McKay's office, my first hemorrhage. A hemorrhage from the lungs is always frightening, and this was a very bad one and my first. They got me to the infirmary at once, but there behind me in Dr. McKay's office was the card stained with my blood and saying that nothing ailed me. I was not allowed to speak for twenty-four hours, and my thought, once the hemorrhaging had stopped, was contained in two words, which ran through my mind, over and over again. "I've won. I've won." What had I won? Well, for one thing, I'd won my release from going on with my work for that Secondary Credential. All that could be forgotten, and forgotten also the need to leave Liberty at all. I could go back there, back to my stranded sofa and the school library and the mountains, blue over the green barley.

When at the end of twenty-four hours I was permitted to whisper, Dr. Stegner, the head physician at Oakland State, came to see me.

"When did you first see Dr. McKay?" he asked.

"In December."

"What course of treatment did she prescribe?"

"Not any. She didn't know what was wrong with me."

"Did she ever X-ray you?"

"No."

This, I began to learn, was the crux of the case against Dr. McKay. For there was one. She should have X-rayed me. She should have known that in cases of far advanced tuberculosis, and that was what I had, the already deeply infected system pays no attention to the introduction of one or two more bacilli. All of its forces are massed elsewhere—there are no guards left to repulse border attacks of unimportant skirmishers. But by this time my mother had arrived, alert, knowledgeable, and energetic.

"My poor little girl," she said, "this woman doctor has killed you."

I wasn't dead yet, but as I heard the talk around me I began to understand that in another year or two I might very well be so. And listening to my mother's talk, I began to agree with her. Dr. McKay had robbed me not only of health, but also of a promising career—I had been poised upon the edge of something unusual. I was training myself for service. I had remarkable talents. And now all was denied me, and for this denial I could blame Dr. McKay. I did. She had cut me down in mid-career through her ignorance. What did the campus think of its hero now? For the campus had heard of Dr. McKay's mistake. And the Board of Regents! My mother said it was her duty; that she owed the steps she was taking to some other poor girl who might suffer as I had through Dr. McKay's medical incompetence. I thought it was a matter for her to decide, and besides, I was far too ill to have or want any say in such decisions. I was sent, as soon as I was able to be moved, to a sanatorium near my home in Southern California.

I had been there four months when I saw Dr. McKay again. At the beginning of the visiting hour on the first Saturday in October, the nurse on duty came to my room.

"Dr. McKay to see you," she said.

I had no chance to refuse to see her—though I don't know that I would have refused if I'd had the chance—for Dr. McKay followed the nurse into the room and sat down by my bed.

She had changed a good deal; she appeared little, nondescript, and mousy. She had stopped shaping her eyebrows and painting her nails. I suppose I had changed, too. With the loss of my fever, I had lost also all my show of exuberance and life. I lay there in the hospital bed looking, I knew, as sick as I really was. We stared at each other without words for a time.

Then I said, to say something, for she continued silent, "How are things at Oakland State this year?"

"I'm not at Oakland State. I was fired."

I hadn't known it. I was surprised and dismayed, but for a heartbeat—in a heartbeat—I experienced a flash of that old outrageous exultation I had known in her office. I was, in spite of everything, for a second, well and strong and tender in victory. Though what my victory was, I sick and she fired, I couldn't have told.

"I'm sorry," I said. I was. It is a pitiful thing to be out of work.

"Don't lie," she said.

"I am not lying," I told her.

She didn't contradict me. "Why did you do it?" she asked me.

"Do what?" I said, at first really puzzled. Then I remembered my mother's threats. "I had nothing to do with it. Even if I'd wanted to, I was too sick. You know that. I had no idea you weren't in Oakland this year."

"I don't mean my firing—directly. I mean that long masquerade. I mean that willingness to kill yourself, if necessary, to punish me. I tell you a doctor of fifty years' experience would've been fooled by you. Why? I'd never seen you before. I wanted nothing but good for you. Why did you do it? Why?"

"I don't know what you mean."

"What had I ever done to you? Lost there in that dark library, dreaming of being a doctor, saving my money and finally escaping. How had I harmed or threatened you that you should be willing to risk your life to punish me?"

Dr. McKay had risen and was walking about the room, her voice, for one so small, surprisingly loud and commanding. I was afraid a nurse would come to ask her to be quiet. Yet I hesitated myself to remind her to speak more quietly.

"Well," she said, "you have put yourself in a prison, a fine narrow prison. Elected it of your own free will. And that's all right for you, if you wanted a prison. But you had no right to elect it for me, too. That was murderous. Really murderous." I began to fear that she was losing control of herself, and tried to ask questions that would divert her mind from the past.

"Where are you practicing, now?" I asked.

She stopped her pacing and stood over me. "I am no longer in medicine," she said. "I'm the librarian in the high school at Beaumont."

"That's not where you were before?"

"No, it's much smaller and hotter."

"It's only thirty miles—as the crow flies—from Liberty, where I used to teach. I'm going back there as soon as I'm well. It was a mistake to leave it." She said nothing.

"I really love Liberty," I said, "and teaching. The big fields of barley, the mountains. There was an old sofa in the schoolyard, where I used to sit. It was like a throne. I thought for a while I wanted to get away from there and try something else. But that was all a crazy dream. All I want to do now is get back."

"I wish you could have discovered that before you came to Oakland."

I ignored this. "Don't you love books?"

"I had better love books," she said, and left the room.

As it happened, I've never seen her again, though I get these cards. I didn't go back to Liberty four years later—when I was able again to teach. I got this other school, but somehow the magic I had felt earlier with the children, I felt no longer. An outdated little schoolroom with the windows placed high so that neither teacher nor pupils could see out; a dusty schoolyard; and brackish water. The children I teach now look so much like their predecessors that I have the illusion of living in a dream, of being on a treadmill teaching the same child the same lesson through eternity. Outside on the school grounds, my erstwhile throne, the sofa, does not exist. The mountains, of course, are still there—a great barrier at the end of the valley.

Just across the mountains are Beaumont and Dr. McKay; and I am sometimes heartened, standing on the packed earth of the schoolyard in the winter dusk, as she suggested, to think of her reshelving her books, closing the drawer of her fine-till, at the same hour. We can't all escape; some of us must stay home and do the homely tasks, however much we may have dreamed of painting or doctoring. "You have company," I tell myself, looking toward her across the mountains. Then I get into my car to drive into town, where my mother has all this loveliness waiting for me; a composition, once again, that really includes me.

Child
of the
Century

Mary Putnam Young died in the town of Merritt, California, on June 16, 1947, at the age of seventy-eight. She was buried three days later at ten in the morning in Rose Hill Cemetery. By two that afternoon, her son and only child, Oliver Putnam Young, aged forty-seven, was in the law offices of King, Flaherty, and King in search of legal advice.

Maurice Flaherty, brother-in-law of the older King and uncle of the younger, a man about Oliver's age, came out of an inner office to see him. "I'm sorry about your mother," he said. The two men had grown up together in Merritt and knew each other well. "I couldn't get to the funeral, but Jane intended to go."

"Yes," said Oliver, "she did go. I saw her there."

Though Flaherty was surprised to have Oliver come in so soon after the funeral, he bethought himself of something suitable to say. "No matter how old we are, these things always hit us hard," he said. After this statement he waited a moment for some response. When none was forthcoming, he continued. "Well, Oliver, what can I do for you? Something about your mother's will?" Although Oliver had managed Young's Drug-

224

store for twenty-five years, his mother had retained its owner-
ship.

"No," said Oliver, "it's nothing about Mother. It's about
me."

"You?" asked Flaherty with surprise.

"I'd like some legal advice about my birth."

"About your birth?" Flaherty repeated. The afternoon was
warm, and he seemed quite unable to concentrate, staring in a
bemused fashion at two mud daubers as they wove a pattern
of indecision about the open window of the stuffy little room.

"You know when I was born," Oliver said. "The day it was."

Oliver didn't remember the day, of course, but remembered
the September afternoon when he had first been told of that
day. He had been playing in the back yard, making corrals for
his herds of animals. He had a flock of innumerable sow bugs,
almost as many ladybugs, five grasshoppers, two stinkbugs, one
potato bug, and four flies. He had removed the wings from the
flies, and they were quite as tractable and earthbound as the
sow bugs and far more so than the ladybugs and grasshoppers,
which came and went at will over the dirt walls of the corrals
he had built.

"Come in, Oliver dear," his mother called.

"I can't," he called back.

"Can't?" asked Mrs. Young, surprised. " 'Can't' isn't a word
my little boy knows."

Oliver sometimes had the confused feeling—he had never
got over it—that there were two Olivers: himself and the other
Oliver, who was his mother's little boy.

"I can't," he yelled again. "All my bugs will get away."

"Bugs!" exclaimed Mrs. Young. "Bugs aren't things my little
boy would play with."

"I am," Oliver, the Oliver who was not his mother's little
boy, shouted.

"Come here at once," his mother ordered.

He went reluctantly onto the porch and saw that his mother had a pitcher of lemonade and a plate of cookies on the wicker porch table, as if she expected company. "Mother," he protested, "all my bugs will run away."

"Animals that belong to my little boy," his mother assured him, "will not run away."

They had, though, Oliver remembered. All of them except the sow bugs, which he had not cared for anyway, and the flies, which were dead.

"Wash your hands and face and put on a clean blouse," his mother told him. "I've something important to talk to my little boy about."

He washed and washed, until he reached the comfortable stage of having forgotten what he was washing for. Then he pleasantly practiced opening his eyes under water and, tiring of that, scooped water into one ear and tilted his head to see if it would run out the other. His mother came and put an end to these experiments. She dried him, buttoned him into one of his best blouses, and sat him on a chair by the wicker table. When he had finished eating his two oatmeal cookies and had drained his glass of lemonade, his mother pulled his chair closer to hers and pointed to the large scrapbook she held on her lap.

"Do you know what book this is, Oliver?"

"No," he said.

"Read what it says," his mother told him.

Though he was only six, Oliver had been sent to school when he was five and could read after a fashion. Haltingly, he pronounced the words printed on the cover of the scrapbook, "The Baby of the Century."

"Do you know who the Baby of the Century is, Oliver?" his mother asked.

"No," said Oliver.

His mother then opened the scrapbook and, pointing to a large, time-yellowed newspaper picture of a baby, said, "Read this, Oliver." With her forefinger, she guided his eyes to the proper line.

" 'Oliver Putnam Young, Baby of the Century,' " he read.

"My little boy, Baby of the Century," his mother said.

It was then, at that moment, Oliver sometimes thought, that the heaviness of after years had first descended upon him; there on the porch, looking at this picture and hearing the peculiar, throbbing note in his mother's voice.

He had even attempted to escape what was personal in the situation by speaking not of the baby, but of the century. What a century was he had no idea, unless perhaps an animal, something like a centipede. "What is a century?" he asked.

"A century," his mother told him, "is a period of a hundred years, and you, Oliver, were born at the exact minute the twentieth century was born."

"Were you born in the twentieth century, too, Mother?"

"Oh, no," his mother said. "I represent the nineteenth century; but you, Oliver, are the twentieth century."

The two mud daubers in the offices of King, Flaherty, and King hovered about the upper slats of the Venetian blind covering the top half of the window. Maurice Flaherty shooed at them, but they paid no attention to him.

"You remember when I was born?" Oliver asked.

"I sure do," Maurice Flaherty answered. "The stroke of midnight, January first, nineteen-hundred."

That was the truth—not ten minutes or even ten seconds before or after, but exactly on the stroke of the hour, so that his first wail had mingled with the sounds of the bells, guns, whistles, firecrackers, and pounded milk pans with which the residents of Merritt were celebrating the arrival of the new century.

The fact that his birth had occurred at this hour had seemed, first to his mother and then later, unhappily, to Oliver himself, significant, a portent of something. But of what? Oliver's mother had taken for granted that it was a portent of success for her son, and of no ordinary success either. Her little boy, who had been born on January 1, 1900, would, she felt, equal in some way the promise of the new century.

She early searched her son for intimations of the direction in which this success would lie; but the "Century Baby," as the newspapers had called him, was in no way unusual. In appearance, he was a large-headed, silky-haired, tallow-colored baby, and he became a medium-headed, silky-haired, tallow-colored boy. The little boy, as later the grown man, had shallow, saucer-shaped indentations at the temples, and when he was troubled, which was often, a forked vein like a plum-colored tree spread across the center of his forehead. His silky, straw-colored hair did not, even as he grew older, develop enough body to permit him to sweep it upward into a pompadour of the kind other boys his age were wearing, and though he became a large boy for his age, he did not become a strong one. He was willing, even anxious, to excel in games; but his muscles were soft and spongy, and they did not, however much he willed it, respond so quickly and reliably as those of other boys born on less auspicious dates.

This troubled him, but it did not trouble his mother. She had no idea that a child sent into the world simultaneously with the twentieth century was destined to become a mere jumper, runner, or ball tosser. Indeed, the fact that Oliver was incompetent at games convinced her anew that he was no ordinary boy and that Fate was looking after her own—making certain that hours which might otherwise have been wasted in tree climbing and ball tossing would be free for training of another sort. But of what sort?

It was of this training that Oliver's mother spoke on the afternoon she first showed him her Baby of the Century scrapbook. She had noticed that he occasionally hummed. When they were downtown, he would stop to listen to the Salvation Army band, and once she had seen him waving his arms in time to "Three Little Blackberries," a gramophone record of his grandfather's. It seemed very likely that the Baby of the Century was destined to become a great artist, and since no artist, to her mind, was so great as a violin virtuoso, she had begun to see Oliver against a backdrop of velvet curtains, silky hair falling over his fragile temples, bow arm lifted.

"Would my little boy like to play the violin?" she asked.

This question had seemed to Oliver to lead away from the Baby of the Century talk, which embarrassed and depressed him, and in his relief he at once said, "Yes."

"I thought so!" his mother exclaimed joyously. She ran into the house and brought out a violin of a size suitable for a six-year-old. "There," she said, handing the instrument to Oliver, who took it gingerly in his arms. "Always remember this hour, Oliver, the hour when you first began to make music." And then, more practically, "On Saturday, Professor Schuyler will come to give my little boy a lesson."

Professor Schuyler came for four years and three months. Then he departed. On the day of the Professor's departure, Saturday, December 17, 1910, he entered the Youngs' living room singing the song Oliver had heard him sing for four years and three months. It began "O Lily up and Lily down and lay them on the side wheels," and went on Oliver knew not how, for this was all the Professor had ever sung.

229

"How is our young Paganini today?" the Professor asked that December afternoon. Sometimes he asked, "How is our young Ole Bull?" and other times, "How is our young Mozart?"

But Oliver did not mind. He knew the Professor asked these questions because of the set of books about the lives of great musicians his mother had bought. Oliver had not minded either the four long years of practice. They had given him an excuse for avoiding what was even more painful than the music lessons—the games in which he could not excel; they had made his mother happy, and they had brought the Professor, who interested him and never called him Child of the Century.

The Professor was a tall man with a dark, seamed face. Each Saturday he drove to the Youngs' in a buggy drawn by a dapple-gray horse. In the whip socket of the buggy, the Professor carried the butt end of a broken whip. Oliver had never seen him use this stump on his horse; but sometimes, after a lesson, the Professor would linger for a few minutes in his buggy meditatively scratching his back with the whip stump.

The Professor quite often spread a large handkerchief over his face while he listened to Oliver practice. Once when Oliver's mother had discovered him thus, he had said, without so much as lifting a corner of the handkerchief to provide himself a peephole, "The ears resent the eyes." Hearing this, Mrs. Young had tiptoed from the room.

There were times, however, when Professor Schuyler did not have Oliver practice at all, but played for the whole of the lesson period. He would stand, on these occasions, by the front window, his eyes on the rise and fall of the green or sallow grass in the vacant lot across the street, while Oliver listened to the sounds cascading from his violin. Oliver did not associate these sounds with music. They reached him simply as feeling, as an audible expression of the heaviness that almost continuously filled his chest and was the result both of his love for his mother and of his conviction that, in spite of everything he could do, he was a disappointment to her.

About his own playing, Oliver had a variety of feelings; but what he most often felt was despair. He simply could not make the notes he saw before him come forth from his violin as music. Some barrier in his hands or mind, or both, prevented it. Still, no one reproved him—neither his mother nor Professor Schuyler—and playing on the afternoon of December 17, 1910, Oliver was consoled by a thought that had often consoled him before: perhaps his terrible sense of failure and insufficiency was the true sign of the great artist. Perhaps it was with just such a feeling that Mozart had practiced. Perhaps what he felt about his playing was exactly what a Child of the Century, destined to be a great violinist, should feel.

The lesson that afternoon went worse than usual. Professor Schuyler early retired to his handkerchief; but Oliver, even without those black eyes upon him, was unable to put three notes together properly. He stumbled, misplayed, broke down completely, started over. Finally, after producing a whining, sniggering sound so strange as to rouse the Professor from behind his covering, Oliver, out of his embarrassment and despair, cried, "Mozart—Mozart was pretty mad, too, I guess, when he made mistakes like that."

At that name, Professor Schuyler leaped to his feet and attempted to throw his handkerchief to the floor. But it would not throw; it floated. "Mozart," he said. "Mozart. As long as it was your mama who had these ideas, it didn't matter; but if you've got them, too, it's time to call a halt." Professor Schuyler then took Oliver's violin, threw it into the fireplace on top of the smoldering eucalyptus logs, broke the bow over his knee, and sent it to join the blazing instrument. "Boy," he said sternly, "you can no more play the violin than a pig can sing. And while there's no harm I can see in a pig's trying to sing, calling himself a nightingale is another matter entirely, conducive to craziness in the world, and a sign it's time to call a halt."

That afternoon Oliver heard for the first—and last—time the next line of the Professor's song. "O Lily up and Lily down," the Professor sang, "and lay them on the side wheels, the river feels the boat go round but that's not what the boat feels." Gently he closed the front door behind him, climbed into his buggy, scratched himself briefly, and drove away forever.

After that, everything was better for a while. Oliver's mother, naturally, was angry with Professor Schuyler for destroying her son's violin. However, she was able to recover some of its cost by refusing to pay him for Oliver's final lessons. She had nothing to say to Oliver except that, since there were no competent teachers in the neighborhood, she was afraid he would have to give up his musical training.

The next two years, Oliver's twelfth and thirteenth, were, he afterward thought, the happiest of his life. He was permitted, for the most part, to do as he liked, and there was very little, or at least he heard very little, Child of the Century talk. The Youngs at that time lived near an arroyo, which, dammed at one end by a Pacific Electric embankment, held during the winter and spring months a considerable body of water. From this pond Oliver fished up tadpoles, water dogs, even an occasional small turtle. These he kept in glass jars on the back porch, and he enjoyed standing before them in a kind of pleasant stupor, watching their easy, fluid movements.

One evening, shortly after his twelfth birthday, he caught a small green snake by the pond side. He took it to the house to place with the other inhabitants of his menagerie. While he was arranging its home on the back porch, he heard his mother speak from the kitchen to some unseen guest in the living room. "Oliver, you know," she said, "is going to be a great scientist."

There was some reply Oliver could not make out. Then his mother went on, "I was so foolish for a while, so old-fashioned. I hampered my boy so. I was determined he should be a violinist, but his heart was just not in it. At heart he really has never been anything but a scientist. Exactly what we should have expected of a child of this century, of course."

Hearing these words, Oliver lost all pleasure in his thin, coiling snake. The old heaviness, the old responsibility began once again to fill his chest. He started to tiptoe from the porch; but his mother, catching sight of him, called him back.

She was delighted when she saw what he had in his hand and hurried them, unhappy snake and boy, to meet her caller. "See!" she cried. "What did I tell you? A born scientist!"

Oliver was not a born scientist; but except for the nervousness and self-consciousness his mother's expectations aroused in him, he might, by unrelenting effort, have made himself a scientist of sorts. But the burden of this expectation, coupled with his barely average ability, kept him below average in all his science classes in high school. And it was this poor scholastic record, together with his unhappiness and sense of failure, that caused him, in 1917, to enlist in the army. Since he was underage, it was necessary for him to have his parents' permission. He had expected his mother to weep, protest, perhaps even refuse her permission. Instead, she was pleased and enthusiastic.

"I had hoped my boy would want to do this," she told him. She placed her hand on his soft, light hair—she had to reach up to do this now—as if she were bestowing a benediction. "This is a crusade, Oliver, a holy task of liberation. Perhaps it was for this you were born."

Mrs. Young kissed Oliver and sent him forth. But she was unable to believe that he had been born to serve as a pharmacist's assistant in a hospital in New Jersey, or that his work was of much importance in the holy task of liberation. His destiny must still lie ahead.

Oliver went home from the army at nineteen, large, rather slope-shouldered, with attentive, watchful eyes. He felt he was missing something, and the strain of looking for it showed in his eyes and in the frequency with which the plum-colored tree spread across his forehead. He enrolled at the state university and, because he could think of nothing better to do, continued as a science major. His two years in the army had not improved him as a student, and the accident in which he was hurt was the result of some volunteer experimentation he was carrying on in the hope of persuading his chemistry professor to raise his grade. He lost the thumb and forefinger of his left hand, and for a time it was thought he would also lose his life.

When he began to recover, his mother sat by his bedside and traced with her gentle fingers and espaliered vein on his forehead. "Science is dangerous, Oliver," she said in her gentle, surprised voice. "My boy might have been blown up, destroyed. He wasn't born for that. Promise me, Oliver, that you will give up science. I had no idea that science was dangerous."

Oliver gave up not only science, but also college. He had lost two years in the army; he lost another year as a result of his accident. When he was well enough to be up and about, he entered, at the age of twenty-one, his father's drugstore as his assistant.

Because of his illness, perhaps, his mother seemed content, at the time, for him to be so employed. Since Oliver did not dislike the work, his discontent was inexplicable. Then, to his unhappy consternation, he discovered that the hope that, during his younger years, his mother had cherished for him had become a part of his own make-up. He would have supposed that his many disappointments would have cured him of his mother's disease of hope. As an artist, he had ended with his violin blazing like any piece of kindling in the fireplace; as a soldier, with the neat pills rolling out from under his trained and obedient thumb; as a scientist, with a part of his hand lost.

Were these experiences not enough to prevent him from beginning anew a search for some means of expressing his uniqueness? What uniqueness had he other than the date of his birth and the persistence of his mother's belief in him? Yet these, evidently, were enough. The only difference was that in him his mother's disease took a new course. He no longer expected to find in the outer world any sign of the uniqueness of Oliver Putnam Young. His kingdom would be interior, known only to himself and one other. It would be a kingdom of love.

It was natural that, as he was dreaming of love, love soon particularized itself. When Pauline Mercer came into the drugstore with her bronze-and-rose skin, her short, daring haircut, her air of being at home in the world, she was immediately dearer to him than anything he had dreamed. Though the dreaming he had done, filled as it was with shreds of Tennyson and Mrs. Browning, scenes from *The Ordeal of Richard Feverel*, remembered snatches of his mother's conversation, conditioned the manner of his loving.

Afterward it seemed to him that nothing he had said or done for the whole of the time he knew Pauline Mercer had any connection with what he wanted to do or say, but only with the pattern of loving his dream had formed.

For his first date with Pauline, he rented at the local garage the largest and fanciest car available. He did not consider his father's model worthy of either Pauline or his dream. He was unfamiliar with the big car and drove it awkwardly and self-consciously. The front seat was bisected, and he and Pauline sat far removed from each other, formal and dignified, like chauffeur and footman in a vehicle conveying royalty. Pauline somehow got the idea that the car belonged to Oliver's father; and since in Oliver's dream a young man's father would own such a car, Oliver let her think so.

For the rest of the ride his mind tossed about, alternating between two courses of action equally impossible: persuading his father to buy a car of similar make or admitting to Pauline that he had, for all practical purposes, lied. While he was still painfully concerned with this problem, they passed a carnival, a gay eruption of glitter and sound into the spring night.

"Let's stop," Pauline cried, clasping Oliver's arm with both hands.

This pressure made Oliver tremble, and for a minute he let himself think of the pleasures of the carnival: the Ferris wheel, the chute-the-chutes, the photographer's booth—all permitting, if not requiring, that the escort's arm be about the girl. But his dream of love would permit nothing so unpremeditated and simply pleasurable. He was taking Pauline to a hotel for dinner, the proper place for the beginning of a stately and romantic courtship.

He drove into Los Angeles, where, unused to city traffic, he so entangled himself at an intersection that a policeman had to extricate him. In an effort to impress Pauline, he talked back and was given a ticket. From then on, his stomach, out of nervousness, rumbled violently. To his sensitive ear, its reverberations were audible above all the city's sounds. To muffle this internal clamor, he tooted the horn whenever an internal spasm seemed imminent. He thus arrived at the Ambassador in a burst of horn blowing. The doorman came to the car at a brisk trot, anticipating, after so precipitate a summons, a large tip. When he received none at all, he turned away muttering.

The Ambassador's dining room frightened Oliver. He had

never eaten in so luxurious a place, and he had no idea what to do: how to get rid of his hat and overcoat, how to get a table, what to do when he did get one. Because it seemed uncourageous to hang diffidently upon the fringes of the crowded dining room, waiting to be noticed, he took his hat and coat in one hand, grasped Pauline's elbow sharply with the other, and made for an empty table. He was turned back by a waiter, who rid himself of a day-long accumulation of spleen by speaking to Oliver as if he were something contemptible, a beetle he would crush.

They were seated, finally, near the doors to the kitchen, where the uproar of cooking and serving made conversation difficult. This was a blessing for Oliver, since what he had to say, following the pattern of his dream, was foolish. The menu arrived. One-third of it he could not read; two-thirds he could not pronounce. With a little finger, pink and curling as a newly boiled shrimp, he pointed to various items. After these had arrived and he had eaten of them, Oliver felt better, though filled with a gnawing shame for his mistakes and ineptitudes. He sat silent amid the din, his maimed hand exposed on the table.

Pauline touched it with gentle fingers. "That must keep you from doing a lot of things you'd like to do," she said.

Oliver, who was sensitive about his hand, removed it from the table. "Yes," he said. Then, with evasive melancholy, "One thing in particular."

"What is it?" Pauline asked. "Something you wanted terribly to do?"

"Something I could do," he said, pensively understating.

"Don't you like to talk about it, Oliver?"

"I never have talked about it to anyone else," he said, truthfully enough.

"Because it makes you sad?"

Oliver nodded. "But you're different."

"What was it, Oliver?"

"Play the violin," Oliver answered, emerging, to his own consternation but according to the dictates of his dream, as hero and thwarted artist.

"Oh, Oliver!" Pauline's bronze and rose became rosier with sympathy. "How terrible!"

Oliver said nothing.

"Could you—could you—play well?"

Oliver nodded. "They'd told me so," he said. Then suddenly, above the clamor of china, "My old teacher used to call me a young Mozart. He was only joking, of course."

The words Oliver heard himself speaking could not have surprised him more had they been issued from the empty air beside him. "You fool, you fool," he told himself. "You darn fool. Can't you even tell the truth?" No, he could not; or, rather, he was. He was telling the truth of a world in which he had spent more time than in Merritt; he was telling the truth of the Child of the Century, of that other Oliver, his mother's boy.

"Oh, Oliver," Pauline said again. "How did it happen? Or can you bear to think of it?"

Oliver looked desolate, but managed to speak. "Research," he said.

"Chemical research?"

Oliver nodded.

"About the war?"

"Ultimately," Oliver answered.

For a moment there was a lull in the kitchen clatter, and the music of the dance orchestra spread across the dining room. It lapped about them, warm as a summer tide and as unlasting. Oliver rested for a second on its cresting surface. Then the tide ebbed, ran backward, exposed the kitchen behind them, the bill on the table, the falseness of everything he had said.

On the way back to Merritt, Oliver was too occupied with his remembrance of this falseness to proceed according to dream. When he left Pauline, out of his natural, unplanned misery, he kissed her.

Next evening, carrying the most elaborate box of chocolates in stock at Young's Drugstore, he called at the Mercer home. Pauline and her thirteen-year-old brother, Stanley, were in the back yard pumping in a swing, which hung from the scaly branch of an old pepper tree. After they got the swing to its maximum height and then let it die, Stanley, a well-trained young brother, remembered he had a date.

Pauline, who had been standing in the swing, now sat in it and, swaying gently, looked up at Oliver's package. "Merchandise!" she exclaimed.

Oliver handed her the box of chocolates. "Can you ever forgive me?" he asked.

"Forgive you?" Pauline said, surprised. "Forgive you for what?"

This generosity shook Oliver. "For kissing you." He went on earnestly, "I want you to know that I respect you just as much as if you hadn't let me, and that I know you're not in the habit of letting a fellow kiss you on his first date." This was a thoroughly planned speech, and Oliver expected good results.

Instead, Pauline jumped to a standing position in the swing and began to pump furiously. Oliver could see her white underpants, or at least the blue embroidery around the edges, but he realized that this display was in no way coquettish.

"Beat it," Pauline yelled. "Go on, get away from here, you goop. Go on home."

In spite of this bad beginning, Pauline went with him for

more than a year. Oliver continued to make awkward, impetuous love and to retreat from this love-making with self-hate because it did not fit the pattern he had earlier laid down. He was lost between two worlds, unable to be one thing or another, still hunting the kingdom of love wherein the uniqueness of Oliver Putnam Young might find expression. He knew well enough that Pauline was the person who should inhabit this kingdom with him and that every day he made it more impossible for her to do so.

In the summer of 1922, Oliver bought his car, a new, fashionable roadster. One August evening, after a movie in Merritt, he and Pauline sat parked on the rim of the reservoir in the hills behind the town.

"I don't know why you put up with me," Oliver said morosely.

"I don't know either," Pauline answered lightly. "You're an awful goop."

"No, honestly," said Oliver, "why do you?"

"I guess it's because sometimes I think there's something kind of neat and sweet about you, Oliver, way down deep inside, where I don't see it very often. But I think, maybe, if I wait long enough, it will get to be all of you."

"Neat and sweet?" asked Oliver. "What do you mean by that?"

Pauline couldn't or wouldn't say, and that very evening Oliver convinced her, finally and completely, that this neatness and sweetness, whatever it was, was deep inside him, indeed, and that no matter how long she waited it would never be all of him. They sat for some time not talking, listening to the plop of carp and catfish in the waters below them, watching the headlights of cars swing like luminous antennae up the incline leading to the reservoir.

Pauline took a cigarette from her purse. She tapped it, with newly gained competence, against the back of her hand. "Give me a light," she said.

"I've asked you not to smoke, Pauline," Oliver told her reproachfully. He had. The girl he had imagined himself wooing, the girl of whom he had read and heard his mother speak and about whom he could quote snatches of poetry, did not smoke.

"So you have," said Pauline. She struck a match on the side of her Oxford and lighted the cigarette.

"Throw that thing away!" Oliver ordered.

Pauline's response was to inhale so deeply that tears filled her eyes. But she was laughing when she said, "Try and make me."

Oliver took her wrist and said, "All right, I will. Drop that thing." It had started as fun; but once it had started, Oliver had to win. The man dominated. That was part of the dream. "Drop it," he said, increasing his pressure on her wrist.

Pauline was still laughing. "Who says so?" she asked. She reached over quickly with her hand and got hold of the cigarette, holding its burning end toward her palm. "Fooled you," she said.

Oliver grasped her hand and turned her fingers inward, so that the live coal of the cigarette, very rosy and pretty in the darkness of the summer night, came nearer and nearer the flesh of her palm. "Drop that cigarette," he said, "or you'll be burned."

Pauline had stopped laughing. "You can't make me. There is nothing in this world you can make me do, Oliver."

Oliver forced the cigarette closer to her palm. "I can," he said. "I can, too."

As the live coal touched her hand, Pauline lunged backward, but did not let go of the cigarette.

"Drop it! Drop it," Oliver first commanded, then pleaded.

But Pauline would not drop it. Her fingers gripped the

cigarette as if it were a dear possession her hand would hold firmly, even in death.

"Drop it," begged Oliver.

Pauline said nothing. There was a peculiar smell in the car, and Oliver suddenly released his pressure on Pauline's fingers, jumped out of the car, and ran to the edge of the reservoir. There he washed his face, and more especially his hands, over and over again in the cool water. He let the water slide between his fingers and across his palms as if he were the one who had been burned. When he went back to the car, Pauline was gone.

She never spoke to him again. He saw her next day on the street in Merritt, her hand elaborately bandaged. He tried to stop her, to ask her forgiveness; but she looked at him without a flicker of recognition. When he phoned her, she hung up. One day outside Young's Drugstore, he detained her with a hand on her arm while he begged her to forgive him, to talk to him. She stood quietly enough, unresponsive as a lamppost, looking downward. When Oliver saw that she was looking at a white, puckered, craterlike scar on the palm of her hand, he never again attempted to stop her or speak to her.

The next year, September 18, 1923, he married Loretta Olsen, a tall blonde girl, thin and shy, but with a slow, pleasant smile. As the falseness of his dream had spoiled him for Pauline, so Pauline had spoiled him for Loretta. He continually asked Loretta to be what she could not: careless, jaunty, easygoing, unself-conscious. He asked her, in fact, to be Pauline. Asking this, he missed all of what she had: her quiet humor, loyalty, sensitiveness. He wanted none of these things. He wanted Pauline. Without Pauline, he began to pity himself; he, Oliver Putnam Young, with no place to bestow his uniqueness, no one with whom to share that kingdom of love for which he had been born and in which he was to find the meaning of his life.

In 1924, Oliver's father died and Oliver's first child, a daughter, was born. Oliver's mother asked that the child receive her name, and though Loretta thought Mary Loretta was a pretty name and gave her mother-in-law sufficient recognition, the baby was called Mary Putnam.

Oliver's mother no longer spoke directly to him of her expectations for him. But her belief was unshaken. Oliver often heard her speak to her namesake, as the child grew older, of the remarkable circumstances of his birth and of what it portended. It was obvious, however, that she was reconciled to the fact that her son might not distinguish himself as she had long anticipated.

Oliver, during the twelve years, 1924 to 1936, which saw the birth of his children, began to wonder if it was not his destiny to be a father. To live in these young people, to guide and educate them so they would be an ornament to the age in which they lived—what greater task could any man have? But he was too self-centered to find expression in the life of any other human being, even a child of his own. The hope the date of his birth and his mother's belief had grafted on him could not be fulfilled vicariously. He must himself do something, be something, continue his search for a means of saying whatever it was he had been born to say.

About the time his oldest child, Mary, was fourteen, the boy, Oliver Junior, twelve, and the baby, Paula, two, Oliver made an important decision. He decided that the mistake he had made in his search was this: he had expected that his gift, whatever it was, would find its expression in conjunction with others. As a violinist, he had been dependent on an audience; as inhabitant of the kingdom of love, on a woman; as a father, on his children.

It was the strangeness to him of his own children, his inability to express himself in or through them, that finally opened his eyes. Why had he not understood from the beginning that his gift was a lonely one? Not only one that would never have outward recognition, but also one that would exist and develop without reference to other human beings. An interior grace, needing for a stage only his own soul; for approbation, nothing more than the plaudits of his own conscience. Integrity, compassion, unselfish high-mindedness—these, he told himself, had always been the world's highest goals, and he had been a fool to content himself with lower.

No wonder he had failed in his earlier efforts! The goals he had chosen had all been unworthy of him. Now, expecting nothing more—or less—than the development of his spiritual nature, he would be free of the fear of disappointment in the world. What did it now matter if to undiscerning eyes he appeared to be no more than the small-town proprietor of a small-town drugstore? He would know better.

For a time, Oliver had a brief resurgence of hope. But it was very brief. He discovered, in the first place, that he was in a bad business for the practice of probity and the development of his spiritual nature. His customers were in the habit of buying over and sometimes under the counter at Young's Drugstore articles not congruent with that practice or that development. At first, Oliver resolutely removed these articles from his stock. When he began to lose valued customers, he realized that, however much he might desire a sphere of spiritual isolation where he could grow toward perfection, in his work he was tied to his customers. He replaced the articles, divorced himself spiritually from the drug business, and withdrew into a larger world. But the events of the larger world came seeping inward to invade his security. His son suddenly was taken ill and died.

Oliver's mother never recovered from the shock of her grandson's death, though her final illness was much later and of short duration. Oliver was called to her bedside on the afternoon of Thursday, the twelfth of June, and she died on the night of the sixteenth. As he sat by her bed during those five days, he was aghast at the unspoken accusations he directed toward her. There she lay, once so lovely and commanding, now gaunt, broken, without power, almost without speech. It was the time, if ever, for a son's compassion and love. Instead, Oliver thought: You put a burden upon me that I should never have been asked to bear. You expected too much of me, and you expected the wrong things. You put one set of ideas in my head, while you built up, before I was born, a world in which none of those ideas would work. You are to blame for it all.

His mother, as if she had heard him speak, opened her eyes. "Oliver," she said in her weak, loving voice, "my son."

"Yes, Mother," said Oliver.

His mother made a movement of her hand in his direction, and Oliver took her hand in his. It was a cluster of fragile bones against his plump palm.

"My boy," she said tremulously, "never forget—when you were born—or what I expected of you—will always expect. You won't forget, will you, Oliver?"

"No, Mother," said Oliver. But in his mind he was saying: Die, die. Release me. Let me go in peace. Let me be free of the burden of your expectations.

And when, three days later, his mother did die, he felt nothing but a wonderful lightness and well-being. Never forget when I was born! he exulted. Never forget what you expected of me! That is exactly what I'm going to do at the first possible minute. Forget the whole thing.

During his mother's funeral service, he said to himself again and again, "Free, free." The emotion this word gave him was so great and obvious that people mistook it for the sorrow he did not feel. For reasons of decency, he lingered after his mother's interment, speaking to her friends and relatives.

An old lady about his mother's age said to him, "I'm your mother's second cousin, Jennie Rideout. You don't remember me, but I'll never forget you. You were born on the stroke of midnight, January first, nineteen-hundred. 'Baby of the Century,' they called you. Your mother expected great things of you. We all did."

Oliver walked away from her without a word, drove his family home, had a bite to eat, and went at once to Maurice Flaherty's office.

Flaherty repeated the words with relish. "The stroke of midnight! The Baby of the Century! Right here in the flesh!"

"I intend to change all that," said Oliver.

Flaherty was a black Irishman, red-cheeked in the afternoon. "What is it you want changed? The flesh?" he asked, tapping Oliver's paunch.

Oliver drew away irritably. Now that there was only this one matter to be taken care of, he was impatient of delay. He pushed aside Flaherty's hand. "What I want changed," he said, "is the date of my birth."

Flaherty sat down on the edge of the heavy, golden-oak table and looked up at his friend. "What would you like?" he asked ironically. "About twelve years removed? Oliver Putnam Young, born in 1912 and now thirty-five. Is that what you want?"

"Don't be a fool," Oliver said. "All I want is that January first, nineteen-hundred business killed. Put me back a day; put me forward a day. That's all I ask."

Flaherty cocked his head. "You know I can't do that, Oliver."

"Why can't you? Fix it up so I will never again have to write, 'Oliver Putnam Young, January first, nineteen-hundred,' and hear some fool say, 'If it isn't the Child of the Century himself.' Make it legal. Authorize it, notarize it, witness it, whatever it takes."

"It can't be done," Flaherty said.

"Why can't it? People have their names changed every day. What's the difference?"

"The name," said Flaherty, "is a matter of chance. The birth is an actual happening in time."

"It's a matter of chance, too," Oliver argued, "most of the time."

"Now, look here," said Flaherty, "I know law. I've practiced for a quarter of a century, and there is no possible way a birth date can be changed. That I'm certain of."

Oliver bleakly fingered his empurpled forehead. "I'm stuck, then, am I?" he asked.

Flaherty stood up. "Insofar as your birth date goes," he said, "you are stuck."

Without another word, Oliver turned, opened the frosted-glass, gilt-inscribed door, and went out. Flaherty watched his friend's shadowed outline diminish down the corridor.